WITC...

MATHIAS THULMANN, THE relentless witch hunter, is back. Accompanied by his brutish henchman Streng, he travels to Wurtbad, hot on the trail of an unhallowed book and pursued by the evil vampire Sibbechai. However, an outbreak of plague locks down the city and threatens the life of the intrepid witch hunter. Meanwhile, an old nemesis from Thulmann's past is hatching a diabolical scheme, the townspeople are hostile, the local authorities have their own hidden agendas and that's not all. Where there is plague, there are always rats...

C. L. Werner, author of the popular Brunner novels, pens this thrilling tale of gothic fantasy and action. Darkness and insanity threaten, and the only thing standing between humanity and damnation are the witch hunters!

A WARHAMMER NOVEL

WITCH FINDER

C. L. WERNER

*Dedicated to Ray Bradbury, who provided
encouragement when all was despair.*

A BLACK LIBRARY PUBLICATION

First published in Great Britain in 2005 by
BL Publishing,
Games Workshop Ltd.,
Willow Road, Nottingham,
NG7 2WS, UK

10 9 8 7 6 5 4 3 2 1

Cover illustration by Stefan Kopinski
Map by Nuala Kennedy.

A CIP record for this book is available from the British Library

ISBN 1 84416 161 7

Distributed in the US by Simon & Schuster
1230 Avenue of the Americas, New York, NY 10020, US.

Printed and bound in Great Britain by
Bookmarque, Surrey, UK.

See the Black Library on the Internet at
www.blacklibrary.com

Find out more about Games Workshop
and the world of Warhammer at
www.games-workshop.com

THIS IS A dark age, a bloody age, an age of daemons and of sorcery. It is an age of battle and death, and of the world's ending. Amidst all of the fire, flame and fury it is a time, too, of mighty heroes, of bold deeds and great courage.

AT THE HEART of the Old World sprawls the Empire, the largest and most powerful of the human realms. Known for its engineers, sorcerers, traders and soldiers, it is a land of great mountains, mighty rivers, dark forests and vast cities. And from his throne in Altdorf reigns the Emperor Karl-Franz, sacred descendant of the founder of these lands, Sigmar, and wielder of his magical warhammer.

BUT THESE ARE far from civilised times. Across the length and breadth of the Old World, from the knightly palaces of Bretonnia to ice-bound Kislev in the far north, come rumblings of war. In the towering Worlds Edge Mountains, the orc tribes are gathering for another assault. Bandits and renegades harry the wild southern lands of the Border Princes. There are rumours of rat-things, the skaven, emerging from the sewers and swamps across the land. And from the northern wilder-nesses there is the ever-present threat of Chaos, of daemons and beastmen corrupted by the foul powers of the Dark Gods. As the time of battle draws ever near, the Empire needs heroes like never before.

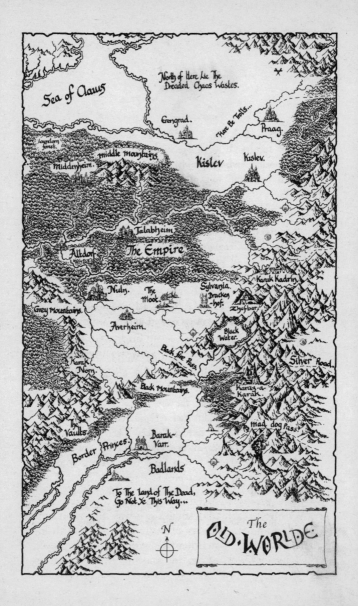

PROLOGUE

GREY CLOUDS HOVERED above the tiled rooftops of the city, stretching across the horizon like a gigantic shroud. A chill wind stirred the air, an unseasonably early harbinger of the coming winter. From the brick chimneys of every house and hovel, thin serpents of smoke slithered upwards, adding to the already dingy atmosphere, blotting out the sun's feeble efforts to smile down upon the streets of Wurtbad.

The narrow lanes that wound their way between the sprawl of the city were subdued, despite the masses of grim-faced men and women. With winter threatening an early advent, the people of Wurtbad were eager to gather provisions for the harsh months ahead. Bakeries and wine shops bustled with commerce, and rang out with the clink of coins changing hands. But there was little conversation. Each tradesman's eye was narrowed with suspicion and fear. Cloves of garlic, pots filled with fragrant flowers and parchment seals marked with prayers to Shallya, goddess of healing and mercy, marked most doorways. The threat of winter was still some distance away. But the threat of plague was already upon Wurtbad.

The disease had appeared in the harbour districts first, the miserable little ghettos to which dockhands and labourers slunk back once their day's toil was at an end. Foul black boils festered upon the victim's skin until, at last, they burst open, weeping brown pus. The sick and dying would linger for weeks, their bodies becoming ever more grotesquely infected until there was no nourishment left in their wasted frames to sustain the disease. Then they expired. It was an ugly, loathsome death, of a kind that the city's doktors and scholars, even the temples of Shallya and Morr, had never witnessed before. But it was not all the victims had to bear. To the terrifying stigma of the disease was added the horror of the unknown.

Sinister shapes stalked the streets now. Strange figures born from the city's despair. One such apparition prowled that part of the city that had been given over to brothels and taverns. The stranger wore a heavy brown topcoat about his tall, elongated frame. On his head sat a wide-brimmed hat, it was battered and twisted, stained by the tainted rain from the smoke-befouled clouds. His gloved hands held a long, steel-handled walking cane and a dingy leather satchel. But his most distinctive feature was the mask that shielded his face from the elements – a mask of oiled leather with a long, bird-like beak, stretching out from beneath the shadow of his hat. Its smoky lenses were glazed, like the eyes of a vulture, hiding the human orbs that peered from behind them. The faint smell of lilac suggested itself as the stranger passed, seeming to exude from the bird-like bill.

The stranger was a plague doctor, one of the only men in Wurtbad with the courage to venture into the homes of those brought low by the blight. One of the only men greedy enough to make their suffering his business.

He reached the end of an alleyway, his steps frightening a starving cur from where it hid beneath a staircase. His mask turned upward, his eyes studying the red slash painted upon the doorway above the steps – the sign that the Blight had struck. Without hesitation, the plague doktor ascended the stairs, rapping upon the portal with the steel crown of his cane.

Shuffling steps told of movement, and the portal shuddered inward as its warped frame was pulled inside. The grimy face at the door considered the strange apparition with an expression between hope and terror. The plague doktor did not wait to be admitted, forcing the occupant to retreat before him. The interior was dingy and decrepit, dirt and debris piled against its cracked plaster walls. A small corridor branched off from the foyer while a rickety wooden staircase wound its way upward.

'Who is sick here?' All humanity in the doktor's voice was smothered by layers of leather and sheepskin.

'Four floors up,' the concierge was quick to reply, stabbing a finger at the ceiling. The doktor's mask rose to follow the gesture, then fixed its lifeless lenses on the grimy little man. The concierge loudly swallowed the knot in his throat.

'This is the third visit I have paid to your household,' the doktor stated. 'Infection has perhaps taken hold.'

'She's no kin of mine!' the concierge protested hastily. 'A common whore, like the others!' His cry was desperate, as though denying any relationship with the infected woman might spare him from the disease itself.

'You will show me to her room.' The concierge's face grew more pallid beneath its layers of grime as he hurried after the visitor. 'I should like to examine everyone who resides here,' the plague doktor said. 'If the blight has appeared here three times, others are likely infected.'

'Is that really necessary?' the concierge gasped.

'It is not you who pays the cost,' the doktor consoled the little man, seemingly oblivious to the reason for his concern. 'And it would be better than contracting the blight yourself.' The concierge nearly tripped on the stairs as he forgot which foot he was using.

'That – that isn't – I couldn't…' the concierge stuttered. The doktor paused on the stairway. He looked down from the upper step as though he was one of the gargoyles crouched upon the cathedral of Sigmar.

'Do not discount the possibility,' the doktor asserted. 'After you have shown me to the woman's room, I suggest you retire to your own. I shall examine you when I am done.' His leather glove creaked as he made firm his grip upon his cane. 'All it will cost is a little time, and a little silver.'

The concierge swallowed again, and hurried to conduct the visitor to his appointment.

'REMOVE YOUR CLOTHING,' the muffled voice intoned from behind the mask. Vira Staubkammer raised a slender hand to her breast, her fingers lighting upon the strings that dripped from her bodice. The plague doktor did not seem to notice, his gaze swept the room, studying its dingy squalor. Shabby excuses for a wardrobe and dressing table were visibly crumbling. There was a reek of dirty straw from the small bed-frame, its mattress supported by sagging ropes.

The woman might once have been considered possessed of beauty, but long years of squalor and shame had cheapened its bloom. Her mouth was too accustomed to false laughter and hollow pleasure, her eyes were pits of emptiness that had seen far too much ugliness in her short life. What remained in her shapely figure, in her long dark hair, was only the illusion of what stirred longing in the blood of men. But it was enough to suit her needs; enough to serve men who would pay for the tattered reflection of that which they desired.

'I am not accustomed to this,' said Vira, her voice struggling to assume its normal bold haughtiness. 'I am paid to remove my clothes. *I* have never paid for the privilege of removing them myself.'

'You should change your bedding,' the plague doktor said, completing his inspection of her room. He strode past the young whore as she opened her bodice, exposing the pale flesh beneath. Oblivious to her partial nudity, he set his bag down upon the table. 'All sorts of ill humors can gather in such squalor.' He removed a set of gruesome picks and bone-scrapers. Vira blanched as she saw the ugly instruments, her face turning almost as white as her bodice. The mask turned to regard her once more. Vira quivered before its vulture-like eyes. She would have been more at ease to see lust, despair, even hate, in the man's face, but the mask betrayed not the slightest hint of emotion.

'Extend your arms,' the plague doktor ordered. 'Hold them to either side.'

'It is only a cough,' Vira protested even as she obeyed. 'I was out late… a friend who was too eager to wait to reach indoors. It will pass.'

'Perhaps,' the muffled voice mused. Vira shuddered as the man strode from the table, a long, needle-like lance in his gloved clutch. The plague doktor circled her slowly, as though he really were a vulture circling some carrion before feeding upon it. The lilac scent exuding from the mask's leather beak filled her lungs. Vira cringed as the cold tip of the lance touched her skin, prodding her to raise her armpit. From the corner of her eye, she could see the mask nod up and down. What had he seen, she wondered?

'I fear that Herr Kemper is something akin to a biddy,' Vira said, silently cursing the prying concierge who saw fit to send for this man. It was only a minor cold, she was certain of that. That it could be anything more was too horrible to contemplate.

The plague doktor strode back toward the table. Vira watched with relief as he began to drop the sinister instruments back into his bag. The vulture-like mask turned toward her once more. 'Lower your arms and restore your clothes.' Vira breathed an audible sigh of relief, hurrying to comply.

'I am well then?' she dared to ask, unable to hold back the relief. The doktor removed a small bottle from his bag.

'Perhaps,' he repeated. 'There is no outward sign of the blight about you, but this cough disturbs me. It may signify an imbalance among your humors.' He held the tiny bottle in his gloved hand.

Vira felt a wave of unease as the plague doktor approached, beyond even her earlier trepidation. Her eyes fixed on the clouded glass clutched in his hand. 'What is that?' she asked.

'Medicinal vapours,' came the answer. 'They will restore the harmony of your body's humors. You should have a rag at hand, I fear. And I do hope you did not spend too much for your breakfast.'

The young woman suppressed a cough and smiled nervously. 'What must I do?'

Although she could not see his face, she seemed to sense the plague doktor smiling as he pulled the clay stopper from the bottle.

'Just breathe deeply,' he told her. 'The vapours will do the rest.'

THE PLAGUE DOKTOR slipped into the shadows of an alley beside the brooding brickwork of the Black Sleep tavern. In the darkness he removed his outer garments, carefully folding his topcoat and hat before slipping them into his bag. He undid the small bronze clasp that held his mask against his face, inhaling deeply as he freed himself of the lilac odour. The pomander within the bill of his mask would need replacement when next he went abroad, but it was a small expense when weighed against the great work in which he was engaged.

It was a lean, elderly man who emerged from the alleyway, tapping on the cobblestones with his steel-tipped cane, frosty white hair standing out in the flickering lamplight. The old man smiled politely as a pair of burly ruffians emerged from the Black Sleep, stepping aside with an elaborate gesture as they swaggered into the night. His mouth pulled into a quiet sneer as he watched them fade. He would not have to linger amongst such squalor for long. Very soon his work would be completed and his name ranked amongst the immortals, as the greatest mind of his time

The old man paid little heed to the Black Sleep, his eyes not dwelling on the boisterous crowd inside the tavern. He strode away from the bierkeller, toward a small stairway set against the wall nearest the bar. Lingering for a moment, ensuring that he was not observed, he slipped down the stairs.

He soon found himself within the Black Sleep's cellar, surrounded by casks of ale, beer and wine. The old man cast one more cautious glance over his shoulder. Satisfied that he was still alone, he walked to one of the casks, sliding his body into the narrow space between the huge barrel and the cellar wall, then worked his way along until he reached a narrow gap. A length of black cloth hung against the wall. He lifted it and entered the crude, burrow-like tunnel it concealed. Hesitating for one moment, he lit a tiny lantern he found resting within a niche in the earthen wall of the tunnel.

He had not proceeded far before he was greeted by a diminutive figure bearing a lantern similar to his own.

The old man peered down at the small shape, noting with amusement its awkward, spider-like gait. The lamplight performed further malevolent tricks on the little creature's disordered features.

'Your work went well, herr doktor?' the gargoyle's shrill voice enquired.

'As well as might be expected,' the old man replied. 'I treated a half-dozen this day. I shall send our friends to collect two of them. They will make rather interesting subjects for my studies.'

The old man handed his bag to his minion, the tiny creature nodding his malformed head. It was a gruesome combination, he thought, a head large enough for a full-grown man rising from the shoulders of a halfling. But one could never be certain of what exact form his studies would take – nor, indeed, of what shape the objects of his studies might choose to manifest themselves in. At least he had been able to prove that halflings were not completely immune to what ignorant men called 'Chaos'. And poor little Lobo has proving a most enthusiastic servant, since he believed only the great Herr Doktor Freiherr Weichs could ever cure his affliction.

A sound in the darkness caused Doktor Weichs to turn about, his feverish eyes peering into the shadows. As the scuttling noise repeated itself, the doktor slowly lowered his lantern. His new friends were not over-fond of the light, nor was it was wise to upset them. A trickle of fear ran down Weichs's spine. The kind of stark, mortal terror that even the Templars of Sigmar had failed to wring from his corrupt soul. The stink of mangy fur, the reek of sewer filth, exuded from the dark. Once again, Weichs heard the scrabbling of claws on the earthen floor of the tunnel, the soft chittering of inhuman whispers. They weren't supposed to be here. Skilk was supposed to keep them away!

Weichs cringed as he sensed something drawing near. Red eyes gleamed from the shadows, reflecting the dim light from his lantern. Beside him, Lobo emitted a moan of fright. The scientist fought to compose himself. He knew these creatures had senses far beyond those of a man, that they could smell fear dripping from a human body. They were drawn to any sign of weakness, any taint of frailty. The doktor remembered the bag he had given to Lobo. That was what had drawn them. It was the odour within. He should have known. Should have expected. Should have prepared for them.

The red eyes were not looking at him now; they had shifted and turned toward Lobo and the bag. Weichs gained an impression of whiskers twitching in the dark, of a rodent's muzzle sniffing at the air. Of furred lips pulling back, exposing inch-long incisors. Beyond the first set of eyes, he now saw others gleaming within the tunnel.

'You are most punctual,' Weichs stated, his voice echoing loud. The red eyes instantly turned back upon him. 'I had not expected you so soon.' He fought to keep his timbre calm, struggled to impose a note of command. 'Grey Seer Skilk is fortunate to be served by such capable and noble followers.' Weichs noted the eyes flinch as he spoke the name of Skilk, his sense of smell registering the unpleasant musky odour that exuded from the shadows. If they didn't understand anything else he said, at least the vermin had recognised the name of their inhuman priest.

'I need you to collect two more subjects…' Weichs held up his hand, displaying two fingers. He knew from previous experience that the creatures could see far better in the dark than even a dwarf. They would not fail to notice the gesture, any more than they would miss the lilac scent that led them to their victims. Again, the chittering gnawed at the shadows, making the doktor's flesh crawl as their ghastly voices clawed at his ears.

'Yes-yes,' a sharp voice hissed from the darkness. 'Man-meat find-take. Grey seer like-like!' Slowly the gleaming eyes withdrew back into the darkness. Weichs heard the sound of verminous paws pattering their way down the tunnel. The scientist lifted the lantern again, throwing its door wide open, revelling in the warm comfort of its illumination.

'Back to the laboratory, Lobo,' he ordered. The halfling nodded his oversized head, limping back down the tunnel, struggling with the doktor's heavy bag. Weichs watched him for a moment, then cast a nervous glance after the retreating red eyes, suppressing another shudder. His dealings with the skaven always filled him with dread. He could see their envy and hatred of the entire human race burning in their eyes.

Weichs fought back his loathing. It was immaterial what he felt, or what the skaven felt. All that mattered was his work. He needed a safe place to conduct his studies. Skilk had provided that. He needed subjects for his experiments. Skilk was able to provide that, also. But most of all, he needed warpstone, and that too was in Skilk's power to provide.

Yes indeed, the world would soon come to know the name of Doktor Freiherr Weichs.

One way or another…

CHAPTER ONE

THE SUN SLOWLY sank into the west, its last rays smouldering like a dying ember behind the gaps in the grey
clouds. Night would soon fall upon the land, strength-
ening the shadows and heralding the supremacy of
darkness. Travellers upon the road would hurry to find
sanctuary, however mean and humble, to huddle about
warm fires and hide behind locked doors, praying that
the horrors of Old Night would pass them by. The eyes
of such men were ever on the lookout for the flickering
lantern of a roadside inn or coaching house, seeking the
welcoming watchlight as keenly as they did the
approach of some denizen of the dark.

No such eager hope turned the heads of the two men
now riding slowly down the old dirt road. They had seen
too often the dread shapes within which Old Night
clothed itself. Their fears could never hope to conjure an
apparition as frightful as those that walked the corridors
of memory. And they had seen that there was no safety

from darkness behind locked doors or beside roaring hearths.

The foremost of the two horsemen was a squat, stocky figure, his bulk straining at the weathered mass of a leather tunic reinforced with steel studs. A simple scabbard, the surface scarred where some marking had been crudely removed, swung from his hip. The sword held within was unremarkable, like any that might have been issued to the Empire's many armies. Like the crossbow holstered on the saddle of the rider's horse, it was the simple but effective tool of a professional soldier.

But the rider no longer considered himself as such. Still, old habits, like bad habits, were difficult for Streng to be rid of. The bearded mercenary lifted the fur water-skin hanging from a strap across his chest and took a deep swallow of something far more vibrant than water. Streng grunted appreciatively, letting the skin fall, the liquid within sloshing noisily as it slapped against his hip.

He preferred beer. It was a much more sociable drink, and it took a vast quantity to put him down. Vodka was a much harsher spirit, and overindulging in its favours could result in assorted aches and bruises, a visit to the local dungeon, or a bill for damages. Still, his time campaigning in the north had taught Streng one unassailable fact – there was nothing better to chase away the cold of winter than a bottle of good Kislevite. He only wished he'd been able to liberate more of it from the wine cellar of the Grey Crone back in Klausberg. Of course, the innkeeper would have noticed the disappearance of more than two bottles. Reikhertz had been a decent enough host, and Streng would have hated to bash his skull in over something as minor as a few bottles of vodka.

He sucked at his teeth, growing thoughtful. There would be a fair bit of coin coming his way when they reached Wurtbad. The Temple of Sigmar's gold was more honest than most he had earned during his brutal life, but it spent just as quickly. The mercenary smiled. He should manage a week of drinking, gambling, whoring and fighting when he reached the city. Assuming, of course, that he stayed one step ahead of the watch. And allowing that his employer didn't have other plans. Streng cast a sour look at the rider following in his wake.

The witch hunter was a black shadow upon the back of his white steed. His cloak whipped about him in the wind that blew from the north, his face hidden beneath the brim of his tall hat. The weapons that hung from the templar's belt were more extravagant than those borne by Streng: a pair of pistols with their dark-stained grips inlaid with gold; a silvered longsword with a gilded pommel sheathed in a dragonskin scabbard. But then, everything about the witch hunter was meant to provoke the onlooker. To evoke feelings of respect and pious terror.

Streng looked away, hawking the aftertaste of the vodka from his mouth and spitting it into the dust. From the arch of his companion's shoulders, the way his chin sagged toward his chest, Streng could tell he was deep in thought. He could well imagine the paths down which those thoughts roamed. For he himself had travelled with Mathias Thulmann, templar of the Order of Sigmar, far too long to deceive himself that his employer's mind was considering cold tankards of ale and hot-blooded tavern wenches.

Well, perhaps Streng might be able to indulge those vices for a day or two. At least when they reached Wurtbad, and before the witch hunter had need of his services again.

'PLEASE.' THE BEGGING voice gnawed at Thulmann's mind, as fresh in his memory as the dark day in which the words had been spoken. 'She is just a child!' The witch hunter could still smell the sorry stench of pig dung and spoiled cabbage, the ugly odour of decay and poverty. 'For Sigmar's sake, my lord, show mercy!'

Thulmann's calfskin gloves tightened their grip on the reins of his steed. How many times had he thought back to that loathsome, black day in Silbermund? How many pleasant moments had that same recollection reached out to kill? The memory was burned into his brain like the brand of some malevolent daemon, forever festering there until he answered the final call of Morr, lord of death.

'For Sigmar's sake, I cannot let her live.' The words had tasted like wormwood as he spoke them, spitting them from his mouth as though they would choke him. The woman had fallen to her knees then, sobbing, wailing, washing the filth from his horse's hooves with her tears.

How many ugly little villages had he travelled through, always one step behind the thrice-accursed heretic he was in pursuit of? And how many times had he arrived too late to bring his quarry to ground? Too late to find anything but the monster's handiwork, like the calling card of a daemon. Thulmann knew that it was no coincidence. His quarry was taunting him, mocking his efforts. Daring the witch hunter to make good the chase.

He thought again of the little girl. How long had she lived? Six summers? Seven? Surely she had seen no more than eight. The child had been kicked by a mule, her tiny leg snapped and broken. It was feared she would never heal, for the break was too complex for the poor farmers of Silbermund to set. The little girl was destined to be a cripple – if she survived at all. But then, one of the gods had smiled down on the village when a traveller chanced to tarry awhile. He was a healer, a man of medicine. His promise was that he would look upon the child, and help her if he could.

Oh yes, the gods had indeed smiled upon Silbermund. The Dark Gods.

Thulmann could see the faces of the farmers, glaring at him from every corner of the square, hate boiling in their eyes. No, they would not challenge him. For they knew it had to be done. But how they hated him for it. And how he had grown to hate himself. Even the girl's father could not challenge him, but instead stood slumped against the wall of the blacksmith's shop. His gaze staring into nothingness. His face twisted in pain.

There were some heretic philosophers and mystics who dared claim that Chaos did not embody the force of evil. They said that it was like fire or water – a worldly force, a force of nature neither good nor evil. Was water evil when the banks of the Reik swelled and drowned a village? Was fire evil when it escaped the hearth and laid waste to the most part of an entire town? Such was their argument. And such men were more dangerous than the vermin who bowed and grovelled before the Dark Gods themselves, for they cloaked their degeneracy behind words like 'reason' and 'science'. They did not fear the judgement of Sigmar because they saw no evil in what they did, even when that evil glared back at them from the darkness of their deeds.

Herr Doktor Freiherr Weichs. That name haunted Thulmann, mocking him from the shadows. He had first learned of this deranged physician from a Sigmarite priest named Haeften. Weichs had been employed by the Baron von Lichtberg to act as physician to his house. It was an appointment that ended in a hideous tragedy.

One of the village girls had been with child, a child sired by the baron's son. To avoid complications, the foolish girl had turned to Weichs, begged him to find a way to undo what had been done. The doktor, may all the gods damn his soul, had prescribed a potion he promised would dissolve the seedling life as harmlessly as it had been created. But that potion had not contained hope. It had contained the seeds of mutation. Of death. The girl's own mother reported what had happened to the village priest, when it became clear to see that the life growing within her belly was no clean thing, but a spawn of darkness.

Haeften had, in turn, informed the temple and they had sent Thulmann to assess the matter. It took some time to determine the cause of the girl's condition. At first, he had thought the seed of the mutation might lie with the father, and so had put Reinhardt von Lichtberg to the test as well as Mina Kurtz. But later, much later, Mina had confessed her shame. Confessed what she had asked Weichs to do. But by then it was too late. The heretic had seen which way the wind was blowing and fled. Thulmann tarried only long enough to dispose of Mina Kurtz, and the unclean life within her. He then set out on the trail of the man truly responsible for the girl's destruction.

THULMANN REMEMBERED CLOSING his ears to the sounds of wailing that filled the air. He had looked toward the pile of wood heaped in the centre of the square; at the stake rising above it; at the tiny form lashed to it. There was a faction of the Order of Sigmar who held that suffering was needed to purge the soul of any who were tainted by Chaos. Sforza Zerndorff was one such man, the late Lord Protector Thaddeus Gamow had been another. They claimed it was necessary to wrench every last scream from a heretic before extinction. For only thus could the witch hunter ensure the soul of the condemned might be pure enough to enter the sight of Sigmar on passing through the Gates of Morr.

The witch hunter stared at the tiny figure. At the little girl slumped against the pole. What crime had tainted this child's soul? She was surely guiltless – a victim of heresy, not a heretic herself. It would take a cruel, calloused soul like Zerndorff not to see that. If a child had to be tortured for the greater glory of Sigmar, then he was not the same god that Thulmann worshipped and served.

Thulmann had commanded the innkeeper to produce his strongest grog, and then had Streng feed it to the child until she fell into a drunkard's stupor. He hoped that it was enough, that she would not regain her senses when the flames did their work.

A child's broken leg. Thulmann wondered at the corrupt mind that could seize upon such misery and exploit it. That could subject a small child to his abominable experiments. Weichs had set the child's leg, then wrapped it in a poultice which, he assured the girl's parents, would speed the healing and ensure the bone would not knit crookedly. Then he had left, words of gratitude following him as he departed the village. Two days later, Thulmann had arrived in Silbermund and asked the villagers if a stranger, a tall elderly man who might be presenting himself as a doctor, had passed their way. His enquiries led him to the child.

The witch hunter shuddered as he remembered that moment – just as he recalled so many similar moments. He'd voiced a prayer to Sigmar that even Weichs would not be so depraved, that he had spared the girl his inhuman attentions. Then, slowly, he had cut the poultice away from her leg. There had been screams then, the girl's parents wailing in horror. Thulmann himself turned pale. He had seen worse things, but never on the body of a child. Coarse black hair covered the flesh beneath the poultice, an unclean growth like the fur of a fly. The contagion was spreading, too, already beginning to creep upwards toward her knee. The fur was an outward sign of the infection, but what other changes might be happening inside, within the girl's mind and soul?

Perhaps the cruel mutation would so completely consume her that she would become no more than an animal, loping off into the woods to join the foul beastman tribes, a lust for human flesh gnawing at her belly.

Thulmann spoke prayers to Sigmar as he cast the iron brand into the pile of burning wooden fagots, but truly did not know if he meant them for the little girl or for himself. The flames had burned quickly, fiercely. The witch hunter had ordered most of the village's store of lamp oil dumped upon the tinder. He doubted if even one of the fire wizards of the bright magic college could evoke fire so swiftly. Yet, even so, it seemed to take an eternity to burn. Thulmann had forced himself to watch, refusing to look away, and once more swore the same oath he had made at each such pyre – that he would find Herr Doktor Weichs and make him pay for his crimes.

THE TRAIL HAD led to Wurtbad. Weichs was known to have been in the city, before he became embroiled in the strange and sinister murders that led to the arrest and execution of the witch Chanta Favna. But the trail was cold now. Ordered by Sforza Zerndorff, newly appointed Witch Hunter General South, Thulmann had been forced to abandon his hunt to investigate the dire events unfolding in the village of Klausberg.

Thulmann forgot the mad doktor for a moment, turning his thoughts to more recent events. Even if Weichs was no longer in Wurtbad, the witch hunter had business there. He had learned that an unspeakable tome of profane knowledge had been hidden in the city, a blasphemous grimoire titled *Das Buch die Unholden*. The foul tome had been the dark secret of the Klausner family and had ultimately brought about their doom.

The book had drawn the interest of a powerful vampire lord, a creature named Sibbechai, one of the ghastly necrarch bloodline. Thulmann did not think the death of old Wilhelm Klausner would be enough to kill the vampire's coveting of the book. For the necrarchs were a breed of vampire sorcerer, existing only to increase their knowledge of the arcane, determined to one day exterminate all living things and create a world of the restless dead. It was vital that the witch hunter should find it first and destroy it. The implications of such a tome in the clutches of a necrarch were too ghastly to contemplate.

Thulmann's mind turned to the fate of the last son of the house of Klausner. Sibbechai the vampire had attacked young Gregor Klausner, left him for dead in the ruin of his father's chambers. When the witch hunter had left, Gregor was still bedridden from his ordeal, but recovering.

Recovering? Thulmann did not want to think about how swift, or how likely, that recovery would be. It had been one of the reasons that drove his hasty departure from Klausberg, more so than the desperate hope of finding Doktor Weichs or the compelling need to destroy *Das Buch die Unholden*. Gregor Klausner had been a noble, courageous man, a comrade who had helped Thulmann to uncover the horror plaguing Klausberg – even though the trail led back to his own house. Gregor had saved Thulmann's life, a debt the witch hunter knew he could never repay. For all signs indicated that Gregor had been exposed to the poison of the vampire. If he had remained any longer, Thulmann would have had no choice but to acknowledge those signs, and to do what had to be done.

There were already too many ugly memories haunting his sleep. Thulmann cursed himself for such selfish weakness, but he would spare himself the destruction and dismemberment of Gregor Klausner if he could. He would return to Wurtbad, make his report to his superiors in the Order of Sigmar, then have Meisser send one of his men to investigate Gregor's condition. Perhaps he would make a full and clean recovery. Thulmann had known men among the Templars who had staved off the infection of a vampire's bite through their faith in Sigmar, and sheer strength of will. Both qualities were strong in Gregor. But, if they were not strong enough, then whomsoever was sent by Meisser would have to deal with the fate of Gregor Klausner.

THE WIND MOANED outside the black walls of Klausner Keep, like the spectral wailing of ghosts. Red-rimmed eyes turned toward the narrow window, discomfited by the sinister sound. There was enough misery and dread within the ancient black-stoned fortress without the elements contributing their own efforts. The woman's soft hands rose, wiping the moisture from her eyes. Miranda had been sitting beside the enormous iron-framed bed for most of the day, maintaining her quiet vigil. At times, she had been joined by Lady Ilsa Klausner, dressed in her black widow's garb, her face drawn and wasted. There was no comfort or solace in her brief visits. She had buried a husband and one son already, and the icy hopelessness that filled her gaze told Miranda she expected to bury another son before much longer.

Miranda choked back another sob. Surely, the gods could not be so cruel as to take away her Gregor? Her brave and noble Gregor. Her kindly nobleman who took an interest in the welfare of even the lowliest peasant of Klausberg. Who had risked his life to do what was right. Surely, the gods would not punish him for possessing the courage to confront the inhuman forces that preyed on the good people of Klausberg?

The young woman sighed. Gregor was dying. He had not taken food for two days now, and had not moved so much as a finger in the last twelve hours. The only sign of life lay in the faint rise and fall of his chest and in the slight rasp of air escaping his mouth. She shook her head in despair, helpless to stop the decline of her beloved, helpless to stop her hopes and dreams from fading into the shadows that reached out to claim him. Miranda gave up her contemplation of the darkening landscape outside the window. Her eyes fell once more on the silent, statuesque figure of Gregor.

He remained perfectly still, but Miranda sensed that something had changed. It took only a moment to realise her beloved nobleman's eyes had been closed before. Now they were open, staring vacantly at the ceiling. She gasped in astonishment, hurrying to the side of his bed.

'Gregor! Gregor!' she cried, reaching out and clasping her stricken lover's hand. The pale flesh was cold, utterly devoid of warmth. Miranda's face contorted with sympathetic pain as she rubbed her own hands against Gregor's, striving to force the warmth of her own body into his.

Gregor Klausner gazed up at the ceiling, his eyes registering only a colourless expanse. Slowly he began to register the presence of the young woman at his side. The warm hands stroking his icy arm. Gregor turned his face toward her. He could perceive the room as a colourless background of light and shadow, the rich tapestries and polished wooden furnishings robbed of their vibrancy. Miranda herself was only a grey shadow, indistinct, as though his eyes could not focus upon her. But most alarming of all were the vivid pulses of crimson that shone from within, a network of rivers coursing through the apparition. Gregor closed his eyes and clenched his teeth.

He had thought it a symptom of his fever – this unreal, unholy delirium that made shadows of the living. He had believed the entrancing light flowing through those shadows a perverse dream, a foul imagining brought on by his injuries and his sickness. Now he knew it was not.

He could see the blood burning within Miranda's body. See it flowing beneath her shadowy form. He could feel the warmth of it reaching out to his chilled flesh, smell its aroma caressing his face. His mouth writhed with anticipation, filling with the phantom taste of salty crimson wine rushing down his parched throat.

Gregor ripped his hand from Miranda's caress, sitting bolt upright in his bed. She reached out toward him, but Gregor recoiled as if from a viper, raising his hands to ward her off.

'Gregor!' the young woman cried again. Emotion clawed at his heart, his face twisting with an agony he had never believed possible. Again Miranda reached for him, forcing Gregor to slip from the bed onto the floor. Miranda hesitated, waiting as her beloved nobleman raised himself. But as he did so he stepped away from the bed, towards the stone wall behind him.

'Stay back, Miranda!' Gregor snarled, summoning up every last ounce of authority. His words arrested her as she made to rise from the bed. 'For Sigmar's sake, stay away!' he added in a piteous tone. The sound stabbed into the young woman, her face contorting in anguish.

'Why Gregor? What is it? What is wrong?' She began to rise once more. Gregor waved her back with a violent gesture.

'Please!' he cried. 'I don't want to hurt you!' As Miranda took one single step toward him, a worried smile formed on her face. Gregor retreated before her approach.

'But you… you would not injure me!' she insisted. 'What is this nonsense that you speak?'

'The vampire, Miranda, the vampire!' Gregor wailed. His back was to the wall now, he could retreat no further. 'It touched me! Its poison is within me!' Miranda froze, her face growing pale as the horror of Gregor's words bore down upon her.

'No,' she dismissed his hysteria. 'That isn't true. You've just been sick. Unwell. The burden of your father's death...'

Gregor buried his face in his hands, his body shuddering as deep sobs wracked his form. 'It is true, Miranda. Hideously, loathsomely true. I am poisoned, corrupted. There is no future for us...'

He looked up at her, watching as the tears rolled down her shadowy face. 'I release you, my sweet. Find a good man. Make a life for yourself. I can give you nothing now.' Gregor turned away, unable to gaze upon her any longer, unable to bear the unspeakable hunger growing within him. 'Only death.' With one fluid motion, Gregor leaped forward, crashing through the glass window, falling into the black of night.

Miranda screamed, racing to the shattered glass and twisted iron fittings. She stared out into the darkness, looking for any sign of Gregor's body. She steeled herself to find it crushed at the base of the keep's wall. But nothing met her gaze, only a few shards of glass twinkling in the moonlight as the clouds briefly released Mannslieb from their grasp.

Miranda withdrew back into the room, weeping, her mind struggling to accept what she had seen and heard. She was startled when Lady Ilsa Klausner appeared, taking her into a motherly embrace.

'He's gone,' was all Miranda could manage to say.

'I know,' Lady Ilsa tried to console her. 'I know. My son died three days ago.'

WITHERED FLESH STRETCHED into a grotesque leer, a look of feral, inhuman triumph. Crimson eyes narrowed with satisfaction, the flaming orbs burning a little brighter from the pits of the vampire's face. It had taken many days, far longer than it expected, but at last its call had been answered. The taint it had placed in young Gregor

Klausner's blood had at last begun to consume him. The strength and defiance of the boy's spirit had surprised the necrarch, for a time it had even worried that Gregor might be able to resist its power, to overcome its venom and sink into a mortal, permanent death.

But the ancient will of Sibbechai had been greater, more than sufficient to devour the man's soul. It was good that there had been such strength within the last of the Klausners. Sibbechai had need of such strength. By the use of its arcane arts, the vampire would add it to its own reserves of power. It was akin to those practices of mortal wizards, who studied light magic and employed small retinues of acolytes to aid them in focusing and empowering their spells. It was so foolish to think that dark magic might not profit by similar means. Of course, there was some danger. The necrarch was not certain of control over its newly created spawn. If Gregor Klausner had not become its slave, then he would certainly try to avenge himself on the vampire. And the magical link between them would work both ways – Sibbecahi would always be able to sense its new progeny, but perhaps Gregor would be able to follow that same bond back to his unclean father of darkness.

The necrarch lifted a shrivelled hand, its black, necrotic flesh clinging to the bones like wet parchment. It pushed upon the heavy wooden lid of its casket, forcing the panel to the floor with a resounding crash. Sibbechai exerted a small measure of power, causing its body to pivot upwards as though fixed on unseen hinges. It was a vain employment of the vampire's black arts, but Sibbechai knew such displays would keep its unwanted ally nervous and uneasy. It did not want the miserable mortal wizard to enjoy a moment's peace while he stood in the presence of one who was a master of the necromantic arts, centuries before the wizard was even a gleam in his father's eye.

Sibbechai's skeletal face considered the dank shadows of its new lair which was a small barrow mound just beyond the district of Klausberg. The vampire's unnatural vision pierced the darkness, exposing every crack in the walls, every pebble lying upon the floor. The figure of a man stood revealed, standing between the vampire and the barrow's opening. Thin and scraggly, his slight figure huddled within the fur-trimmed mass of a heavy cassock, ratty black hair falling about his pale, leprous face. Scrawny hands scratched at the sleeves of his necromancer's robe, and Sibbechai smiled again at the mortal's unease, exposing its chisel-like fangs. The necromancer took a step back, one spidery hand slipping within the sleeve of his grey robe. Then the wizard seemed to collect himself, glaring angrily at the vampire.

'The maggot crawls from its hole, does it?' Carandini's spiteful voice lashed at the vampire. 'I grow weary of waiting, leech. Three days and three nights I have stood here while you rested within your coffin. I will wait no longer!' The necromancer's hand emerged from within his robes, a small, silver twin-tailed comet icon dangling from the slender chain twined about his fingers. Sibbechai recoiled from the holy symbol, but its mocking smile did not wither. It had seen the fear within the mortal's eyes, however bold his words. The necromancer was fearful that he had made a mistake. Fearful that he had allowed the vampire too much time.

'Put that obscenity away,' Sibbechai's hissed. 'As you grow weary of waiting, I grow weary of your childish theatrics.' The vampire turned its head, watching as Carandini returned the tiny icon to a pocket within his robes. Sibbechai responded by stepping down from its coffin, its tattered black robe hanging shroud-like about its spindly frame.

'Your waiting is at an end, necromancer,' Sibbechai pronounced. 'I am recovered from my ordeal, ready to resume the quest we share.' The vampire studied Carandini's pale features. No, the necromancer could not conceal his doubt and fear. But killing him now might not be so easy, a frightened wizard was still a wizard, after all, and even a frightened man may speak a Word of Power. Besides, the recovery of the grimoire had already taken several unexpected turns. The mortal might possibly come in useful, if fate held any more in store. For the time being, it was better to let Carandini live and believe their tenuous alliance still held.

'Where has the book been taken?' Carandini asked. Sibbechai had bargained with the necromancer for its life with the abhorrent *Das Buch die Unholden*. Claiming that it knew where the book had been hidden by the late Wilhelm Klausner, it swore an oath that even the vampire feared to break. Now the necromancer was anxious to have his side of the bargain fulfilled.

'Klausner sent the book to Wurtbad,' Sibbechai said. 'For some reason, he had decided it was no longer safe in Klausberg.' The vampire displayed its lethal fangs, reminding Carandini what the reason for Klausner's desperate action had been.

'Where in Wurtbad?' the necromancer demanded. Sibbechai shook its head, lifting a claw-like finger.

'You are far too eager,' the necrarch said. 'Was it not you who extolled the virtues of patience?' There was venom in the vampire's voice as it remembered the taunting words spoken by Carandini as he kept the vampire from its coffin, as dawn began to break. 'You will discover where in the city when I feel the time is right.'

Carandini's glare was murderous. He could barely restrain his anger at the undead sorcerer. 'How then shall we proceed?' he said at last.

'We shall journey together to Wurtbad, you and I,' Sibbechai hissed. 'It will take two days to reach the city and I shall rest more easily with so devoted a comrade to watch over me during the hours of day. After all, if any harm came to me, you would never know where the grimoire is located. I should think that a poor mortal, whose years are so dreadfully few, would take great pains to avoid losing his chance at eternal life.

'For now, however, you shall need to find us transport to the city. Something big enough for my—' the vampire gestured with its claw towards the heavy wooden casket, '—baggage. And you might bring me back something to fortify myself with. The younger the better. Young blood is so much more sustaining.'

Carandini gave the vampire a last sour glance, then crept back into the gloom. Sibbechai watched the necromancer depart. It would be able to trust the man, for now at least. He would be useful in getting to Wurtbad – Sibbechai had not spoken falsely when it praised the boon of a guardian to watch over it while it slept. It had spoken rather less truthfully about the need to feed. The necrarchs were not slaves to their thirst in the way that other breeds of vampire were. They learned, over time, to subdue and deny their hunger. The oldest of the breed rarely fed at all. But let the necromancer believe Sibbechai to be a slave to its thirst. Carandini might hope to exploit that as a weakness, and when he did, the necromancer would be unpleasantly surprised.

For, in the end, only one of them would possess the dark secrets of *Das Buch die Unholden*. Sibbechai had no doubt which of them it would be.

THE HEAVY OAK door slowly creaked inward as a slender shape crossed the threshold. The shadow paused, ears straining at the darkness for any sign her stealthy approach had been betrayed by the door's rusty hinges. The only sound that answered was a deep rumble of snoring from the large bed that dominated the tiny chamber. The woman's expression transformed from nervous caution to savage, bestial hate. She waited, savouring the moment, letting her eyes become accustomed to the gloom that surrounded her.

The small rooms above the Hound and Hare were owned by the bloated parasite that ran the tavern itself. He rented them by the hour to his patrons, the wealthy merchants and ancient aristocrats who composed Wurtbad's elite, offering them privacy for their night games. Of course, later he would expect a tithe from whichever whore had plied her trade in one of the squalid little rooms, an iron cudgel ensuring his demands were always met promptly and in the correct amount.

Carefully, the woman began to cross the small room. She had removed her boots, so that her footsteps might not betray her, ignoring the wooden splinters that the floor stabbed into her naked feet. Beside the anguish that wrenched at her heart, the slivers of wood were nothing. She glided toward the bed, like some night hag conjured from a fable, glaring at the two figures sprawled among the fur blankets. The woman only gave a scant glance to the lithe shape lying on the left side of the bed – the strumpet who had replaced her seemed of little consequence. Her interest was focused upon the bed's other occupant. The man who had betrayed her.

Manfred Gelt was a wealthy river trader, one of the richest in Wurtbad. It was a boast she had heard oft spoken, but Manfred had the money to back his claim, throwing it away in buckets during his visits. The best wines, the finest minstrels, the richest meals. Even the squalid little rooms above the Hound and Hare, rented not for a few hours but for an entire evening. Manfred was a man who did not like to be rushed in his pleasures.

He had spoken such pretty words to her, such enticing words. Manfred visited her exclusively for three months, promising to one day raise her from the squalor, to make an honest and respectable woman of her. He bought her gifts, putting some substance to his fine words. The woman had heard such fantastic stories before, from every drunken sailor and melancholy soldier she had entertained through the years. But Manfred's stories were different, for he had made her believe. For the first time in her short, hopeless life, she had dared to hope for better things.

The woman glared hatefully at the familiar face snoring upon the pillow, his fat little hands clutched against his breast. She should have known better. Manfred's ardour had started to cool, until at last his roving eye found a prettier face. Yes, she should have known it would end in such a manner, but the woman could not help but feel betrayed.

She leaned down over the bed, a stray beam of moonlight shining through the shuttered window revealing her pale arm and the foul, black boils that defaced it. The woman bent her head towards his slumbering face, lips parting into a hateful sneer. Slowly, she edged closer until her lips were crushed against those of the man she had so stupidly allowed herself to love. As she withdrew, the slumbering merchant sputtered, the pattern of his snoring interrupted. The woman froze for an instant, wondering if he would awaken, then her eyes narrowed, deciding she did not care. What could he do to her now? She was already dead.

Spitefully, the woman spat into the merchant's open mouth, willing the contagion that pulsed through her body to enter her betrayer. Manfred stirred but did not awaken. With a last hateful look at him, Vira Staubkammer slipped back into the shadows. The sound of a creaking door broke through the silent darkness once more. Then the only sounds in the small room were the rumbling snores of the river merchant.

* * *

'YOUR EVENING WAS productive, excellency?' the liveried servant enquired, his arm extended to receive his master's cloak. The first rays of dawn shone down upon the streets of Wurtbad, as the sounds of the city began to stir.

'Most productive,' his corpulent master replied, his meaty jowls lifting into a lewd grin. 'Positively decadent, one might say.' He stalked past his servant, striding into the massive hall. His imperious gaze swept across the tiled floors, the marble columns and the panelled walls, secure in his knowledge that he was master of all he surveyed. 'I should have been born an Arabyan sheik, Fritz, then I should not be bothered with appearances.'

'Of course, my lord,' Fritz replied, hurrying after his master. A pair of soldiers dressed in uniforms of green and white flanked the two men, following them into the enormous hall. Fritz's master noted their approach, dismissing the two warriors with a wave of his fleshy hand.

'So tiresome, these swordsmen,' he proclaimed.

'They are only obeying their orders, my lord,' Fritz responded. 'After all, it is their sworn duty to protect your person and keep you from harm.'

'Perhaps,' sighed his master. 'But they are so terribly common. I should replace them with something much more daring. Some ogres from the Middle Mountains, perhaps, or a company of Sartosan pirates!' The obese figure's laughter faded into a dry, wracking cough. Fritz hurried forward, but his master shook his concerned servant away.

'You should be more cautious,' Fritz said, his voice heavy with worry. The brothels were a breeding ground for all manner of diseases. Every time his master went abroad he courted sickness.

'It is only a trifle, Fritz,' the fat man declared. 'A chill, nothing more.

So saying, Baron Friedo von Gotz, cousin to the Elector Count Graf Alberich Haupt-Anderssen of Stirland, governor of the city of Wurtbad and all its provinces, ascended the marble stairs, withdrawing to his chambers for a few hours of rest before the tedium of his office beset him for another day. As he departed, Fritz could hear the baron's boots echoing upon the tile floor, the steps occasionally punctuated by the sound of coughing.

CHAPTER TWO

CATHAYAN SILKS CLOTHED the enormous bed, its frame
carved from pale Estalian wood. Its engraved surfaces
depicted mermen and other fabulous beasts of the sea
cavorting in a most unsettling pattern of intertwined tentacles and finned tails. Velvet drapes hung from the
canopy of the bed, pulled back and bound to the pillar-
like bedposts by silken cords. Sprawled amid the
opulence was a gigantic mound of humanity. Silk sheets
concealed his nudity, his sausage-like fingers depleting a
platter of soft-skinned grapes with the rapacity of a
Norse berserker in a convent. But even as he indulged his
hunger, the eyes that stared from his bloated face were
apprehensive, drifting helplessly across the visages of the
men who surrounded him.

'Well?' Baron Friedo von Gotz demanded at last, his
voice quivering in anticipation of an answer. The trio of
physicians glanced toward each of their confederates,
praying that one of the others would take the initiative.

The aged individual hovering on the left of the bed, as feebly thin as the baron was indulgent, was the first to blink, clearing his throat with a nervous croak.

'Well,' Doktor Kleist began, seeming to parrot the baron's uncomfortable tone. 'After a careful examination, we must accept that… That they are certainly boils, your excellency.' Kleist's hands spread outwards in a gesture of helplessness. Baron von Gotz growled and sputtered.

'Of course, there are many things that could mean, my lord,' the physician to the baron's right hastily squeaked, trying to forestall the nobleman's distemper. He was a bloated creature himself, as though in emulation of his aristocratic master. His girth strained at the velveteen waistcoat that encompassed his frame. Doktor Gehring felt the baron's hopeful gaze sweep back upon him. 'I should like to lance the pustules again and inspect the humor that is exuded by the wound.' The baron nearly choked on the fistful of grapes he was cramming into his face.

'Filthy leech!' he snapped. 'You've had enough of my blood this morning, you'll get no more.' He swung his attention to the doktor who had yet to speak. He was older than either of the others, his head bereft of hair, his garments simple and devoid of ornamentation. Doktor Stuber maintained a neurotic fastidiousness, keeping his entire body clean-shaven in order to provide no breeding ground for lice and fleas, drinking vinegar every morning in order to thin his blood and prevent it from overwhelming his heart. Popular legend had it that Stuber would burn his clothing after wear, refused to eat any meat unless he inspected the animal before it was slaughtered, and would boil his hands after touching another person to remove any taint of disease. Even now, Stuber was wringing his slender hands before him, as though trying to scrape the contagion from his fingers. Baron von Gotz regretted allowing the physician to speak as soon as his pallid mouth snapped open.

'They could be communal sores,' Stuber stated, with the self-righteousness of a street-corner prophet. 'I have warned his excellency against dallying among the rabble. They are a breeding ground for all sorts of filth.' Stuber visibly shuddered.

'I suggest your attitude become more helpful, herr doktor,' the baron warned, as Stuber's pale features faded to grey. 'I have plenty of room in the dungeons for malcontents. It is wrong to keep a hound in the kennel, he must be free to prowl and hunt.' The fat man's face broadened into a vain smirk. 'After all, even a fine woman like the baroness is not able to fulfil a robust appetite like mine.'

In truth, Friedo's wife had not allowed him to lay a hand on her since he'd bloated into 'something more often seen in a stockyard than a palace'. But Stuber's words gave the baron pause. Was that all that was wrong? Was it simply the mark of some unsightly social disease? Such a minor ailment might seem as welcome as a visit from the Emperor amidst the blight that hung over Wurtbad.

'That may indeed be all it is.' All heads turned toward the speaker, a tall, slender man who had been sitting in one of the leather-backed chairs scattered throughout the bedchamber. He was younger than the physicians, his face dominated by the massive black beard that tumbled down to his chest. A round cap topped his head, the border embroidered with a scrolling gold leaf that matched the rich colouring of his flowing robes. A tall staff of the same metal rested against the wall, rushing into his open hand as he rose from his seat, gesturing toward it. The three doktors grumbled and muttered, unimpressed by the wizard's flaunting of his sorcery. He noted their distaste and smiled, having as little use for them as they for him. It was time to undermine these fawning sycophants. They had misread their patient.

Baron von Gotz was not interested in platitudes and placebos this morning. He was frightened, as they knew he had good reason to be, though none was willing to confirm his fears. For no doktor could offer hope to the baron. That was the sole province of the wizard, who would use it to win favour with his patron.

'It may be all,' the wizard repeated. 'But can we afford to take that risk?' The question cut the fragile feelings of the physicians like a knife.

'And does Magister Furchtegott have some insight that he wishes to share with us?' Doktor Gehring demanded. 'Perhaps boil a few frog-legs into a broth and mumble a few elven words over it?' The comment brought chuckles from his fellow doktors, but the wizard was pleased to note the baron was not laughing. 'The solution to this problem requires scientific method, not arcane rites of dubious merit.' Though Gehring laced his words with scorn and derision, there was no hiding the uncertainty that undermined them. If the wizard's star were to rise, he could well guess at whose expense it would be.

'There are certain rites and spells that have great facility in healing.' Furchtegott's tone was precise and certain. 'Even working their magic against such noxious maladies as Stir blight.' The name of the dread disease chilled the air. The wizard was pleased to note the gleam of desperate hope rekindled in the baron's eyes.

'Forgive me, magister,' Gehring scoffed, 'I was unaware that you had any facility with medicine. I had always understood that the only wizards who made a practice of healing were those of the light order, not the mystics of the gold order.' But the doktor's sneer became an expression of alarm, when he saw the keen interest in the nobleman's eyes.

'Furchtegott, tell me what you need to work your spells,' the baron implored. The doktors began to sputter protestations, but the nobleman waved them away with an angry gesture.

'I shall need some rather expensive material components and, of course, the gracious indulgence of yourself, my dear baron.' Furchtegott struggled not to let the sense of triumph welling up within him become too obvious, though he was not entirely successful.

'Whatever you need, you shall have,' the nobleman swore.

'Oh yes,' the wizard thought, 'I am most certain of that.' Once he had cured the baron of this corruption of the flesh, Furchtegott would play the nobleman's gratitude for all it was worth. He would become the most powerful wizard in Wurtbad – possibly even in the entire eastern half of the Empire. He would have the ruler of a mighty city eating from his hand. Even the powerful Supreme Patriarch of Altdorf could not boast that same degree of autonomy and political influence. With the ruler of Wurtbad under his thumb, Furchtegott would be able to spend the wealth of an entire city to expand both his magical library and his knowledge, far beyond what he had been taught by the gold college in Altdorf.

But a moment of worry tugged at the wizard, his eyes lingering on the ugly boil just visible beneath the folds of fat dripping from the baron's chin. There was the small matter of curing the plague, something even the Temple of Shallya and all of the city's physicians had been unable to manage. Still, they did not possess the genius of Furchtegott. And they were trying to cure an entire city. Furchtegott needed to cure only one man.

True, the healing arts were not the central focus of a school of magic centred on the enchanted properties of gold, the most royal of metals, but Furchtegott had ideas about how to rectify this omission. There were not so many mystics and mages within Wurtbad that the court wizard of Baron Friedo did not know them all by name.

Many of them he counted as his only friends in the sprawling metropolis. Many nights had they discussed theories on the nature of magic, many times had they swapped pieces of occult knowledge.

Furchtegott conjured up one name in particular, an old wizard who no longer plied his trade but had relegated himself to the role of scholar and sage. Even if he no longer channelled the ethereal winds of magic through his old bones, he still owned a most impressive library. And there was one book, in particular, that Furchtegott recalled with a keen interest.

Hopefully, the old sage would allow his friend to borrow the tome. But if destiny decreed otherwise, Furchtegott was certain the baron's authority could make any such request quite compelling.

THE SPRAWL OF Wurtbad was a dark blemish upon the horizon, the first indication to Thulmann that the city was near. However, the witch hunter's attention was directed toward the more immediate activity unfolding upon the road ahead. Several dozen labourers in coarse woolen tunics were busily constructing a small watchtower from timbers they unloaded from wagons. Other men struggled to roll huge stones into the road, the beginnings of what promised to be a formidable obstruction. A large number of armed men were milling about, some of them sharpening their swords, others finding themselves a patch of shade to sit in. Thulmann was mildly alarmed to note that the uniforms they wore were not the colours of some petty baron or count, banishing his supposition that this was some minor noble's attempt to create a toll road. The rough uniforms were the green and yellow of Stirland's standing army, the uniform of the elector count's own troops.

Overseeing the operation was a mounted officer, his powerful build encased within a suit of steel plate. He watched the work crew with a keen interest, while also casting worried glances in the direction of Wurtbad. One of his soldiers, a rangy youth with a quiver of arrows hanging from his hip, rushed over and directed his attention to the two riders now approaching him.

'What do you make of this?' Streng asked, the words slipping from the corner of his mouth.

'No doubt we are about to find out,' Thulmann replied in the same subdued tone. He noted the sound of Streng moving in his saddle. Without turning his eyes from the approaching officer, he instructed his henchman to leave the crossbow where it was. 'Stirland is not a wealthy province. You can wager that any soldier armed with a bow brought it with him when he was inducted, and knows how to use it. I'd rather not end my days as a pin cushion, and I dare say a dozen arrows in your gut may prove an impediment to your drinking.'

The officer rode forward as the archers drew their bows. The raiment of a witch hunter was quite distinct. Thulmann knew there was no question that the officer had recognised him for what he was. It was why the man was riding forward to parlay, rather than chasing them off with a volley of arrows, though it seemed he was keeping that option open to him.

'Good day, templar,' the officer greeted Thulmann, halting the grey gelding he rode at several horselengths from the witch hunter.

'Good day, captain,' the witch hunter replied, noting the oak leaf badges upon the collar over the soldier's breastplate that displayed his rank. 'You look to be very busy here.' The officer's face grew solemn.

'Plague,' he said, letting the menacing word linger on the air. 'I fear that if you have business in Wurtbad you will not be able to pursue it. By order of the elector count, the city is under quarantine. No one goes in. No one comes out.'

Thulmann fixed the officer with a stare that had caused many a warlock or heretic cultist to break out in cold sweat. 'I am on the temple's business. I must go to the city to complete my holy work. You do your uniform credit by your efficiency, but I must ask that you let us pass.'

The officer shook his head. 'Did you not hear me? The city is infested with the plague. Graf Haupt-Anderssen does not want the contagion infesting the rest of the province, if it is not already too late. He has nearly two thousand men setting a cordon around the city and the river patrol is keeping ships away from the port.'

'I fear no pestilence,' Thulmann retorted. 'I am upon Sigmar's business. Surely the will of a god overrides the edict of a mere man, even if he is an elector count.'

'My apologies, templar, but I have my orders.' There was a tone of genuine regret in the officer's voice. 'I can let no one pass through the cordon.'

'Looks to me like you haven't finished setting up your cordon,' Streng piped up, pointing to where the work crews struggled to erect the tower and block the road. The officer shook his head. Sighing, he reached an autonomous decision.

'As you are going *into* the city, and you are a templar, I will not block your path. But I advise against it. The disease is decimating Wurtbad, they say. Hundreds are dead already, and it will only get worse. Especially once food becomes scarce and winter sets in.'

'Nevertheless, that is where my duty takes me,' Thulmann insisted. The officer moved his horse to one side of the road, waving back to his troops to allow the witch hunter to pass.

'A word of warning, templar,' the officer said. 'Once you pass my post, there is no return. My orders are quite clear. Even Sigmar himself will not find his way out of the city until the elector count lifts the quarantine.'

'I DIDN'T LIKE all that talk about plague,' Streng confessed once they were out of sight of the guard's post. 'Are you certain this is a good idea?' Thulmann gave his henchman a cold smile.

'Have faith, Streng,' the witch hunter told him. 'Sigmar protects his servants, perhaps he can spare some protection for you as well. And if that is not comfort enough, consider that, as a result of our activities in Klausberg, you'll be liberating some of the gold from the treasury at Meisser's chapter house.'

'Thin bit of good that will do me if all the whores have plague,' the mercenary grumbled. 'I was in Wissenbad when the Red Pox hit it. After a few months the beer was so scarce that two crowns could hardly buy a pint.' Streng leaned over in his saddle, spitting into the brush beside the road as though to rid himself of the memory. 'We should have gone back to Klausberg and laid low until the plague was done with Wurtbad.'

'We don't have the leisure to waste that much time,' Thulmann said. 'You seem to forget that we are still on the hunt.'

'Weichs?' The witch hunter nodded his head. 'I don't think he'd be fool enough to linger in a city infested by the plague,' Streng snapped back.

'Quite the contrary, the good doktor would probably find the pestilence a perfect cover for his own twisted activities,' Thulmann declared. 'He'd find any number of willing subjects for his experiments if he offered them a cure for the plague. Besides, we have other business in Wurtbad besides picking up the trail of Freiherr Weichs.'

'The book?' Streng sucked at his teeth, considering the unholy tome that brought ruin to the Klausner family.

'It's been safe in Wurtbad this long, surely a few months won't change matters.'

'You forget, the vampire is looking for it too,' Thulmann stated. 'He knows now that the Klausners no longer have it in their keeping. We can't take the chance that Sibbechai may find it before us, and a little thing like a plague isn't enough to keep him away from Wurtbad if he learns the book is there.'

'So where do we begin?' Streng demanded. It appeared there would not be one single night of drunken debauchery before getting back to work.

'You start by securing lodgings for us,' Thulmann told him. 'Don't skimp on stables for the horses. With plague abroad, I want them kept somewhere they are not likely to be slaughtered for their meat by an enterprising stablemaster. Then you will arrange for me to occupy my old rooms at the Seven Candles. I am sure the innkeeper will be pleased to see us back so soon.'

'And what will you be doing while I'm running your errands?' Streng said in a surly tone.

'Our first priority must be to locate Helmuth Klausner's spell book. Towards that end, I think it will be prudent if I visit our friend Captain Meisser. Even an incompetent fool like him must keep a record of licensed wizards operating in the city. The man we are looking for should be on that list.

'At least if he is still *in* the city,' Thulmann added.

FRITZ GOTTER LEANED a bandaged hand against the cold, stone wall as a wracking cough shook his body. The baker lifted his other hand to his mouth when the spasm had passed, hoping not to find blood trickling from it. His hope was in vain. The disease was chewing up his innards as surely as it was disfiguring his flesh. Thankfully it hadn't reached his face yet, allowing him to conceal his malady from his patrons. It was doubtful if anyone would buy bread from a baker whose face was covered in Stir blight boils.

The sickly baker descended the short flight of stairs to the cellar where he kept his supplies. With the quarantine in effect, no more ships were coming into the harbour, no supplies to feed Wurtbad's teeming masses. The demand for food was already rising as people began to stockpile rations against the winter. The quarantine was like tossing oil onto a fire. There was a great deal of money to be made – money that Fritz Gotter could use to pay for the plague doktor's regular visits.

Gotter sniffed at the tunic he wore beneath his apron, wincing at the smell. It still carried the lilac perfume scent left by the doktor after his visit. Gotter disliked the smell, it made him feel like a three-shilling tart down by the harbour. Still, it was a minor inconvenience when balanced against the prospect of a slow and horrible death.

The baker paused on the bottom step, allowing his eyes to adjust to the gloom. He could see the stacks of flour heaped in one corner, a few barrels of honey sitting beside them.

The sound of furtive scurrying made his face twist with disgust. The damnable rats were back. The filthy things were too shrewd to waste their time with Gotter's sawdust-ridden bread. No, they went straight for the flour, and never managed to stumble into the many traps the baker had set out for them. Sometimes it seemed to Gotter that the vermin were almost human in their intelligence.

He picked an old table leg from a small pile of junk beside the stairway, slapping the improvised cudgel into the palm of his hand. He had troubles enough without rats eating away at his income. But there would soon be a few less of the vermin to bother him.

The baker began to creep across the cellar, straining to prevent even the softest noise betraying his approach.

He knew that even in the dim light streaming down from the stairway, he'd be perfectly visible to the thieving rodents. His only chance to catch them would be if they remained occupied with their stolen supper. Gotter glanced down at the floor to ensure there was no clutter underfoot to stumble on. As he did so, the colour drained from his sickly face. A thin coating of dust covered the floor, remnants of the cheap mix that went into his bread. Something had disturbed that dust. There were tracks on the floor, the clawed footmarks of rats, only larger. Much larger.

Gotter peered into the darkness in the corners of his cellar, conjuring up shapes without form or distinction. His mind raced with horrors recollected from childhood, frightful stories told to terrify the unruly child. 'Be a good boy, Fritz,' his mother used to say. 'Or the underfolk will come and take you away.' The baker shuddered, tears rising unbidden to his eyes, blurring his gaze even as they darted from side to side, straining to see every inch of the cellar.

The faint scurrying persisted, and Gotter was certain he could smell something that was not flour nor sawdust nor the mustiness of the room. The stench of mangy fur, of rank verminous breath, of rotting meat caught between sharp fangs. A cough began to gather in his chest. The baker fought to contain the spasm, his eyes on those hideous tracks.

'Sigmar preserve me,' he prayed. 'I'll never take advantage of anyone that lives again. I'll make honest bread with real flour. Just let me make it back to the stairs. Don't let them see me.'

Even as the thought crossed his mind, there was movement among the shadows of the flour stacks. Red eyes gleamed out from the darkness, seeming to peer straight into Gotter's soul. The baker fought to move, tried to turn and flee back up the stairs, but the only response from his paralysed body was the trickle of urine that spilled down his leg.

The shadow began to slink forward. More red eyes winked into existence, glaring at him from the darkness. The cough he had been suppressing wheezed from his mouth in a choking rattle, its strength diminished by the terror surging through his mind. The shape became more distinct as it emerged into the dim light. Gotter tried to look away, tried to shut his eyes, but his body refused to obey even so small a command.

It was the size of a man. Its outlines suggested the basic human form. Tattered scraps of leather and filthy cloth clung to its shape after the fashion of a tunic and kilt. But it was not a man. Unclean brown fur covered most of its form, save where it faded to a mangy white upon its belly and throat. The hands were tipped with sharp claws, like obscene talons. From the creature's hindquarters, a long, naked tail twitched and writhed. Its face was pulled into a long muzzle, whiskers surrounding its nose, huge incisors protruding from its mouth. The red eyes considered him with pitiless malevolence, a spite beyond human comprehension.

The monster stalked forward, its movements cautious. Gotter almost gave a nervous laugh as he noticed the faint white powder staining the creature's muzzle, realising what had been stealing his grain and flour. But his paralysed body was too rebellious to embrace the onset of madness. The skaven raised its face, sniffing at the air. The monster gave voice to a sound part hiss and part squeak. Other lurking shadows skittered forward, revealing themselves as the creature's noxious kin. The first skaven scuttled right up to Gotter, its muzzle sniffing at his clothes. As the ratman hissed, two more of the monsters hurried forward.

A black paw pulled the table leg from Gotter's grasp, while other inhuman hands closed upon his shoulders and arms. Their touch snapped the baker from his paralysis. Gotter kicked and struggled in their grasp, a wretched moan quivering past his lips. But the skaven were unmoved, pulling him into the darkness. The sound of grinding stone rumbled through the cellar. Gotter watched in horror as a portion of the wall fell inward, revealing the black opening of a tunnel.

'Take-take,' the first skaven chittered. 'Doktor-man like-like. Grey seer like-like. Reward much-much.' The other rat-men laughed at their leader's pronouncement. Gotter joined their hideous merriment as his mind broke. The skaven, undisturbed by his madness, carried him forth into the tunnel.

'Fritz has been a bad boy, mummy,' Gotter giggled as the blackness loomed toward him. 'And now the underfolk have come to take him away!'

The baker's laughter faded as the door slowly closed behind him.

CHAPTER THREE

THE SUN RETREATED before the encroaching darkness, relinquishing its dominion like a vanquished prince. Shadows gathered about the narrow streets of Wurtbad, bringing with them the cold chill of autumnal night. People hurried back into the shelter of their homes, abandoning their streets to those bold enough to challenge the dark or rich enough to hire bodyguards. For night brought out the city's predators, its thieves and cutpurses, murderers and housebreakers. The night was their time and decent folk best stayed behind locked doors. With the plague abroad, the ranks of the desperate, the killers and looters, was swollen by wretched men looking not for the price of ale, but the price of bread. The city watch now patrolled in mobs of a dozen and more, and even they kept mostly to the well-lit streets, perfectly willing to allow the human scum to ply their nefarious trades in the side streets and back alleys.

A different sort of scum gathered in the shadows of an old guildhall. Seven men, their garb heavy to ward off the chill of night and black to blend into the shadows, traced patterns into the dust with their feet. They were old hands at villainy – cut-throats, kidnappers and worse. Their catalogue of sin was enough to shame Khaine, the lord of murder, down in his fiery hells. Yet even these men were uneasy, their shreds of conscience sickened by the acts perpetrated upon their own people these last weeks, and the deeds their hated master would still have them do. But the will to survive was stronger, a shackle their loathsome master had wrapped about each of their necks. A bond not one of the seven had either the courage or the decency to break.

The sound of a trapdoor slamming shut startled them. It brought the rogues around to face the archway that yawned at the rear of the meeting hall, behind the rotting remains of a wooden lectern. It was a portal that opened upon shadow, leading back into the old offices and storerooms of the guild. Now it led to the passageway that connected this place to the lair of their master. The thieves cast nervous looks at one another, some fingering the daggers and swords they wore beneath their cloaks. Their unease did not lessen as a tall, thin figure emerged from the darkness. The elderly man wore a heavy brown coat about his emaciated frame, a massive hat covering his head. The thieves bowed their heads slightly as their master stepped into the grey moonlight seeping through the guildhall's grimy windows.

'You are all here,' Doktor Weichs pronounced. 'Forgive my delay, but it is unfashionable for a gentleman to be punctual. As gentlemen yourselves, I am sure you understand,' he added with a withering sneer.

'You have brought it?' one of the thieves almost pleaded, his voice cracking. The other men remained silent, but the question was foremost in their own minds.

'Of course,' Weichs smiled, stepping toward the battered lectern from which the long dead guildmaster once conducted meetings. The doktor's gloved hand removed seven small clay bottles from his coat, setting each upon the pedestal. The man who had spoken took a step forward. The doktor shot him a stern glance. Chastised, the thief retreated, wiping his moist hands upon his cloak.

Weichs studied the desperate yearning within the feverish gazes of the men. He locked eyes with each of them, fairly daring them to rush forward and take for himself that which each needed, to quench the longing that burned within their veins. Finally, Weichs stepped back, waving his hand towards the podium. Like a pack of starving curs, the thieves rushed forward, shoving and pushing one another as they took up the bottles and hastily downed their contents.

When the last bottle had been emptied, Weichs clapped his hands together. A shadow detached itself from the darkness of the archway. Smaller than Weichs, its hunched shoulders were covered by a filthy black robe, its head by a black cowl. It walked with an unsettling motion that suggested the inhuman, an odour of decay clung to it like an unholy aura. From the front of the cowl, a rat-like muzzle protruded, its chisel fangs exposed. Hands covered in mangy brown fur hung from the sleeves of the robe, gripping the wooden box the creature held before it. The thieves backed away as the monster advanced, setting the box down beside the lectern.

'A fresh supply of medicine for you,' Doktor Weichs told his men. 'A fresh supply of medicine for Wurtbad.' Flashes of guilt flickered across the faces of the thieves.

'You know what to do,' Weichs said. The thieves nodded solemnly, hastily producing leather gloves from their pockets. From the linen bags they carried, the men removed strange leather masks. One of the thieves produced a tinderbox and each man came to him to light a hemp match. Another thief handed out small cloth knots that smelled faintly of lilac. Each thief lit the cloth, the smell of lilac intensifying as the fabric smouldered, then dropped the pomanders down the narrow beaks of their masks. With the scent of lilac filling the meeting hall, human faces disappeared behind bird-like visages.

Doktor Freiherr Weichs uttered a sardonic laugh as his plague doktors came forward, removing the bottles of poison the skaven had brought. Each man took one and placed it in the bag he had brought with him. They would spread out, filtering through the city like daemonic messengers. Heralds of hope to the terrified people of Wurtbad, all the while carrying the very doom that those same people feared. There was a sick irony behind such a deceit, such as only a man like Weichs could appreciate.

Of course, there was an even more subtle irony behind his hold over the men. They had been poisoned by Weichs soon after he arrived in Wurtbad, with a foul mixture of crushed warpstone and weirdroot in their beer and ale. A combination almost guaranteed to cause mutation, if it did not bring instant death. Weichs had happily informed these thieves and murderers of what was happening to their bodies, and why. He had told them the only way to protect themselves from total degeneration was with the potions only he could provide. There was no other choice. They had to become his slaves, if they did not wish to become monsters. Weichs chuckled again. There was an even more poetic irony in that the 'medicine' that held them to his will was nothing more than a smaller dose of the very concoction that poisoned them. His plague doktors worked to help him secure subjects for his experiments, little suspecting that they themselves were just part of one grand experiment.

The old man's features disappeared behind those of a bird of prey. The plague doktor reached down into the wooden box, removing the last of the black glass bottles. He turned the grey lenses of his mask upon the rat-man lingering nearby. 'I shall need six tonight,' Weichs stated, lifting his hands and displaying the appropriate number of fingers. The skaven chittered in its own vile language, holding up its malformed hands to display six clawed talons in response. Doktor Weichs turned away, marching from the guildhall with a deliberately unhurried pace.

The skaven's malicious gaze followed the plague doktor's departure. The creature laughed. It had not been deceived. It had smelled the fear beneath the man's calm demeanour. Trickles of saliva dripped from the creature's mouth. Perhaps the time would soon come when Skilk had no further use for the doktor-man.

Hungry thoughts crawled through its mind, the scent of lilac in its nose. The skaven scurried back into the welcoming darkness.

THE WITCH HUNTER and his companion rode in silence toward the city, sensing the grim atmosphere that hung all about them. Despair clung to the walls of Wurtbad, the unspoken dread that hangs over any community haunted by pestilence. The first sign of the corruption was outside the city walls, the great pit that yawned open in what had once been a wheat field. The plague pit had been filled with naked bodies, black robed priests of Morr chanting sombre prayers to sanctify the dead as they were hastily thrown in. Barrels of quicklime edged the pit, the priests tossing shovels of the powdery substance upon each body as it settled. Lit by flickering torches bound to tall poles, there was something spectral about the ghastly sight.

More sinister still had been the two silent, armour-clad warriors who stood guard over the priests and the plague pit. Encased in plate mail crafted from obsidian, they wore a hooded tabard not unlike the robes of the priests. They were the Black Guard, templars of Morr, god of death. Warriors who did not concern themselves with the living, only with the sanctity of the dead. The mere presence of such fearsome knights kept even the most distraught mother from reclaiming the body of her child from the plague pit, and their deadly reputation kept opportunistic grave robbers from plying their trade.

Within the city, the streets seemed even more desolate than Thulmann had remembered them. Sewage and waste had begun to accumulate in the gutters, a sure sign that the dung-gatherers and muckrakers were no longer active. The witch hunter shook his head as he wrinkled his nose at the stench. He had seen enough over the years to know that doktors and physicians were right to claim filth was a breeding ground for disease, and that sanitation was the best safeguard against pestilence. Altdorf's elaborate network of sewers had been constructed because of such concerns, as had those of Nuln. But Wurtbad, once the glittering prize of one of the poorest realms of the Empire, had no such system. Living in squalor, the men and women who cleaned the streets were among those hardest hit by the plague.

'Watch what you're stepping in!' Streng snarled at his mount, slapping its neck in irritation as the hoof squashed against the dirty cobbles. The bearded mercenary displaced his irritation from the animal and back to his employer.

'We were better off in that ghoul-nest Murieste,' the thug spat. 'They'll have to drown this place to get rid of the stink!' Thulmann gave his henchman a tired stare.

'Persevere,' the witch hunter told him. He turned his gaze back around, staring at the street sign the two riders had just passed. A clutch of shadowy figures lurked within the mouth of an alleyway. As Thulmann rode beneath one of the street lamps, and they saw what kind of a man they were shadowing, the ruffians slipped back into the darkness. 'If foul odours are the worst trial we face here, then Sigmar is being exceedingly kind.' Thulmann stared upwards at another street sign. With a slight pull on the reins he brought his steed to a halt.

'We part company here,' the witch hunter said. 'I must go and see Meisser. You go to secure lodgings at the Seven Candles.' Thulmann did not wait for Streng to reply, but carefully turned his horse about. Streng watched his employer ride off, listening to his mount's hooves upon the cobbles.

The mercenary's hand dropped to the purse swinging from his belt. There were still a few pieces of silver in the worn leather pouch. Enough for at least one night of debauchery. A lewd grin began to work its way onto Streng's face. Let Thulmann find his own rooms, the thug decided, he had his own priorities.

Streng looked at the shop signs swaying in the cold breeze, studying the pictures they bore. The ex-soldier had little skill with letters, but an excellent eye for detail and a prodigious knack for building maps within his head. By the signs, he recognised a chandler, a cobbler and a knife maker all in a row. That meant he was in the Griefweg neighbourhood. If he continued along this street, it would eventually connect with Stahlstrasse, and its over-abundance of taverns, brothels and gambling dens.

The Seven Candles could wait. Right now, Streng decided he needed ale, a wench – and more ale.

IT HAD BEEN almost ridiculously easy to slip past the guards on the city walls. With his pallid features, dark attire and the air of morbidity that hovered about him, the soldiers at the east gate had taken Carandini for one of the priests of Morr, returned from dumping corpses in the vast plague pit beyond the city walls. The rickety old cart and the stench of death emanating from the wooden box it carried only added to that illusion. Not that the soldiers would have been able to stop him in any event. Carandini was bringing something much worse than plague to Wurtbad, something that would have destroyed the guards as swiftly and ruthlessly as it had their fellows who maintained the quarantine.

The necromancer shuddered as he recalled the ease with which Sibbechai had killed them.

As the cart rumbled through the silent streets, Carandini heard the soft creak of the box opening and closing behind him. The chill of the night air increased, the reek of death became still more distinct. A grotesque shadow rose above the necromancer, then settled beside him on the seat of the cart.

'North,' the vampire voice rasped. Carandini stared at the monster, trying to read some expression in the fires that shone from the sockets of the ghoulish face.

'That takes us to the waterfront,' the necromancer protested. 'We will not find what we seek there.' Despite a lifetime spent delving into the black arts and the morbid rites of necromancy, despite years of forcing the simulacrum of life into rotting corpses, Carandini winced as the vampire's desiccated lips pulled back, exposing its over-sized fangs.

'First we find a safe place to hide my resting place,' the necrarch hissed. 'I would not want to secure the treasure after so many centuries only to be destroyed by the rising sun.' There was an unspoken threat behind Sibbechai's words. Carandini wondered if the monster intended to turn on him even before they had secured the book.

'Why the waterfront?' Carandini asked, trying to discern the vampire's intent.

'I hear much,' Sibbechai replied, 'even within a wooden box. The soldiers at the gate spoke of plague in the dockyards. The living avoid such places when they can. There will be many buildings abandoned by their cowardly owners. Plenty of places to hide.' A dry laugh, like the death rattle of a man choking upon his own blood, bubbled from the vampire's withered throat.

'Fear not, necromancer,' Sibbechai spat, 'once my grave is safely concealed, we shall find this wizard. Then we shall recover my book.'

THE CHAPTER HOUSE of the Order of Sigmar, headquarters of the witch hunters of Wurtbad and its surrounding districts, was exactly as Thulmann had first seen it several weeks previously. It was a squat, two-storey building with a gabled roof and a plaster icon of the twin-tailed comet looming above the main door, with no sign of the subtle decay and neglect that had started to gnaw at some of the surrounding streets. Leave it to Meisser to ensure the street in front of the chapter house was swept, the gutters mucked out and the walls scrubbed clean, Thulmann told himself. The man should have been a bureaucrat. An entire city rotting away around him, yet he found time to worry about dirty walls and muddy gutters.

A man like Meisser should never have risen to the rank of witch hunter captain. It was a hurried posting, whereby a heretic had been replaced by a lord protector who had himself been a heretic. Thulmann knew there was a faction within the Order of Sigmar that strove to redeem the late Lord Thaddeus Gamow's name, but charges of heresy rang a little too true. Indeed, posting a bullying, incompetent and ineffectual swine like Meisser to such an important rank in one of the Empire's larger cities was hardly the decision a capable lord protector would make. At best, it was an almost criminally stupid decision, at worst an act of sabotage, blackening the reputation of the Order by presenting a back-alley racketeer as its public face in Wurtbad. Thulmann wondered how many such suspect decisions Gamow had made. Certainly enough to make the Grand Theogonist believe the heresy rumours, and Volkmar was not a man to reach a decision without weighing all the evidence.

Still, perhaps there was something providential in Meisser's promotion. He was weak-willed and easily dominated, the kind of man who preferred to let others fight his battles for him. Although Meisser was witch hunter captain of Wurtbad, Thulmann had assumed command of his investigation of the scarecrow murders after deflating his pomposity with a few threats. Like all brutal, incompetent men who were given power only to abuse it, Meisser lived in terror of his superiors and of losing his prestigious position. Thulmann had exploited that fear before. He would do so again to find *Das Buch die Unholden*.

One thing Thulmann had to credit Meisser for was his excellent record keeping. It seemed every detail of every confession ever extracted during his tenure had been saved, to judge by Thulmann's previous inspection. A man with such a rat-trap mind could not fail to have a listing of licensed wizards and mystics among his documents. Wilhelm Klausner might have entrusted the unholy book to just about anyone, but something told Thulmann that his confidant was a practitioner of the arcane arts. There was nothing solid to lead him to such a conviction, only an idea that could not be rooted, however he tried to rationalise it away.

A wizard? Would Klausner really have entrusted a wizard with something as dreadfully potent as this grimoire was supposed to be? No witch hunter trusted those who dabbled in magic, for all magic was born of Chaos, the great enemy of Sigmar and of the Empire. Licensed wizards were barely tolerated but deemed a necessary evil by some, heavily monitored where possible, watched for the first hint of corruption. But Klausner had himself been corrupted, meddling with powers far more sinister than anything a student of the colleges of magic was permitted to call upon. Yes, such a man could very well have given *Das Buch die Unholden* to a wizard, reasoning that only such a man could keep it safe from Sibbechai.

Thulmann extracted himself from his thoughts, reining his horse before the main door of the chapter house. He dismounted, striding to the door, his gloved hand pounding on the stained oak. After a moment, an elderly servant opened the door, staring suspiciously until he recognised the Sigmarite emblems on Thulmann's hat and clothing.

'I've come to indulge Captain Meisser's hospitality,' Thulmann stated, stepping across the threshold. The old servant, Eldred, could not quite hide the smile fighting to appear on his face. After rescuing Meisser's investigation and bringing Chanta Favna to trial, Thulmann had become something of a hero in Wurtbad – not least to the men of the chapter house, who felt he had salvaged their honour along with the investigation.

'Welcome back, Brother Mathias,' the old man said, bowing his head. 'I'll have a boy take your horse to the stable.' The servant reached for Thulmann's hat and cloak, but the witch hunter waved him away. It was, perhaps, a little indulgent of him, but he wanted to present as imposing a presence as he could when he once again set eyes on Meisser.

'You'll find Captain Meisser in his study,' the old man told him. This time the smile couldn't be resisted. 'He has company already. A lady friend,' the servant grinned, hurrying away to arrange the care of Thulmann's steed.

Thulmann looked down the hallway that would conduct him to Meisser's study. A lady friend? Meisser had a decided lack of concern for the plague ravaging his city.

Even for a heretic like Gamow, it was an act of audacity to promote such a reptile to the rank of captain.

Thulmann did not bother to announce himself, but simply pushed open the door of the study. The room was opulently furnished, dominated by the massive wooden desk that sprawled across its centre. Bookcases crammed with folios and loosely bound documents sat at each flank. There had been at least one change to the décor. On the wall behind the desk had once hung a portrait of Meisser himself, which Thulmann had gently mocked upon his last visit. The witch hunter smiled to see that Meisser had had the painting removed.

There had been one other change. Meisser was not alone. Seated behind the desk was a striking young woman, her flaxen hair gathered about her face like the halo of a saint. A glass of wine rested among the clutter of documents across the surface of the desk. The deskwork commanded her complete attention and she did not look up as Thulmann made his entrance. The fawning figure that hovered about her, fetching documents from the shelves, did, however. Meisser looked despondent as he recognised his unexpected visitor.

'Br–Brother Mathias,' Meisser sputtered. 'I– we did not expect you to return so soon.' Meisser's words caused the woman to look up from her work. Her piercing gaze focused upon the visitor, a faint smile appearing on her face.

'Mathias Thulmann,' her soft voice observed. 'This is indeed an honour.' Thulmann removed his hat, handing the garment to Meisser. Meisser stared at it for a moment, before carefully setting it down in an unoccupied chair.

'It appears you have me at a disadvantage,' Thulmann silkily confessed. 'You seem to know me, but I can't remember our having met. I am certain I would not forget such an event.'

The woman rose from behind the desk. She was tall, with clothes more suited to a young rake out prowling the taverns than a woman of her station. Yet the incongruity did nothing to diminish her qualities. Knee-high boots and red leather breeches clung to her long, lean legs. A shirt of soft white fabric, its sleeves sporting the extravagant frills currently in fashion among the nobility, rose above the silver-trimmed belt that circled her slender waist. Above the shirt, she wore a black leather vest, the straps unbuckled where the garment constrained the swell of her breast. About her neck hung a brooch set in snakeskin, the rampant griffin insignia of Igor Markoff engraved upon the gleaming bauble. A heart-shaped face rose above the circle of snakeskin, framed by locks of flaxen hair.

Like a startled spider, Meisser scuttled out of the woman's way. She extended a delicate hand to Thulmann. 'Silja Markoff,' she introduced herself. 'I am the Lord High Justice's daughter,' she added when she saw his eyes grow thoughtful. 'You did a great service for my father by exposing the witch Favna.'

Thulmann lifted her hand to his lips. 'I did only what was expected of me,' he said. 'What my oaths have demanded I do.' A thin smile appeared on his hawkish face. 'So, tell me, what brings Silja Markoff to be entertained by the esteemed Captain Meisser at so lonely an hour?'

Seizing the opportunity, Meisser's nervous voice slipped in before she could compose an answer. 'I have decided to coordinate my current investigation with the Ministry of Justice. Lady Markoff is helping me examine the methods and procedures practised by my men. The Ministry is somewhat concerned that we are being more zealous than efficient in our work.'

Thulmann was quietly impressed. It was the closest to an admission of incompetence he had ever heard from

Meisser. The witch hunter turned his attention back to Lady Markoff. She must have had a very powerful personality to crush Meisser's arrogance so thoroughly. He could well understand why Markoff's daughter could also be his most trusted and capable agent.

'Captain Meisser is convinced that the plague afflicting Wurtbad is not a natural phenomenon,' Silja stated, tossing one solitary crumb of comfort. 'In the event that he is correct, my father wants to assist in his investigation. To that end, I have been examining the records of his investigation so far. Pointing out his errors,' she shot the witch hunter captain a scornful glare, 'and his excesses.'

Thulmann could well imagine. Unable to uncover Chanta Favna and her sorcerous assassin, Meisser had resorted to torturing and executing anyone even rumoured to be a witch, condemning far too many innocent men, women and children to death. It seemed Meisser was making just as little progress with the plague and had resorted to his old tactics of deception. Thulmann's face mirrored the disgust in Silja's eyes.

'That explains my presence,' she said. 'What brings you back to our city, Brother Mathias, at so inopportune a time?'

'My investigation in Klausberg has led me back to Wurtbad,' Thulmann declared simply. 'I had hoped the chapter house might be able to assist me in my labours.'

'Of course,' Meisser replied, far too hastily for Thulmann's liking. The man's motivation was as transparent as the lens of his spectacles. His own brutal investigation had degenerated into such a fiasco that the Ministry of Justice was taking control of it. Meisser now saw a chance of redemption by insinuating himself into Thulmann's work. 'Anything the chapter house can do for you, you have but to ask it.' His servile smile was nauseating. Thulmann was happy that Streng wasn't present. The mercenary would have wasted no time wiping that look from Meisser's face.

'You can help me,' Thulmann said. 'The man I am looking for is probably a licensed wizard.' Meisser nodded his head like an agreeable idiot. 'I want to go over the records of every one of them residing in Wurtbad.' The smile faded from Meisser's face. There were not many wizards in the city, but they were powerful men, and not just in the field of magic and sorcery. They also wielded considerable influence as advisors and helpmates to the big guilds and trading houses. Even Baron von Gotz had a wizard among his court. Hunting down and bringing to justice lone witches and warlocks was one thing, but Meisser was not terribly eager to begin harassing real wizards. The thought of the political scandal the mystics might bring crashing down about his ears made the prospect of fighting Chanta Favna's blade-handed scarecrow seem pleasant by comparison.

'I shall get the documents you require,' Meisser said, his enthusiasm already curling up and dying inside him. The witch hunter captain rummaged about the shelves of the bookcases for several minutes. He returned with a bundle of parchment sheets bound by string.

'We have complete histories of each wizard, at which of the schools of magic he studied, who his instructors were, and his accomplishments after being released from the colleges of magic. We need to know, of course, who it is we are dealing with, should one of these men become corrupted by the dark forces they study and turn renegade.' Thulmann waved Meisser aside, grabbing the stack of papers.

The witch hunter smiled as he read the topmost document. Sigmar was truly going out of his way to assist him. Some names had been crossed out with thick black strokes as the wizards they represented had died or moved out of the city. But one name stood out and Thulmann knew it was the one he was looking for.

'Wolfram Kohl,' Thulmann read. Wilhelm Klausner's steward and accomplice in his acts of heresy had been a man named Ivar Kohl. It couldn't be a coincidence. The witch hunter handed the stack of documents back to Meisser, his finger resting on the name. 'I want to know everything that you know about this man.'

STRENG LED HIS prize away from the Splintered Skull tavern, his arm wrapped about her waist. The mercenary greeted the few men who crossed their path with a predatory scowl that made them increase their pace. He studied the shop signs swaying in the cold night breeze. Getting his bearings, the thug turned his companion toward a narrow alley that opened onto the street. The woman hesitated.

'Just what kind of tart do you take me for?' her shrill, girlish voice demanded. 'I ain't no animal to be rutted in some gutter!'

'I'll wager you've done worse,' the mercenary chuckled, his hand dropping from her shoulders to deliver a playful swat to her flank. The harlot squealed in surprise. 'Worry not. I know a place where the rooms are cheap and the fleas are small.' Streng slapped the woman's backside again. 'Now move your arse along before I lose my patience!' he growled. The woman squeaked in mock fright and hurried into the alleyway. Streng chuckled, following her into the darkness. Their laughter died, however, when his companion uttered a gasp of alarm, then a grunt of pain. Streng hurried forward, drawing his sword from its sheath.

Around the dark corner of the alley, he found the woman sprawled on the cobbles, curled into a foetal position, her arms cradling her chest. Standing over her was a man in a ragged black coat. Streng recognised him as the weak-looking young man who had been entertaining the woman in the Splintered Skull, before Streng had appropriated her. A muddy boot kicked at the woman's back before he turned to face Streng.

'We'll finish our talk in a moment, strumpet,' the rogue snapped. 'After I have words with your lover man.' Streng glared at his foe, taking a few careful steps to place the corner of the alleyway within easy reach. It was all well and good to fight for the honour of a lady, but Streng didn't think his companion had all that much honour – nor was she much of a lady. If Black Coat decided to produce a pistol from his pocket, a quick dive and an even faster sprint would see Streng back on the main street.

'Grew some bollocks, I see,' Streng snarled. Black Coat's face split in a hateful glare. The man's hand fell to his side and Streng braced himself to dive. He almost sighed with relief when he saw his enemy pull a sword from its sheath.

'I don't brawl with scum,' Black Coat announced. 'I kill them.' A murderous smile twisted Streng's features.

'Funny,' Streng growled, 'I've always try to follow the same rule.'

CHAPTER FOUR

A DARK FIGURE detached itself from the shadows, slinking across a black alley to conceal itself in an arched doorway. The heavily cloaked man cast a furtive sidelong gaze back along whence that he came, flicking a stray lock of greasy hair from his pallid, sickly face. Satisfied that he was unobserved, he gave his attention to the ironbound oak door looming beside him. Pale hands fumbled in the innards of a leather satchel, producing a desiccated claw bound in mouldering wrappings.

Strange, unclean words belonging to a tongue known only to the blackest sorcerers slithered from the necromancer's lips. Carandini's eyes blazed in the shadows as the unholy power passed through him. The claw, the dismembered hand of the tomb king Nehb-ka-Menthu, began to scratch at the oak, digging runes and hexes into the wood. Carandini smiled as he read the ancient hieroglyphs. The wizard's house was indeed protected by wards, but they were weak and feeble, wasted by neglect.

How very different from the protective spells the Klausners had woven about their own home. In some ways, the necromancer almost felt insulted, that final victory should be bestowed upon him with such ease.

The claw grew still, and Carandini restored it to his bag. More words dripped from his tongue and the hieroglyphs scratched upon the door flared suddenly into flame. A moment passed and the flames were gone, leaving behind blackened outlines of the symbols. The necromancer removed a small packet of grey powder from one of the pockets concealed within his heavy cassock. The mummy's hand had done its work, calling upon the dread sorcery of the long-dead Nehekhara. The feeble wards placed upon the house were no more.

Carandini cast the powder upon the bronze lock that glared from the side of the door. The necrotic powder worked its fell magic, devouring the metal and the wood surrounding it, corroding both surfaces as though the weight of a thousand centuries had aged them in an instant. The necromancer pushed open the door as the foul, black residue of the lock dripped to the ground.

He stepped across the threshold, into the small parlour that connected the dreary side entrance to the inner chambers of the house. Carandini enjoyed the faint, musty smell of old books and piled dust. The smell of scholarship. For a sorcerer, he believed, it was the smell of treasure.

Thoughts of avarice and power withered within the crooked corridors of Carandini's mind, as another smell overwhelmed the mustiness. The odour of death and decay pounded his senses, his pale skin prickling with goosebumps as an unnatural chill crawled up his flesh. Even the feeble light cast by the streetlamp outside seemed to grow dimmer. Without turning around, Carandini knew there was something standing behind him. Just across the threshold, something tall and gaunt and unholy.

'Do not think to cheat me, necromancer,' Sibbechai's rasping voice snarled. Carandini turned upon his partner, his smug smile fighting against his unease.

'Such a strange peculiarity,' he mused. 'The great Sibbechai, lord of sorcery and the black arts. A centuries-old vampire with the strength of ten men in his withered arms. Yet you stand helpless to enter a simple dwelling.' His smile grew as he considered the curse that was part of the necrarch's taint. So strong was the hate of life within the necrarchs that the creatures were incapable of entering any structure that man made his home.

Some said the curse had been placed upon the vampiric sorcerers by the gods themselves, that the necrarchs might be thwarted in their diseased schemes. Others held that the power that bound them came from a far fouler source – the accursed one, the supreme necromancer, Nagash the Black, that his undying slaves might never again linger among the living and be distracted from their profane studies. That no seed of sympathy might somehow take root within the putrid remnants of their hearts. Whatever its source, no vampire sorcerer could cross any man's threshold unless first invited by one who was already inside.

'Reconsider this folly, mortal,' the vampire warned, its smouldering eyes glowing in the dark. Carandini's bravado flickered as the corpse-like visage snarled at him. Sibbechai's burning eyes seared into the necromancer's brain, driving foreign thoughts into his mind. 'Invite me across,' Sibbechai repeated.

For a moment, Carandini's body trembled, struggling to resist the command that thundered inside his skull. Slowly, the Tilean's lips parted. Against his will, words began to wheeze from his mouth. He tried to force them back down, but they were spoken before they could be stopped. 'Enter this house freely, and of your own accord.'

Like a weary moth, Carandini crumpled to the floor, hands clutching at his throbbing head. The gaunt shadow that had been framed in the doorway swept across the threshold, the vampire lingering only to give its duplicitous companion a further command.

'Wait outside and keep watch,' Sibbechai hissed. Carandini turned his face to glare at the monster. The vampire bared its fangs in a bestial snarl. 'Beware, necromancer. Your usefulness is now diminished. Soon you may be at the end of it.'

Carandini managed to linger long enough to watch the vampire pass through the far door and into the hallway beyond. Then, compelled by the necrarch's will, he crept back into the street.

The necromancer's thoughts were black. His hand continually closed about the tiny bottle of holy water sewn into the sleeve of his cassock. It would have been much easier to take the book from Wolfram Kohl, both for himself and for the doomed wizard. Now they would both have to face the vampire. After Sibbechai's recent display, Carandini was less certain than ever about his chances against the necrarch.

MATHIAS THULMANN STALKED the deserted night streets like a hound that scents the nearness of its prey. Wolfram Kohl. Brother of Ivar Kohl. Student of the amethyst college in Altdorf. Amethyst, that school of wizardry closest of all to the forces of dark magic and necromancy. The witch hunter had thought Wilhelm Klausner an idiot to entrust a potent work like *Das Buch die Unholden* to a wizard, but he must have been mad to entrust it to one who was practically a necromancer already.

How many years had Kohl been in possession of the forbidden text? How many years had the wizard spent studying its abominable rites and blasphemous incantations? According to Meisser's records, Kohl had suddenly stopped practising the arcane arts five years ago. Amethyst wizards were in high demand, for their profane spells could call upon the spirits of the dead to communicate with the living. For the bereaved, one last moment with a departed loved one was worth any price. When he turned his back on his art, the wizard ended a very profitable series of séances. Thulmann knew even wizards placed some value on gold – if only to fund their arcane studies. Wolfram Kohl must have had a good reason to quit his trade. Was it to devote himself body and soul to studying Helmuth Klausner's unholy spellbook?

Thulmann kept one eye on the men following him through the lonely streets. Bearding a wizard in his lair was always a dangerous proposition. Supernatural powers could give the wizard prior warning of a witch hunter's approach, while an infinite number of spells and wards could be called upon to protect him and bring harm to his enemies. Not a few witch hunters refused to pursue such a course without a wizard of their own, to fight magic with magic. It was particularly common in Altdorf, where the colleges of magic and their students were readily available. Thulmann had always found such tactics unconscionable. Even more so now, for it was alarmingly similar to the heresy that had consumed the Klausner line. He preferred to put trust in his courage, and faith in the grace of Sigmar, not the unclean spells of conjurers.

Even so, he would have felt better with more men. After discovering the existence of Wolfram Kohl, Thulmann had ordered Meisser to round up every available witch hunter. But only five could offer their services, the others strewn about the city conducting investigations on Meisser's behalf. Two were not unknown to Thulmann, his comrades in arms at the conclusion of the scarecrow murders, who had helped to surround the hovel of Chanta Favna. He could be certain they would stand firm if his worst fears about Kohl proved well founded. There were two apprentices who seemed cut from the same cloth, but then he had seen expensive equipment and exhaustive training shatter before the powers of Old Night too many times. The last was the elderly warrior priest Father Kunz, attached to the witch hunters by the Wurtbad temple of Sigmar.

His sixth conscript from the chapter house was less agreeable. It was only natural that Witch Hunter Captain Meisser should volunteer to assist. Indeed, the wily Meisser had suggested that matters may become politically difficult for the visiting witch hunter, should he refuse. The balding Meisser, with his piggish eyes, was an indifferent swordsman – doubtless even more so with one arm still injured from his encounter with Chanta Favna's automaton. Still, Thulmann was somewhat relieved by the offer, if only because it seemed Meisser was more concerned for Thulmann's welfare than he himself.

The reason for Meisser's concern walked with all the dignity of an emissary from the royal court of Bretonnia, her hobnail boots scratching on the cobbles as she unerringly picked out the cleanest places to set her feet. Silja Markoff had insisted upon accompanying the witch hunters, stating that her role as liaison between the Ministry of Justice and the Order of Sigmar demanded no less. Thulmann was of a mind to refuse, but swiftly relented when he considered the politics involved. He was in no mind to play games with the ministry when his quarry was so close at hand. Besides, Silja Markoff had brought her bodyguards with her. Thulmann recognised that two highly-trained soldiers from the Ministry of Justice may well have their uses.

A sharp curse made Thulmann turn around. A faint smile flickered on his face as he saw Silja wipe something from her boot. It seemed her unerring footwork had at last deserted her. The witch hunter sighed as he watched the woman discard her soiled handkerchief. When they arrived at their ultimate destination, he hoped she at least would have the good sense to stay out of the way.

'You are wise to keep an eye on her,' Meisser whispered from beside him. 'She's trying to weaken the order here in Wurtbad, to subvert our authority on behalf of her father.'

Thulmann arched an eyebrow, staring intently at Meisser's swinish face. There was no mistaking the innate cunning he saw there. 'Indeed,' he mused. 'She's told you as much, has she?'

'Actions speak more loudly than words,' Meisser stated. 'She's been a thorn in my side ever since the quarantine was established. Getting in the way. Hindering the investigation.' His tone became indignant. 'As though secular authority has any power over our order.' Meisser's clammy hand gripped Thulmann's arm, pulling him closer. The witch hunter looked back to see the suspicious, disapproving look that Silja directed at them.

'You might not know it, Mathias,' Meisser confided, 'but you are very highly thought of in certain circles. Our uncovering of the witch and her scarecrow impressed not a few of Wurtbad's notables.' Thulmann fought to control his disgust as Meisser referred to *their* tracking down of the witch. It had been Thulmann who discovered the fiend behind that series of ghastly murders. Left to his own devices, Meisser would have continued torturing and executing innocents until the return of Sigmar. 'Not a few regard you as some sort of hero.' Again, the cunning gleam entered Meisser's eyes. 'Now, if you were to protest this unprecedented intrusion into our order's affairs, I am certain some action would be taken.'

'So that's it,' thought Thulmann. 'Get me to fight your battles for you.' He detached Meisser's hand and stepped away. 'Captain Meisser, I've not been back in Wurtbad long, but it seems that there are a great many people here who feel the city needs to be protected from the Order of Sigmar.' His withering hiss of contempt silenced any retort. 'But who, Captain Meisser, is going to protect the Order of Sigmar from *you*?'

As Thulmann left the insulted captain to brood on his scorn, he took a backward glance at Silja Markoff. She nodded respectfully at the witch hunter as their eyes met. Thulmann returned the gesture.

He looked out on the city's horizon to the distant artisans' quarter. Wolfram Kohl's house would be found there, and his quest to destroy *Das Buch die Unholden* would soon reach its conclusion. After so much darkness, so much doubt, the prospects were finally starting to look brighter.

THINGS WERE STARTING to look very bleak, the mercenary decided, as he beat back the blade of his enemy. Streng's relief that the young tough he'd insulted had equipped himself with a sword rather than a pistol, had quickly evaporated on his discovery that the rogue was more than proficient. Streng's left arm bled from where Black Coat's sword had glanced off his flesh. The cut in his side was deeper. Streng knew that if he didn't stem the blood seeping through his armour, it would not be long before he had no strength to lift his own blade.

'Where's your glib tongue now?' Black Coat was sneering, parrying Streng's retort with an insulting degree of ease. 'Isn't it funny how all the bravado drains out of a man once he starts to soil his breeches?'

Streng growled at his antagonist, his sword managing to slip past his enemy's guard and scrape along his forearm. Black Coat gasped in pain, flinching and transferring his blade to his uninjured hand. Streng grunted with satisfaction. Black Coat might be skilled, but he was no veteran duellist. He was allowing his over-confidence to make him sloppy, his sword making flashy attacks that left gaps in his defence.

'Don't like the sight of blood, eh?' jeered Streng, mustering his strength in the brief respite his enemy had allowed. Black Coat's face contorted into a look of such intense rage that Streng was reminded of a Norse berserker. With a bestial snarl, the youth leapt to the attack once more.

Streng blocked it with his own blade, letting Black Coat's charge carry him forward, so that the faces of both men were scant inches from each other. Streng hawked phlegm into his mouth and spat the foulness in his adversary's face. Black Coat recoiled in disgust, momentarily blinded as he wiped the spit from his eyes. He still managed to block Streng's retaliation, the mercenary's sword ringing as it crashed against Black Coat's parrying blade. But the attack was only a feint. With a savage kick, Streng's heavy boot smashed into Black Coat's knee, breaking the joint with an ugly popping sound.

Black Coat spilled to the cobbles like a sack of grain, a dry shriek ripping through his lungs. Streng was on him in an instant, his boot attacking the side of the youth's neck, choking the scream as it snapped. Black Coat's body writhed in silent pain until Streng's sword slashed downward into his spine. The mercenary had seen far too many mortally wounded men muster enough strength to finish off their killer. The thug's cold eyes watched as the spasms that wracked Black Coat's broken frame gradually subsided. Only when they had stopped did Streng let his sword drop, hands clutching at the gash in his side.

With a moan of pain, he crashed to the street. The mercenary tore a strip from his undershirt, prodding it

into the gap that Black Coat's sword had slashed through
his leather armour. The cut wasn't deep, it had missed
any vital organs, but it could prove no less fatal if he did
not stem the loss of blood. He'd have to get the harlot to
help him, to send her for a chirurgeon. Streng turned his
face back to where he had seen Black Coat kicking the
woman. He groaned in disgust, but not surprise. The
whore had not lingered to see who would emerge victo-
rious from the back alley duel. She was probably already
spending Streng's money in some tavern.

'Well,' Streng spat at the corpse lying beside him. 'The
way I see it, you owe me a debt.' The thug grunted in
pain as he rolled onto his side and crawled over to Black
Coat's body. Bloodied hands pawed through the dead
man's clothing. Streng grinned as he removed a small
purse, its contents jingling with coins. He was less certain about the purpose of the leather mask he found
hidden under the black coat – a long, hook-nosed object
that reeked of lilac. Streng tossed it aside and continued
his search, removing a small linen bag from the dead
man's belt. It contained a bottle. The smile that greeted
the discovery of the money pouch echoed across the
thug's harsh features. But as he removed the bottle from
its wrapping, the smile faded. The dark glass vessel was
empty, but it was not this that alarmed Streng. There was
an air about it, a taint that Streng had experienced many
times since pledging his service to the witch hunter. It
was the stench of sorcery, the cold chill of black magic.

Streng hastily replaced the bottle within its wrapping.
The witch hunter would want to examine it, to know
more about the man who had carried such a talisman.
The mercenary pawed once more at the corpse. He
recoiled in horror as his probing hand discovered a massive, wormy growth that sprouted from the dead man's
belly. No simple mugger or cutpurse, he was something
unclean. The dead man had been a mutant! In a frenzied

motion, Streng scraped the blood from his hands with the dead man's coat.

The mercenary gathered the bottle and the strange leather mask from the cobblestones and painfully lifted himself to his feet. Thulmann might even see fit to give him a bonus for his troubles. The thought cheered his dark mood somewhat. With one hand trailing along the wall of the alley to support him, Streng slowly made his way back to the street. Between the witch hunter's bonus, and what he had looted from the mutant's corpse, he'd have a grand time once he was back on his feet again.

Allowing, of course, that he was able to find a healer before he passed into the arms of Morr from loss of blood.

MATHIAS THULMANN PAUSED outside the door of the wizard's dwelling. The stench of magic was in the air, the noxious taint of unnatural power. Even the most untutored of men could have sensed it. The unseen aura of sorcery was what made even the lowliest animal loth to approach the domicile of a wizard. Thulmann stared up at the looming façade of the house, watching the flicker of a streetlamp cast eerie shadows upon a plaster gargoyle. His expectations were uncertain, but he looked for some outward sign of the corruption that raked its spectral claws against his nerve endings. It was more than the foulness and decay that characterised the magic of Amethyst wizards. An older, darker energy seemed to crawl from the very walls of the house. Thulmann had wondered if his fears were correct, if Wolfram Kohl had been fool enough to dabble into the forbidden power that had been entrusted to him. Now it seemed he had his answer.

The witch hunter did not have long to ponder his fears, before Meisser's swaggering frame squirmed his way past him. The captain's hand gripped the brass knocker that sprouted from the front door and delivered a sharp, imperious report. Meisser called out sharply, 'Wolfram Kohl. By the authority of the Temple of Sigmar, you are commanded to open this door.'

An animalistic snarl of frustration hissed from Thulmann as he shoved the meddler aside. Any chance of taking the wizard unawares was now completely lost. 'Idiot!' he spat at Meisser, drawing one of his pistols from its holster. Without hesitation, Thulmann fired the weapon into the lock, his boot smashing into the ruined mechanism. The door crashed inward. Thulmann stepped inside, shouting back to the startled men who had been following him.

'Three of you.' he snapped. 'Around to the sides and back. Make certain he doesn't slip away.' Without waiting to see who would execute his commands, Thulmann raced into the shadowy hallway.

THE HALLWAY OPENED upon a large parlour, its wooden floors furnished with heavy rugs, its walls concealed behind shroud-like drapes of black cloth. A small fire slowly smouldered within the fireplace that separated the drapes, a claw-footed couch and a cluster of chairs arranged about the hearth. The witch hunter's eyes darted across the chamber. He noted the crystal decanter standing upon a small table, and the glass goblet shattered on the floor beside it, a pool of Estalian brandy slowly seeping into the rug. A richly upholstered footstool had been kicked onto its side, and the rugs around it were clearly disordered. Someone had quit his habitat in a most reckless fashion.

Thulmann took another step into the parlour, fingers wrapped about the grip of his pistol. His eyes studied the room, his ears keen for any sound. But only the soft crackle of the fire competed with his breathing. Thulmann's eyes narrowed as he observed the flicker of the flames. The sound of footsteps intruded upon him. Meisser and Silja appeared at the parlour's entrance, each with an underling hovering behind them like a shadow. Thulmann lifted his hand, motioning for them to keep silent.

Removing his calfskin glove, he reached toward the draped wall. He could feel the faint touch of cold air caressing his palm, confirming his observation that the fire was reacting to a draught. Thulmann gripped the drape, pulling it toward him, exposing the doorway it concealed. He had known, of course, that the hidden walls would hide a number of doorways, a simple measure by the wizard to disorient any unwelcome visitors without calling upon sorcery. The wizard also would have known that a draught from an open door would make a secret portal much easier to find. It was either careless or maliciously deliberate. Did the wizard intend for his unwanted guests to follow after him?

'Two of Meisser's men are watching the sides of the house,' Silja whispered. 'One of mine is watching the back.' Thulmann tugged the black drape from its fastening, letting the heavy fabric crumple to the floor. The witch hunter glanced down at his pistol, assuring himself the hammer was still primed, the flashpan secure. He bestowed a grim smile upon Silja.

'I don't think our sorcerous friend intends to escape,' he told her. The words brought a nervous sweat beading onto Meisser's forehead.

'What – what does the swine hope to accomplish then?' Meisser asked. It was one thing to stalk a wizard when the roles of hunter and prey were clearly established. For all his political machinations, Meisser was uncomfortable when things became too complicated.

'There is only one way to find out,' Thulmann observed. He placed his hand upon the half-shut portal. The door creaked inward. Finding no sorcerous flame in the darkness, the witch hunter ducked into the opening. He found himself in a narrow hallway, with doors spaced across its length. Ahead of him he saw another chamber, the dim flicker of firelight dancing across its walls. Thulmann's gloves creaked as his grip on his pistol tightened and his steps grew hurried. In the flickering light he could see bookcases, their shelves bulging with leather-bound tomes. Behind him, he could hear the others follow.

It was Wolfram Kohl's library, of that he had no doubt. It reached upward for two storeys, every inch of wall space consumed. A wrought iron staircase wound its way upward from the centre of the room to merge with the narrow walkway that provided access to the upper tier. Against one wall, a bronze brazier, its bed of coals covered by a crystal hood, provided intermittent illumination. Thulmann stepped inside, eyes prowling amidst the shadows.

His gaze fell upon the broken, ragged thing lying upon the walnut desk that reposed near the room's north wall. Its sombre robes were in keeping with the grim raiment of an amethyst wizard, its pallid skin and weak frame the marks of a scholar. Its face resembled that of Ivar Kohl. The man Thulmann had been so anxious to subdue before he could unleash the profane lore of *Das Buch die Unholden*. Kohl's back was snapped like a twig, his neck twisted like that of a slaughtered hen.

Thulmann stared at the body, for once in sympathy with Meisser. Things were becoming complicated again, and he did not like it. Like an arrow hurled by Sigmar himself, Meisser's records had pointed the way to Wolfram Kohl. But now, the arrow was broken.

From the corner of his eye, Thulmann saw a withered apparition appear from the shadows around the bookcase. The gaunt, unspeakable form lunged at him with impossible speed. Talons, black and hard like the backs of beetles, reached for Thulmann's throat. Instinct saved the witch hunter's life, as he threw himself over the desk, spilling the ruined corpse of Wolfram Kohl onto the floor. In his wake, claw-like hands splintered the wood of the desk, shredding it as though it were paper.

Thulmann rolled onto his back, aiming and firing his pistol in one smooth motion. But the instincts of his attacker were just as keen, the silver bullet passing within inches of its skull-face as the monster dodged aside. Torn paper exploded from the far side of the room as the shot burrowed into a bookcase.

'Again you place yourself between me and what is mine!' the vampire snarled, eyes blazing from the pits of its face. 'You shall not do so a third time, witch finder!' it spat.

Sibbechai! By what dark and unholy arts had the creature been led to Wolfram Kohl's door? It removed even the faintest doubt that *Das Buch die Unholden* had been entrusted to the late wizard. But such logical reasoning would mean little if Thulmann was to allow his throat to be torn out. He ripped his sword from its sheath, glaring defiantly at the undead abomination. A wary quality entered Sibbechai's expression, for the necrarch remembered the weapon well. Vampire and witch hunter glared at each other, each waiting for the other to make the first move and the first mistake.

'Shoot!' Silja's quivering voice cried out. 'Kill it!' Thulmann looked past the vampire to see her standing just inside the room. Behind her, Meisser and his two witch hunters were dragging pistols from their holsters. Their movements may as well have been those of men wading through a bog. To the vampire, they might as well have been standing still.

The monster spun around, a snarl ripping through its withered lips, its shroud-like robe whipping the air. Sibbechai prepared to lunge at its new foes when Father

Kunz's elderly face appeared behind the witch hunters. A small, silver twin-tailed comet icon flew from his hand as his mouth moved in prayer. The holy symbol was swatted aside with disgust by the vampire, but Sibbechai hissed in pain, acrid smoke sizzling from its dried flesh where it had touched. A deeper malice blazed from the vampire's eyes.

With a roar and a crack, the bullet from Meisser's pistol slammed into Sibbechai's chest, knocking the vampire back. The other witch hunters added their fire to the small fusillade, both shots smashing into the vampire's withered frame. Sibbechai curled its torso toward its midsection. A wracking, malevolent laugh oozed from the vampire. Straightening, it smiled at the men who were shocked by the vampire's vitality.

'Think your common pig iron is enough?' Sibbechai spat. Before the vampire could demonstrate its undiminished strength, Thulmann leapt upon it from behind the desk. The templar's momentum drove the steel of his sword deep into the necrarch's body, impaling its midsection. Sibbechai roared in agony, clawed hands grabbing Thulmann's shoulders and flinging him across the room. The witch hunter crashed against one of the bookcases, head ringing from his violent impact.

The vampire staggered away from the desk, twisting its body in a desperate effort to release the sword embedded in its flesh. Seeing the monster's weakened condition, Silja and her bodyguard charged forward, blades gleaming in the flickering light. The back of one hand smashed into the woman's chest, hurling her backward as though kicked by a horse. Claws ripped the face of her guard, his sword falling as he tried to push his ruined eyes back into his skull. The two witch hunters hurrying to support Silja's attack met similar resistance. One man lay in a pile of limbs and gore, his belly ripped open by the vampire's supernatural strength, the other was fortunate to escape with a fractured collarbone.

Empowered by the scent of blood in the air, Sibbechai's claws closed about the weapon trapped in its flesh. With a savage growl, the vampire ripped it free, pulling its length from the side of its body. Smoke rose from the wound as Thulmann's blessed sword clattered to the floor. The vampire's smouldering gaze burned as the witch hunter slowly rose. Then Sibbechai's eyes darted toward the hallway.

'Don't let it escape!' Thulmann shouted, but the vampire was already in motion. Like a thunderbolt of darkness, Sibbechai swept into the corridor, swatting Meisser aside like an irritating insect as the captain fumbled to reload his pistol. Father Kunz, striking at the monster with his staff, was rewarded with a torn throat. From deeper in the house came the sound of shattering glass, punctuated by a short scream from outside. As Thulmann staggered across the library to recover his sword, he knew it was already too late. Once more, Sibbechai had disappeared into the night.

Thulmann looked at the carnage all around him. Silja Markoff had crawled over to her injured guard, doing her best to help bind his mutilated face. One of Meisser's men was dead, the other a groaning heap of pain. Father Kunz lay in the hallway, dying noisily as he choked upon his own blood.

Meisser was struggling to bind a gash running along his leg, a clumsy operation with one arm still bound in a sling. Thulmann took a step toward the injured man, pausing to lift Meisser's pistol from the floor.

'That… a vampire!' Meisser gibbered. He had been an apprentice when last he encountered the foul undead in a tomb outside Carroburg. He had thought, or hoped, that he need never encounter such a being again. Politicking and scheming had become his vocations, in prosperous villages and great cities, not unhallowed tombs and ruined castles. But it seemed the undead were not content to remain in their own grisly habitat.

'Yes, a vampire!' Thulmann agreed, venom filling his words. He angrily tossed the lead bullet Meisser had been ramming into his pistol at the wounded man. 'Congratulations, captain, you've learned something this day! There is good reason for the Order of Sigmar to instruct its servants to use bullets crafted of silver, blessed by a priest!' Thulmann pulled Meisser to his feet, forcing a cry of pain from the older man. He could practically read Meisser's mind – silver bullets were an expensive piece of ostentation, why arm his men in so costly a fashion when the money might be better spent buying favours at court?

'I am of a mind to finish what Sibbechai started,' Thulmann spoke, his voice cold and murderous. The witch hunter turned his head, feeling eyes upon him. Silja Markoff's expression was perhaps even more horrified than before. He released his grip, letting Meisser crash back to the floor. 'I need your men, captain. All of them. If you found hunting down a witch an entertaining distraction, I'm certain you will find tracking a vampire's grave even more stimulating!'

Thulmann strode from the library, not trusting himself to remain near Meisser. Already he could hear the surviving guards from outside rushing into the wizard's parlour. He would need them to carry the wounded and the dead from the library. Then they would help him burn every scrap of paper in the room. There was no time to search it thoroughly. Even now Sibbechai would be gathering its strength to return. If *Das Buch die Unholden* was there, it would be consumed with the rest.

Either way, Thulmann knew, the vampire would soon be hunting him. Sibbechai would demand revenge for the events of this night.

But one thought troubled him even more than the vampire's ire. If it hadn't been able to retrieve *Das Buch die Unholden* from Wolfram Kohl's library, then exactly where was the book?

FURCHTEGOTT LOOKED UP from the mouldering pages he had been consulting. The wizard was happy that he hadn't eaten a large supper. The very substance of *Das Buch die Unholden* was abhorrent enough – bound in what looked like tanned human skin, the skull of some horned reptile fixed upon its cover, its parchment of human flesh written upon in blood – but the spells he had been deciphering were enough to sicken the most jaded murderer. They were designed to combat disease and plague, but it seemed to Furchtegott the cure was even more abominable than the sickness. Still, the wizard was taking the pragmatic view of a healthy man. Somebody with Stir blight coursing through his body would no doubt see things differently. Still, it was probably better if Baron von Gotz didn't know the secrets of the magic that his court wizard would employ on his behalf.

The wizard stared again at the ugly symbol that festered upon the page. It was like a crumbling scab, three intertwined circles each pierced by an arrow. Furchtegott knew enough about the proscribed gods of Chaos to recognise the symbol of one of the most dreaded: Nurgle, the god of plague. The ugly blemish seemed to writhe upon the page as he said the name of the lord of pestilence. The wizard dismissed the impression. There were no real gods, dark or otherwise. Chaos was simply a force, a power that men clothed in superstition because they did not understand it. Were not the winds of magic simply a manifestation of this energy? All magic owed its power to what men called Chaos.

No, there were no Dark Gods. Only petty men who used their dark imaginings as an excuse to oppress others. *Das Buch die Unholden* was only one more grimoire, the spells he had deciphered not so different from those he had been taught in Altdorf, once they were stripped of references to the Dark Powers. Its spells would help him to cure the baron, placing his patron deeply in Furchtegott's debt. Which was exactly where he wanted him.

The wizard searched the list of material components he would need to work the spell. Many of them he could find easily enough. Others would be more difficult. He was especially nervous about the 'maggots from a sick man's belly'. Those, he realised, he would need to collect himself.

Furchtegott also realised it would be a long time before he could face anything approaching a large supper.

CHAPTER FIVE

THE EARLY MORNING sun peeked through the clouds that hung over Wurtbad. Slowly, like some wounded beast, the city began to stir. Doors made fast against the hours of darkness were unbolted, shutters swung open to admit the fragile grey light of morning. Bleary-eyed men emerged from their homes to face whatever labours the day held for them. The sound of traders carting their wares from storehouses to places that could yet afford their goods rattled from the main streets of the city. There was feed and straw to be taken from warehouses to the stables scattered across Wurtbad, wine and beer to be doled out to the taverns. The world of commerce had yet to be consumed by the disease that infested the city. Only the prices had changed, thus far. It would be weeks before most merchants became bold enough to raise their prices extortionately, before their greed devoured their decency.

Mathias Thulmann walked the early morning streets with a heavy tread. Twice he nearly spilled himself into the gutter, his tired boots keeping poor purchase on the dew-slick cobblestones. After the battle in Wolfram Kohl's library, Thulmann had gathered the rest of Meisser's witch hunters, telling them what needed to be done. Little more than an hour later, the wizard's home had been reduced to a mound of smoking rubble. He wanted to believe that the Klausner book had been destroyed along with the wizard's other possessions, but a grim foreboding warned him against it.

Beside him strode the slender form of Silja Markoff, her stately gait impaired by the limp that betrayed the injury dealt by Sibbechai. Thulmann had tried to induce the woman to return to her father, to nurse her bruises, but she brushed away his concerns.

'Your ambition is showing,' Thulmann commented, as they turned the corner onto the thoroughfare that led to the Seven Candles inn. 'You needn't worry about any influence Meisser has with me. I can assure you that the fool has none.' A harsher quality entered the witch hunter's voice. 'I can also assure you that I am not easily manipulated.'

'Forgive me, Herr Thulmann,' said Silja. 'I am better acquainted with Captain Meisser and his creatures. I had assumed that all witch hunters were spineless cowards content to allow others to do their fighting. Unfortunately, that presumption is rather at odds with your own character. I have much pondering to do before I can make further assessment.'

'You speak candidly,' Thulmann said. 'But spend not too much time taking my measure. I am just a humble servant of Lord Sigmar, nothing more. And don't be too hard on your templars, many of them are good and honest men. If they seem less, the blame lies in their leadership.'

The witch hunter stumbled, his fatigue overcoming his balance. Silja grabbed his waist, steadying the tottering templar. Thulmann gave his companion a weak smile. Silja removed her grip as she found him steady once more.

'You need your rest, Brother Mathias,' she stated. 'You'll do no one any good if you are dead on your feet. And believe me, you *are* dead on your feet.' The witch hunter turned to face the young woman. Her remaining bodyguard, several steps behind them, also came to a halt, making no move to close the distance between himself and his charge.

'Two things, Lady Markoff,' Thulmann's silky voice snapped. 'First, there is much to be done and no one else to do it. The day will not last forever. Only an idiot would attempt what we need to do after the sun has set. Second, you should call me Mathias. Saving my bruised hide from a vampire entitles you to at least that much. Leave "Brother Mathias" to simpering cretins like Meisser.'

'Very well, Mathias,' Silja replied. 'But tell me why you take so much responsibility onto your shoulders? Surely you are not so conceited as to believe yourself the only one in Wurtbad capable of that which needs to be done?' Thulmann shook his head.

'I've seen enough to know there's a brain inside that pretty noggin of yours, even if it doesn't have the good sense to keep out of a vampire's reach,' Thulmann told her. 'But you are not of the Order of Sigmar. You are an agent of the secular authority, not a representative of the temple. The only men trained to find the vampire's hiding place are the witch hunters, and they will not follow you. Besides, you are just as tired and bruised as I am.' He lifted his hand, forestalling Silja's protest. 'Don't let Meisser fool you, there are decent, intelligent men under his command. It is a cruel jest that they must be subordinate to such a scheming toad, but the gods will have their amusements.'

'If there are such men,' Silja insisted, 'then put one of them in charge.'

Thulmann sighed, shaking his head. 'Meisser will let me run things because I'm an outsider. Frankly, the swine is afraid of me. If I put one of his own in charge, Meisser will undermine him and take command himself.' His voice grew sombre. 'Four men will be buried today because of that parasite, another will probably be crippled for the rest of his days. I'd say Captain Meisser has already made a great enough contribution, would you not?'

Thulmann began to walk away. Silja hurried to keep pace. 'Last night, after the vampire escaped… ' She stared into her face. 'You wouldn't really have… '

'Killed him?' Thulmann let a humourless sound rumble from his throat. 'By Sigmar I wanted to. But that would have been purely selfish. It would have been on account of my hate, not justice for the men who died for his stupidity.'

'Different motives, but the same end,' said Silja.

'No,' he corrected her. 'The reason that a man acts is as important as the deed itself. Nobility of purpose may excuse the blackest deeds, hate and greed may foul the proudest accomplishments.' Thulmann smiled as he saw the sign of the Seven Candles inn at the end of the street.

'My rooms are here,' he told Silja. 'We'll gather up Streng and hurry back to the chapter house.'

'This man of yours has some skill in these matters?' Silja enquired.

'Perhaps not skill, but certainly experience,' Thulmann said. 'We have faced these monsters together. I can trust him to stand his ground. Not everyone has the courage to confront the undead, much less go searching in cemeteries for their hiding places. I want Streng with me.' He paused to consider his words. 'That is, if his hangover hasn't left him in a state even less fit than my own.'

'You make him sound very gallant,' Silja observed. Thulmann paused again, casting an appraising eye over Silja Markoff's figure.

'When you meet him,' he warned her, 'watch his hands.'

EVEN IF THE threat of plague did not hover over the dock-yards, Carandini suspected the foul reek of the fishmonger's shop would have kept inquisitive souls at bay. The Tilean was, he had to admit, rather impressed by his undead associate's choice of hiding place. Vampires did not see the world the way living creatures did. Only in places where the aura of death was great did they find any degree of comfort. Graves and mausoleums were more 'real' to such beings than the cities and towns of the living. It was only among such surroundings that they could find even the shadow of comfort and ease.

And Sibbechai was cunning. The necrarch knew it might become the hunted rather than the hunter, and had prepared for that possibility. Certainly, a rundown fishmonger's hut was the last place Carandini would expect to find a dread lord of the night, sleeping away the daylight hours.

The necromancer slipped into the hut, a single-room hovel filled with debris and rubbish. He navigated his way twixt the heaps of fish bones, cracked masonry and splintered wood. When the business had failed, it seemed its neighbours had adopted the building as a dumping ground. Of course, thanks to the plague, there was no one left in the vicinity to continue the practice. At the back of the room, Carandini found the small trap-door. In the past, he supposed, the little cellar had been used to smoke fish. Certainly the smell rising from below seemed to bear out his theory.

The vampire's coffin filled most of the small cellar, pushed close against one of the walls. It was locked from the inside, another precaution Sibbechai had adopted of late. Carandini was more than a little irritated by the monster's fear and distrust. That it was well founded only made the necromancer's annoyance greater.

Sibbechai had failed to secure *Das Buch die Unholden*, Carandini knew. The vampire had fled the wizard's house in haste, not triumph. If the book had been there, then the witch hunters had destroyed it. Carandini had considered confronting them, but common sense had prevailed. The necromancer had lingered outside long enough to see the witch hunters set fire to the place. He had also seen them remove a body that had all the appearance of a wizard. He wasn't sure if it was they or Sibbechai who killed the sorcerer, nor did he much care.

Carandini unfolded a large sheet of leathery skin, setting it down upon the dank cellar floor. From a pocket he produced a bottle of ink, with more than a little dead man's blood in its substance. He set the withered claw of the mummy Nehb-ka-Menthu upon the sheet, dipping each of its fingers in the ink. The necromancer looked at Sibbechai's coffin. If Wolfram Kohl had told the vampire anything before he died, the sorcerer would soon know it. The spirit of the dead wizard would tell him – as he would anything else that he had neglected to disclose to the vampire.

Knowledge was power, and Carandini had every intention of regaining the upper footing in his alliance with Sibbechai.

At least until he found a safe way to dispose of the vampire.

THULMANN HAD BEEN given one of the topmost rooms by the proprietor of the Seven Candles, the very best in the house. The innkeeper had not been entirely pleased by the witch hunter's return, but, with plague abroad, his rooms were already empty. At least custom could not suffer any further.

They found Streng sprawled upon a massive canopied bed. Thulmann was not unduly surprised. It was not the first time his underling had appropriated his master's lodgings to impress some buxom tavern wench. A few sharp words would serve to reprimand the thug, at least until the next time he became drunk enough to forget his place. Silja sensed his irritation.

'If there is a reason you've commandeered my room,' Thulmann snarled acidly, 'then I would hear it.' The sound of his employer's voice caused Streng to stir. As he disturbed the sheets drawn about him, Thulmann could see the ex-soldier's side was covered in bloodied bandages.

'It would seem your drunken carousing has caught up with you,' the witch hunter snapped. Streng reached for the wine bottle on the floor beside the bed. Angrily, Thulmann kicked the bottle, sending it rolling across the room. 'You look as though you've had more than sufficient,' he declared. 'I warned you that I'd have need of you soon, and here I find you in a drunken stupor, broken up in some tavern brawl!'

'Have a care, Mathias!' Streng protested. 'You know it takes longer to knock me off my feet than a few hours, even if they were serving Bugman's best!' With a groan, the mercenary sat up, blinking his eyes to clear his vision. He blinked again when he spotted Silja Markoff just inside the doorway. 'Well, now I see why you're so cross!' he grunted. 'And here I was thinking you were all prayers and sermons! Nice eye, Mathias,' he added with a lewd wink, bringing colour to Silja's face.

'Mind your tongue, you misbegotten mongrel.' Thulmann ordered. 'And get that filthy carcass of yours moving, if you expect to get paid. Sibbechai is already here in Wurtbad and we're going to find his lair.'

'You maybe, but not me,' Streng grinned back. 'Dok-tor says I should stay off my feet for a few days – maybe even a couple of weeks.' The mercenary coughed dramatically. 'Much as I'd like to risk my neck fighting that gruesome blood worm again.' Streng's face pulled back into a proud and arrogant smile. 'Besides, I've already had a run-in with some nastiness,' he boasted, pointing to the far corner of the room. Thulmann's brow furrowed as he saw the strange leather object lying where Streng indicated. Looking closer, he found it to be a curious, bird-like mask, the bill of its beak stuffed with a pomander that reeked of lilac. Beneath the mask was something even more interesting – a small, dark glass bottle. Thulmann picked the bottle up carefully, sensing the fell energies gathered about it. It was empty save for a crusty residue on its bottom and sides. A sickly reek, like old vomit, rose from within.

'It wasn't a bar brawl,' Streng explained. 'I saw this sin-ister character creeping around the back alleys. I knew there was something wrong about him so I followed to see what mischief he was up to.' The mercenary had decided Thulmann didn't need to know the particulars of the encounter.

'That looks like the masks worn by the plague doktors,' said Silja moving up to examine the garment.

'Plague doktor?' Thulmann asked.

'They're healers, or so they claim. They haunt the plague-ridden districts, offering to cure those who've contracted the Stir blight,' she elaborated. 'Charlatans mostly, preying upon the poor and the sick, taking what little they can offer in exchange for water potions and quack remedies. My father would have had them impris-oned but feels the public outcry would be too great. They may offer the sick false hope, but they are the only ones to offer them any kind of hope.'

'Hmmph,' grunted Streng. 'That's all well and good, lady, but the one that knifed me was more than some quack healer.' He looked over at Thulmann. 'He was a mutant. And if that bottle he was carrying don't stink of black magic, I'm a Solkanite monk!'

Thulmann stared at the dark bottle, relieved to release it from his grip and set it back on the floor. 'A mutant masquerading as a healer,' he reflected. 'Carrying a bottle of… ' he hesitated. What had been in the bottle, leaving behind it so hideous a taint? Poison? Something worse than poison?

Streng lurched forward on the bed, pain and fatigue forgotten for the moment. 'You're not thinking… '

'We lost track of Weichs in Wurtbad,' Thulmann said. 'There's no reason to believe he's moved on. If this is really what it appears to be, it stinks to the Chaos Wastes of Herr Doktor Freiherr Weichs.'

'Who is this Doktor Weichs?' asked Silja. Thulmann removed his cloak, bundling the noxious black bottle within its folds.

'I'll explain that to you on the way.' Thulmann pushed Silja toward the door. Behind them, Streng rolled to the side of the bed, reaching for his boots.

'Give me a few minutes Mathias, and I'll be with you,' the mercenary said. He looked around the room for where he had thrown his breeches.

'Go over to the chapter house and keep an eye on Meisser,' Thulmann told him. 'Don't worry, if I learn anything I'll send for you.' It was a promise the witch hunter intended to keep. As much as anyone, Streng deserved to be there when Weichs was finally brought to justice.

'Where are we going?' Silja demanded as Thulmann ushered her back down the main stairway of the Seven Candles.

'Where we may be able to learn more about these plague doktors of yours,' Thulmann told her. 'Something

I've learned is that when you want to find out about a healer, you don't ask the healthy, you speak with the sick.' The witch hunter extended his arm for Silja to precede him. 'I am still something of a stranger to Wurtbad, Lady Markoff. If you would please lead the way.'

'But where am I leading you?' Silja asked again.

'To meet some of your plague victims. The hospice of Shallya. But if I am correct in my readings, then your city is beset by something more terrible than any plague.'

A WILD-EYED, half-human thing grinned from behind the bars of its iron cage. Sometimes it would laugh, other times it called out random words in a shrill, sing-song voice. Mostly it moaned and cried. Doktor Weichs took it as a sign, perhaps, that the man's senses had not completely deserted him when the skaven fell upon the wretch. An insane subject was of very limited value to Weichs, enabling him to study only the physical effects of his experiments. But he was as interested in the mind as in the body. The ideal subject was one whose mind was strong enough to accept what was happening to it and still manage to endure. Naturally, such men were rare.

The doktor's laboratory was a network of caves, old warrens that the skaven no longer used. Skilk had said something about a conflict between two local warlords that resulted in a decrease in the population beneath Wurtbad. As with everything else the skaven priest said, Weichs accepted the story as a half-truth. In any event, Skilk had given the abandoned warrens to his human confederate. The grey seer had propounded it was much safer for Weichs to labour down below, where none of his fellow men might accidentally stumble onto his work. Again, it was nothing more than a half-truth. Weichs was more convinced that Skilk wanted him where the skaven could closely monitor his experiments.

For all their bestial appearance, he had to keep reminding himself that the mind of a skaven was as sharp as that of a man, and more devious and conniving than the most degenerate Tilean robber-prince.

The old warren was hundreds of yards in length, but narrow, with a low ceiling that sagged in places to within six feet of the floor. Crude wooden pilings had been erected in places to support the weakened roof, while in some corners the cavern had been allowed to collapse, a jumble of broken stone and shattered earth. Dozens of small tunnels opened onto the warren.

In his exposure to them, Weichs had learned that perhaps the only sensation that ruled the skaven more than hunger was fear. The vermin were loth to linger in any place that was without at least half-a-dozen boltholes and escape routes. Many of the tunnels led into dead ends or hideously ingenious traps, others twisted and turned until the traveller found himself back where he had started. But the majority connected back to the main network that burrowed beneath Wurtbad. Weichs had navigated only a few of these, and there were only two or three he could follow without becoming hopelessly lost. It was yet another tactic by which Skilk kept him isolated and under his control.

A large number of the openings in the walls were shallow, only a few feet deep at most. These had been the individual dens where the skaven had made their nests. Now they served Weichs as cells in which to contain his subjects, each blocked by a framework of wooden bars. Flickering torches were set in sconces before each of the cells, their inmates visible at all times. Weichs doubted any of the wretched creatures would possess either the strength or drive to attempt an escape, given the mixture of debilitating herbs and meagre rations he provided them with. But he didn't believe in taking undue chances.

The central section of the cave was dominated by a maze of wooden tables, upon which were assembled every piece of alchemical apparatus Weichs had been able to describe for his skaven assistants. The skaven had displayed fiendish cleverness, covering their thefts by setting fire to the workshops of their victims. Alchemists were forever dabbling with materials of a dangerous nature, so no one was truly surprised when their homes suddenly burst into flame in the dead of night. A quiet chill crawled down Weichs's spine when he considered how many other 'accidents' were actually the fruit of mankind's ancient rivals.

Weichs strode past the bubbling alembics, the smoking clay vessels arranged about the brick athenor that the skaven had dragged down stone-by-stone from the surface. One of his less intelligent human assistants was engaged in working the bellows that supplied heat to the brick furnace. Weichs paused to assure himself the man was not too enthusiastic in his labours. Too much heat might spoil the mixtures slowly boiling away in the clay bottles.

The plague doktor paused at intervals to inspect the glass pelicans whose narrow beaks fed into one another, refining and distilling the substances boiling within them. A grizzled skaven snout leered at him from above the heavy iron press. Small green-black stones were placed beneath the press and ground by the ratman into fine black powder.

Such a small thing, yet the warpstone dust formed the very life-blood of his experiments. It could be combined with other substances, the mixtures refined until their disparate parts became a single whole. Given the right combination and conditions, the noxious properties of the warpstone could be controlled. Negated. Reversed. Or so Weichs was convinced. The ancient alchemists and warlocks had experimented with what they had called wyrdstone, and written much about its curative abilities. But they had guarded their secrets too well, neglecting to pass on the vital knowledge of how they conquered the corrupting influence of the stones.

Weichs turned, feeling eyes upon him. A leprous visage quickly shuffled back into the darkness of its cell, a shapeless tendril that might once have been an arm covering what could only mockingly be called a face. The doktor shook his head solemnly. The combination he had used on that woman had not worked, the mutating effects of the warpstone had not been conquered. She was degenerating more each day, like a worm shrivelling under the hot summer sun. Still, even her dissolution might teach him something. There was always something to learn, if one but had the wisdom to observe.

His theory was sound, no power on earth would convince Weichs otherwise. If an Arabyan fakir could render himself immune to the poison of an asp by controlled exposure to the same poison, then why could not men be made immune to a much greater poison by similar means? The power that men called 'Chaos' was not some daemonic malevolence, as superstitious idiots continued to preach, but a natural force which man had not yet been able to adapt to. Were the high mountains evil because their snows caused frostbite, or the deserts evil because their sun burned the skin? Men had simply been forced to adapt, to cover their feet in fur boots or their bodies in silken robes. And men would learn to adapt to the mutating force of Chaos, to protect their bodies from its power just as they had from the frost and the sun.

Weichs drew near the ironbound table upon which his newest subject lay strapped. The old man's pinched face twisted into a scowl of disapproval. He'd expected the conniving raconteur to be made of sterner stuff, but the wretch hadn't even been able to withstand the shock of abduction by the skaven. After a minor application of a warpdust ointment to his skin, the baker's wits had deserted him entirely. Weichs stared at the lustreless eyes that gazed blindly at the roof of the cavern, listened as infantile mutterings dribbled from his mouth. The plague doktor uttered a black curse and turned away.

What good would it serve if he at last unlocked the secret he sought, found a way to render men immune to mutation, if the cure left them drooling idiots. Weichs snapped his fingers. Lobo leapt up from the small wicker chair in which he had been resting. The misshapen halfling scurried forward at his master's summons, changing direction as Weichs stabbed a finger at the cabinet that housed his equipment. Lobo hurried, swiftly removing a crystal decanter and a glass.

Weichs took the halfling's burden silently, charging his glass from the decanter. Estalian brandy, looted from the cellars of a baronet in Ostland, was one of the few vices the doktor allowed himself. The rich liquor helped him to think, to ease his anxieties and doubts. Idly, he wondered if he might not relocate to the arid hill country of Estalia one day and thereby ensure a plentiful supply of the spirit.

A foul smell disturbed Weichs's repose. The plague doktor looked up, noting with dismay the quivering, cringing shapes of his skaven assistants. The ratmen were cowering behind their apparatus, rodent faces hidden behind glass tubing and lead vessels. The foul smell had come from them, an instinctive by-product of the fear that gnawed at their greasy hearts. Weichs suspected there were many things that could cause the skaven to vent their glands of noxious musk, for they were a slinking, skulking people, but he knew of only one such thing that would visit his workshop.

A trio of skaven stalked through the maze of cages, tables and alchemical machinery. Two of them, the largest skaven Weichs had yet seen, muscles rippling beneath their sleek black fur, wore crude armour about their bodies, the metal plates pitted by rust, and on their backs they wore coarse black cloaks. A saw-edged sword hung from a rope tied about each of their waists, the steel so rotten with filth that Weichs suspected any man struck by it would die from infection long before he expired from his wounds.

Between the two black-furred killers strode a third skaven. The ratman hobbled forward on a gnarled staff, the crown of which was tipped by an ugly triangular iron icon representing the loathsome god of the ratmen. The ratman's frame was crook-backed, crushed by the weight of age. A black robe clothed its body and about its neck was a vibrant collar crafted from scraps of multi-coloured fur. Weichs knew the morbid story behind that garment – each scrap was a trophy, torn from the throat of a rival or enemy. The skaven's fur was grey speckled with black, fading into pure black upon his paws, as though the ratman wore fur gloves.

Grey Seer Skilk lifted his face, whiskers twitching as he inhaled the pungent odours of the workshop. Weichs felt a tremor of fear stab through him, thankful he did not have any musk glands to vent. The skaven were unsettling enough, but the grey seer was even more grotesque. Great horns erupted from the sides of his head, two curling tusks that framed the sides of his skull like that of a ram. Weichs had understood the skaven to be free from the more extreme forms of mutation – a remarkable thing for creatures exposed to raw warpstone on an almost continual basis – yet the first time he had laid eyes upon Skilk he had been forced to reconsider his belief.

The sorcerer-prophet halted only a few feet from Weichs, the bleary red eyes glaring at the human physician. 'Not rest!' Skilk's thin voice hissed. 'Work-work! Find-learn, yes?' The grey seer's nose twitched again, at the decanter still gripped in Weichs's hand. The doktor smiled weakly, arresting the motion before he acciden- tally displayed any teeth – a gesture the skaven used among themselves as a sign of aggression.

'Estalian brandy, grey seer,' Weichs explained. 'Perhaps you might forgive a man his humble vices?' Skilk bobbed his head up and down, the closest the creature ever came to displaying excitement. Weichs realised woe- fully that, before much longer, the ratman would deplete his dwindling reserves. Sighing regretfully, Weichs prof- fered the decanter. The grey seer did not bother to take the glass offered with it, thrusting his pale pink tongue down the neck of the bottle like a fleshy cork. Wriggling his tongue, Skilk let the fiery liquor trickle down his throat. When a quarter of the bottle had been drained, Skilk withdrew, handing it back to Weichs. The doktor fought to keep the disgust from his face. 'No, I want you to have it, grey seer. Take it with you back to your bur- row.' Skilk stared at Weichs, suspicion glowing in his eyes, but then made the sharp chittering that passed for laughter among his kind. Weichs wasn't stupid enough to try to poison Skilk.

'Progress?' Skilk hissed as he handed the decanter to a bodyguard. 'Make-find potion to cure-heal?' The grey seer looked pointedly to a huge iron cage at one end of the workshop. Its inmate was a huge, malformed thing. It could have passed for a troll. No one would imagine it had been a cooper only a few weeks before. It was the most glaring of Weichs's failures.

'Not yet, grey seer,' Weichs admitted. 'Great discoveries are not made overnight. There is progress, but we must not expect miracles.' Skilk's eyes narrowed as it digested the words. Weichs understood the skaven were just as eager to harness the healing properties of warpstone as he was, to eliminate disease and infirmity among their kind. A part of him shuddered to consider the horror of a skaven race not regularly culled by pestilence and plague. Even if he succeeded in his experiments, he might be eliminating one threat to mankind only to replace it with an even more terrible one.

'Time,' Skilk snarled. 'Always doktor-man want-take time!' The skaven bared his teeth, his naked tail lashing against the earthen floor. 'Skilk tired-sick, doktor-man. Progress. Now-soon.'

'I'll need more warpstone,' Weichs retorted as the grey seer turned to leave. 'More test subjects, better than those with which your people have been providing me.' Skilk continued to shuffle toward the tunnels, his bodyguards following behind him.

'Doktor-man get all-much need-want,' Skilk asserted. 'Take-fetch more man-people, take-fetch all man-people. Progress, doktor-man. Now-soon, Skilk need-want progress.'

Skilk's threat lingered long after the skaven priest's departure, like a black cloud filling the cavern. The skaven's demands were increasingly persistent and impatient. Weichs suffered no illusions as to what his fate would be when the grey seer's equanimity reached its fragile limits.

Shuddering, he lifted the glass of Estalian brandy and downed its contents in one quick swallow. Somehow, the expensive spirit was less satisfying than it had been only moments ago.

THE FAT FORM on the bed stretched his arms, a deep, throaty laugh rumbling from his immense frame as he felt strength and vigour flowing through his limbs. Only last night he was so weak that he'd been reduced to allowing a servant to feed him. Now he felt rejuvenated, restored.

He wrinkled his nose at the pungent reek of the salve that the wizard had smeared over his body. Vile muck, but it had done the trick. He'd been too tired and weak to protest the wizard's methods in the small hours of the morning; now he was jubilant that he had not. There was no denying that Furchtegott knew his business. Baron von Gotz swung his head around, smiling broadly as he met the gaze of his court wizard.

'By Sigmar, Taal and Manann, you've done it!' the baron roared. 'I can feel the health thundering through my veins!' He turned his eyes to the ashen faces of his doktors. The three men looked at the floor, the ceiling, anywhere that did not force them to meet that stern gaze. 'Hex-mongers! Take your damn leeches and get the hell out of my city!' The physicians quivered in their boots, turning their hats in their hands. Furchtegott felt triumph surge through him. These men had tried to humiliate him, now it was they who were feeling the sting of scorn.

'But your excellency,' Doktor Kleist spoke, his tone timid. 'The city is under quarantine. We cannot leave.'

'Then rot in the dungeons with the other traitorous vermin!' the fat baron snarled. 'You'd have had me weak as a kitten and dead within a fortnight! Science! Doktors! Bah!' The baron waved his bloated hand, motioning for the guards scattered about his chamber to lead the physicians away and for one of them to come near.

'Lord Markoff is waiting in the other room,' von Gotz said. 'Tell him I would see him now.' The baron waved the soldier away, turning his attention back to Furchtegott.

'You are a wizard's wizard,' the baron chortled. 'A wizard among wizards! I am going to have you knighted. No, a lordship! You deserve it more than half of those simpering maggots at court!'

'That is very kind, excellency,' Furchtegott replied. The wizard's earlier sense of victory was beginning to fade. He didn't like the look in the baron's eyes. They were bleary, unfocused. The boils had not receded, still visible beneath the layer of reeking salve the wizard administered a few hours earlier. There was no denying that the baron seemed healthier, but he certainly looked no better. Furchtegott decided he'd better consult *Das Buch die Unholden* as soon as he was able to detach himself.

The door to the baron's chamber opened once more, admitting the wizened figure of Wurtbad's Lord High Justice, Igor Markoff. The magistrate wore his crimson robes of state, the golden griffin of the Ministry of Justice displayed proudly upon his breast. Markoff bowed his head respectfully to his sovereign.

'I understand that you are feeling better, excellency,' Markoff said. There was doubt in the magistrate's voice. He could see the sickness marking the baron's exposed chest and arms, smell the disgusting stench wafting from his body. These were not the traits of good health.

'Quite well, Igor,' von Gotz replied with a smile. He waved a hand to a trembling servant boy. The youth stepped forward, retreating as soon as the baron had removed the silver platter from his hands. Von Gotz tore into the roast squab with savage gusto, wiping grease from his jowls as he paused to continue his conversation. 'You can help me to feel even better,' the baron said.

'Whatever I can do to serve,' responded Markoff. Von Gotz chuckled as he heard the servile reply, but then grew serious, peering into Markoff's eyes.

'You will clear out one of the keeps. The one on Muellerstrasse would probably serve best,' he pronounced. 'Clear it out and then gather up every one of these plague stricken dregs you can find. Herd them there and keep them there.' The baron smiled even as Furchtegott and Markoff opened their mouths in horror. 'We'll lock this sickness under one roof, contain it there. That's how we'll best this plague. There'll be no one left loose to spread it.'

It made a brutal kind of sense, but the barbaric cruelty of the baron's plan stunned the sensibilities of those who heard him speak.

'And you will do one more thing,' he declared. 'There is a brothel with a tavern's name, the Hound and Hare. You will round up everyone there and remove them to the Muellerstrasse keep. Then you will burn the brothel to the ground.' Von Gotz ground his teeth together as he imagined his revenge against the place that nearly killed him. 'I don't want two pieces of wood left nailed together or a single brick left intact.' He waved his hand, dismissing the Lord High Justice.

Furchtegott glanced nervously at the bloated figure of his patron. 'Excellency, I must be retiring also.' Von Gotz nodded.

'Yes, by all means.' he laughed. 'You've had a very busy morning and no doubt need your rest.' Von Gotz waved again, dismissing his wizard. He watched as the golden robed mystic hastily withdrew through the door, hurrying back to his tower to begin his next sorcerous enterprise. As well he should, for the wizard would not find the gratitude of Baron Friedo von Gotz either lacking or transitory.

Von Gotz's smile faded as the buzzing of a fly disturbed his thoughts. The baron looked askance, watching with revulsion as the insect crawled across his shoulder. Drawn from its pesthole by the pungent smell of Furchtegott's salve, the baron decided. His fat hand slapped against his shoulder with a sharp crack. Von Gotz stared at the smeared ruin of the fly staining his palm.

Looking aside to ensure that his servants were not watching, the baron lifted his hand to his face and licked the remains of the fly from his polluted skin.

* * *

THE TEMPLE OF the Lonely Sacrament had existed since the earliest days of Wurtbad, founded by pilgrim priestesses from the great temple in Couronne. The structure was long and low, filling a broad expanse of Wurtbad's old city district with its surrounding groves and gardens. Its outer façade was largely devoid of ornamentation, only the marble doves that topped the buttresses supporting the temple walls proclaimed the deity that was worshipped within. It was not the way of those who followed Shallya, goddess of healing and mercy, to announce their faith with garish displays and raised voices. Like the dove that was their emblem, they were quiet and content, secure in their faith. Those who had need of the goddess would find their way to her temples without expensive statues and cyclopean architecture.

There were many in Wurtbad who had need of the goddess now. The Stir blight had ravaged entire districts, devouring entire households. The secular doktors and healers had thrown up their hands in frustration, unable to combat the sinister malady. Most now refused to even try, fearful that they themselves might fall prey to the pestilence. For those who had been abandoned to the plague, there was only one place to turn to, one place that would not turn them away.

The halls of the temple were now filled with the sick. Wretched bodies had been crammed into every available space. An air of misery and disease hung about its interior, an aura of hopelessness utterly at odds with the white walls and alabaster floors. In times of plague, even the grace of a goddess was taxed to its limit.

Mathias Thulmann made his way through the crowded halls, keeping his eyes fixed upon the corridor itself, blind to the sorry figures, deaf to the moans and cries that echoed through the temple. He was no healer. There was nothing he could do to help these people. He was a warrior, for that was his calling. If he could make a stand with sword and courage, he would never abandon an innocent soul. But against something as nebulous and spectral as a plague the witch hunter felt the sting of his helplessness.

Silja Markoff and her bodyguard followed him. Thulmann was impressed by the woman's courage in following him to this place of disease and death. He knew it must be even worse for her to prowl these halls of misery. To him, these were pitiable unfortunates. To her, they were her people.

The high priestess of the temple was conducting services in the main chapel, a simple ceremony culminating in the release of a white dove from a small cage. The bird fluttered upwards, vanishing through the open window at the top of the chapel's lofty ceiling. With the ritual completed, the other sisters departed to continue their ministrations to the sick. Sister Josepha nodded solemnly to the templar and his companions.

'Your faith in the protection of Lord Sigmar does you credit,' Sister Josepha told Thulmann, her old face suggesting an owl as she peered from under her white hood. 'Or else your need is great. I was told there were questions you would ask of my supplicants.' A hardness entered the woman's eyes. 'I should warn you that I will not have these people abused any further than they have been already, not even by one of Sigmar's witch hunters. These people have begged the mercy of Shallya and such protection as her temple can provide.'

'Then how do we proceed, sister?' Thulmann asked. Sister Josepha smiled back at him.

'Your Captain Meisser would have made demands, you ask questions,' she said. 'That impresses me perhaps more than it should, but I am all too familiar with demands of late. The aristocrats demand that we turn away the poor; the nobles demand that we turn away those with the plague. Everyone seems to want the blessing of the goddess, but no one wants to share that blessing with those who need it most.' The priestess grew thoughtful for a moment, then looked back at Thulmann. 'How do we proceed?' she repeated. 'I shall hear these questions you would ask. Then I shall decide if others can hear them.'

Thulmann removed the garish leather mask he had been carrying in a linen sack. He held the bird-like mask upward so that Sister Josepha might see it better. The priestess nodded her head sadly.

'So, these plague doktors have finally come to the attention of the Order of Sigmar,' she mused. 'I hoped that they would. I have heard much about them, and little of it good. They are like vultures, preying on the dying, feeding off their desperate need for hope. Shallya venerates all life, but I must confess to believing men like that have no right to live.'

Thulmann nodded in sympathy, understanding well how she must feel.

Suddenly, a great commotion sounded from the entrance of the temple. Thulmann could hear harsh voices barking orders above the cries and shrieks of the sick. Sister Josepha hurried to find the source of the disturbance, her recent guests following after her. Soon, they found themselves fighting their way through a press of panicked, fleeing bodies.

The source of the disturbance was a body of soldiers dressed in the livery of the Ministry of Justice, supported by an even greater body of troops wearing the green uniform of the city guard. The soldiers were brutally herding every person they could out of the temple. Thulmann could see a large number of wagons strewn across the gardens into which the soldiers were loading the sick.

'What is the meaning of this outrage?' demanded Sister Josepha to a soldier wearing the bronze pectoral insignia of a captain. The officer forced himself to meet her withering gaze.

'Order of the Lord High Justice,' he said, pulling a sheet of parchment from his belt. 'All those who have been infected by the Stir blight are to be taken to Otwin Keep. Those orders encompass all those within the temple.' The high priestess staggered back, shaken by this violation of her temple's sanctity. Mathias Thulmann stalked forward.

'Surely those orders do not include the sisters?' It was not a question but a challenge. Before the captain could respond to Thulmann's words, they were answered by Sister Josepha.

'We will go with them,' the old priestess stated. 'These people are supplicants of the Temple. If they are not allowed to remain here, then what grace and solace the temple can provide shall go with them.' The captain nodded reluctantly, shouting an order to his men to allow the sisters to board any wagon that still had room. For a moment, Thulmann could see deep self-loathing in the captain. A man bound by oath and duty to execute orders he found contemptible.

'I can assure you that my father will hear of this,' Silja snarled, demanding the captain's attention for the first time. The officer's face turned ashen as he saw her.

'Begging your pardon, ladyship, but these orders *are* from Lord Markoff,' the captain repeated.

'Then you may be doubly certain that he will hear of this,' Silja hissed, pushing her way past, daring any of his soldiers to even think of stopping her.

Thulmann followed after her. There were a great many matters unfolding in Wurtbad that he was uncertain about, but one of which he was as sure as the Ulricsberg.

He was glad that Silja Markoff was on his side.

CHAPTER SIX

THE WITCH HUNTER stormed through the doorway of the Wurtbad chapter house like a thing possessed. The hideous cruelty he had witnessed at the Temple of Shallya gnawed at his brain, worrying at his thoughts like a dog chewing on an old bone. Mingled with feelings of frustration, anger and impotence was another emotion that disgusted him more. A deep and profound guilt.

Ruthless, merciless as the baron's edict had been, Thulmann understood it. It was as if a battlefield chirurgeon were cutting away an infected arm from a wounded man, killing the part to save the whole. Baron von Gotz had decided to sacrifice those already infected by the plague in an attempt to save those who were not. There was no question that relocation to the chill darkness of Otwin Keep was anything but a death sentence, but, the colder, more pragmatic part of Thulmann's mind told him the sick supplicants of the Temple were as good as dead already. But still, the decision to brush aside the lives of so many people who did nothing to warrant their destruction was one Thulmann believed he could never make. He secretly hoped there would have been enough humanity left in him to reject such a course of action.

Thulmann canvassed the entry hall of the chapter house. All at once his distemper found something other than his guilt to direct itself toward. A dozen men dressed in black were standing about the hall, armed for battle. They cast surly looks at the pale figure slumped in a chair near the door. This bearded warrior held a loaded crossbow across his lap, beads of sweat dripping from his forehead. Streng turned his head as Thulmann entered, nodding weakly at his employer.

'By all the daemons!' Thulmann snarled. 'What is going on here? Why aren't you looking for the vampire's grave?' His eyes burned into the face of every witch hunter, causing some to look away with shame burning on their cheeks. 'One of you shall answer me!' he demanded.

'Unless someone has appointed you witch hunter captain of Wurtbad,' a voice snarled back, 'then I don't believe you have any right to abuse my men.' Thulmann turned his head to see Meisser stalking forward. A bandolier of pistols now crossed the templar's chest. Meisser had changed his apparel, adopting a uniform as dark and nondescript as that of his men save for the pectoral medal that hung from a chain about his neck, a twin-tailed comet engraved upon it.

'You are a guest here, Brother Mathias,' Meisser went on. 'I suggest you start behaving like one.'

Thulmann gritted his teeth. He should have expected something like this. He'd made it clear to Meisser the previous night that he wasn't going to help him in his power struggle with the Ministry of Justice, told him in no uncertain terms he considered him a dangerous incompetent and a disgrace to the holy name of Sigmar. True, he'd lost control of himself following the fight with Sibbechai, assaulting and abusing Meisser in front of his own men. That was the kind of mistake that could make the scheming witch hunter captain show his teeth – an assault on his distorted ego. Thulmann had compounded his mistake by giving Meisser time to brood over his injured pride, to allow the reptile to muster the vitriolic venom that substituted for courage in his character.

'Why are these men not looking for Sibbechai?' Thulmann growled through his clenched teeth. Meisser set his good hand on his hip and snorted a contemptuous laugh

'Why should they?' he replied, defensive. 'It is not our task. The Order of Sigmar is concerned with protecting the lives and souls of the Empire's citizens. When a citizen has been corrupted by dabbling in proscribed magic or communion with profane deities, it is also our duty to seek them out and make them repent their crimes.' A smile spread across Meisser's swinish face. 'Sigmar is the benevolent god of our glorious Empire, watching over every living subject that walks our land. This creature, this vampire, is one of the restless dead. Therefore it is not our problem. Sigmar is a god of the living. Morr is the god of the dead. I have informed the temple of Morr about this creature and they are thus compelled to investigate the matter. It is their jurisdiction, after all.'

'*Scum.*' Thulmann spat. 'You filthy, conniving vermin. You cower behind words twisted beyond their meaning, like some snail slinking behind its shell! It is the duty of any servant of Sigmar to combat every menace to his Empire and his people, whatever form or shape it might take. How have you the gall to say the vampire is not our concern?'

Meisser retreated from the violence of Thulmann's outburst, until there was half a room between them. 'You must not try to involve the entire order in this personal vendetta of yours,' Meisser declared. 'The Raven Decree of 2345 made the clear distinction that the temple of Morr is to handle such matters.'

Thulmann shook his head in disbelief. How long had the filthy maggot burrowed through his books to dig up that piece of history? 'The Raven Decree states that no templar is to violate the sanctity of any field of Morr without first notifying his priesthood,' the witch hunter snarled. 'It was never intended to place the responsibility for hunting and destroying the undead under the sole authority of the priests of Morr.'

'Be that as it may,' Meisser said, not wanting to continue an argument he could not win, 'the priests of Morr are looking for your vampire now. This chapter house has more pressing matters with which to concern itself.'

A sharp stab of suspicion cut its way through Thulmann's anger. What was the purpose of Meisser's game? Clearly he had lost all taste for riding Thulmann's coattails after he beheld the grotesque monster that the templar was hunting, but what scheme had he put in its place? Thulmann found himself wishing that Silja had accompanied him back to the chapter house. With her knowledge of Wurtbad's politics, she would surely recognise what Meisser was plotting.

Meisser smiled again, mistaking silence for a submissive retreat. 'We are to help the baron's men clear out the ghetto. Round up every plague-stricken dreg and send them to Otwin Keep,' he added with a touch of pride. 'That is, if you will tell your man to stand down and let us get about our work.'

Streng looked up at Thulmann. 'I don't have your way with words,' the thug grunted. 'Had to find a way to keep them here until you showed yourself.' The witch hunter relieved his henchman of his crossbow. Meisser's smile broadened, but it died when Thulmann swung the crossbow in his direction.

'I've had a taste of the baron's edict, captain,' he said. 'The Order of Sigmar will smell better for staying clear of it. I'd expect a true officer to recognise that fact.' Thulmann directed his words at Meisser, but his gaze swept the faces of the other witch hunters. He'd read the situation correctly – none of them had any taste for Baron von Gotz's draconian command. Now he'd give them an alternative. 'I believe last night's ordeal has taxed you greatly, captain, and under such strain and fatigue you are not yourself. Since that is the case, I must temporarily assume your duties as my own.'

'Khaine's blood, you will!' cursed Meisser, his face livid. The witch hunter captain reached for one of the pistols hanging from his chest. The other Wurtbad templars sprang into motion, pistols and hand crossbows appearing from beneath cloaks or inside leather holsters. None of them was pointed at Mathias Thulmann. Face twisted into a scowl, Meisser let his hand fall away from his weapon.

'It seems I already have,' Thulmann pronounced, looking across the room at the men who pointed weapons at their former commander.

'Traitors! Heretics!' Meisser roared.

'Brother Mathias is right, captain,' a white-headed witch hunter named Tuomas stated. 'You are not yourself. You need a reprieve from the burden of command.' The consoling words did nothing to soothe Meisser's ire.

'You are all apostates!' he snarled. 'Sigmar's grace has deserted Wurtbad, Chaos walks the land and we are all damned to the Pit.' Meisser spun about on his heel, stalking back to his study.

'He took that rather well.' Streng grinned weakly as he watched him leave.

Thulmann paid no attention to his underling. He had read the feelings of the men correctly – pious, zealous men who chafed under the leadership of an inept scoundrel like Meisser, who had been ready to abandon ship as soon as an alternative presented itself. Thulmann gave the witch hunters their orders. Enough time had already been wasted, Sibbechai's lair had to be found before darkness descended upon Wurtbad once more.

But there was another concern just as pivotal. Six of the witch hunters would coordinate with the priests of Morr and help them in the hunt for Sibbechai, but he needed the other half-dozen for something perhaps even more important for the city. The second group were to enter the ghetto, not to aid the baron's soldiers but to look for any sign of the plague doktors, and to capture one if at all possible. If what he suspected about them was correct, what he asked of the second group might prove no less dangerous than the vampire hunt.

One last task had been saved for himself. The bottle Streng found would have to be examined. Thulmann had a grim premonition that he already knew what he would learn from it.

WITHIN THE CONFINES of his study, Witch Hunter Captain Meisser sat and brooded. His authority had been usurped, as good as stripped from him. He'd been a fool to think he'd be able to use someone like Thulmann. He'd seen his kind before, self-righteous lunatics so certain in their own beliefs that they hurl aside all worldly concerns. What did such men know of the balance of power? What did they understand of the constant struggle to maintain the authority of the Temple in the face of secular greed and manipulation?

Apostates and fanatics. The late lord protector had seen his worth, known the value of his appreciation for politics. Of course, there were ugly rumours circulating about Lord Gamow now, rumours of heresy and worse. The witch hunter rose from his seat and nervously poured himself a glass of wine. He almost jumped out of his skin when he turned around and saw a messenger boy standing in the doorway.

'How did you get in here?' Meisser demanded.

'The man in the red shirt was giving orders to everybody,' the boy explained. 'Nobody paid any attention to me.' He stepped toward Meisser, extending the letter he carried. The captain took it cautiously, as though it were a live serpent rather than a sheet of parchment. The wax seal upon the letter stared back at him.

Meisser broke the seal and hastily read the letter's contents. A smile spread its way across his features as he quickly finished the last of his wine. A summons. From Baron von Gotz himself. Requested by name, in fact.

'Play your games, Thulmann,' Meisser thought. 'You will find I'm much better at them than you are.'

'WE CAN'T LET the vermin live.' The murderous words were spoken in the softest whisper, yet sounded loud as thunder in Gregor's ears. His hearing had been improving, to such a degree that every moment was a tiny piece of suffering, like a hot knife stabbed into his brain. He could hear everything. The rustle of grass as he stepped upon it, the click of termite legs as they burrowed through the walls. He could hear the steady pulse of the men's hearts. He could hear the blood as it pounded through their veins.

They were smugglers, these men. Gregor had found the city of Wurtbad under quarantine, surrounded by a ring of soldiers with orders to let no one in and no one out. But the eyes of mortal men are weak in the night. Gregor's eyes were no longer those of a man. He had seen the bright red glow of the warmth exuded by the smugglers as they prepared to break the cordon. They were skilled villains, old hands at deceiving the servants of the law and the elector count, and this was not their first excursion into the forbidden city. But Gregor was something less than a man now. He had become a very part of the darkness itself, in a way even the blackest outlaw would never be. He'd confronted them as they prepared to scuttle along the old drainage ditch that would conceal them for the first leg of their journey.

Skorzeney, the half-Kislevite who led the small group had been alarmed, naturally, but shrewd enough to know that a fight was the last thing he could afford. The soldiers of the elector count were everywhere and the sound of conflict would be sure to bring them running. He had smiled, a cunning, faithless smile, and agreed to Gregor's compromise, his demand to be taken into the city. Shrewd to the last, Skorzeney had handed Gregor some of the grain sacks he and his men were smuggling into Wurtbad. The ditch would not conceal horses or mules, the only goods the smugglers could carry was what they themselves bore. Skorzeney was happy to put his unexpected and unwanted visitor to work.

Gregor had expected the men to turn on him. In truth, they could do nothing less. The money he had promised to pay them was a lie, and the peasant rags he wore betrayed that fact. But more importantly, Gregor would now know the smuggler's secret route into the city. He could betray it to the authorities. Worse still, he could go into the smuggling business for himself. Skorzeney had the look of a killer about him. Perhaps he would decide to murder Gregor even without good reason.

Gregor stood in the shadow of the old tannery the smugglers had converted into a storehouse. He had to acknowledge that the men knew their business – crawling along ditches and culverts, a sack of grain lashed to each man's back, until they reached a small storm drain set in Wurtbad's outer wall, a metal grill far less sound than it appeared. The tannery stood only a few blocks from the wall, the tall tower of the horse trader's guild obscuring all view of the tannery from the nearest gatehouse.

'A quick stab, just under the ribs,' Skorzeney was telling one of his subordinates. 'Something a bit extra for the butcher. Won't be too long before even long pig becomes a delicacy around here.'

The other smuggler laughed nervously, then turned, regarding the spot where Gregor leaned against the wall. He approached the stranger, trying to maintain an air of casual ease.

'Come along, old beggar,' the smuggler said. 'You can help me sort the goods we just brought in. Get it ready for distribution. Boss says that's part of the deal too.'

He was a man who had killed before with no taint of remorse or regret. The same look of casual indifference was on his face now. But Gregor could hear the quickening of his pulse, the soft slither of steel against leather as he drew his dagger from its sheath. Before the smuggler could even blink, Gregor's cold hand grabbed his, twisting it upward and snapping his wrist. The smuggler fell, screaming in agony and horror, scurrying away from him.

'You'll not find me so easy to murder,' Gregor stated in an almost aloof tone. He still leaned against the wall. Except for the broken, screaming thief crawling away from him, he might never have moved at all. The half-dozen other smugglers drew swords, but their show of force was half-hearted. Skorzeney took a step forward. Gregor could see the thoughts behind the man's cold, vicious eyes. If he let Gregor go, his gang would break apart, his men no longer respecting and fearing their leader. Fear was pounding in his veins, just as it was in those of his men, but he could not allow it to rule him.

'A fair trick,' Skorzeney conceded. 'A little elf in you, perhaps?' He feigned a thoughtful look, then spoke once more. 'I was rash in my decision. You're more than you appear, friend. I might be able to use a man like you.'

Gregor stepped away from the wall. 'No, _friend_, I've business in this city that presses upon me. Step aside and pray our paths cross no more.' Indecision flickered on Skorzeney's face, then passed as he noted his adversary's unarmed state.

'I can't allow that. You've seen too much,' Skorzeney said. 'And I don't think you'll be able to repeat that little trick against a proper sword.'

There was no further warning. The smuggler sprang forward, slashing at Gregor's belly. Too fast for the eye to see, Gregor dodged aside, the smuggler's sword cutting only through air. Disbelieving, Skorzeney attacked again, chopping at Gregor's neck. This time, his enemy did not leap aside. Cold hands caught the flashing blade in a grip of steel. Skorzeney's eyes were wide with horror as he heard his sword snap under the pressure of Gregor's unnatural strength. The look was frozen on his features as Gregor drove the broken tip of the blade into Skorzeney's throat.

He staggered away as Skorzeney fell. Stared at his hands in shock, horrified by the inhuman power they held. He'd seen only one creature with such strength, the power to break steel with its bare hands. How much longer, Gregor wondered, before he became what Sibbechai was? He looked back on the man he had killed, as the bright, glowing crimson drained from his body, beckoning to him with its promise of warmth and life.

The young man fell upon his hands and knees beside the body, his face inching toward the filthy floor of the alley. Gregor stopped himself, self-disgust and revulsion beating down the obscene compulsion.

Like a human crab, Gregor scurried backwards from the expanding pool of blood. He looked into the dying face of Skorzeney and groaned in horror. As life fled the body it was becoming more distinct, clearer to Gregor's twisted sight. It was as if a veil had been pulled away, exposing that which lay beneath. The body became more real to Gregor in death than it had been in life.

The other smugglers had fled into the night as soon as their leader had fallen. Yet even as they hurried through blackened streets and dark alleyways, they could hear the long, anguished, inhuman howl from outside the tannery. It was the cry of the lost and the damned.

THE SUN HAD barely disappeared beneath the horizon when a chill imposed itself on the small cellar. A coldness that had nothing to do with the onset of night. A shadow rose from the heavy wooden casket. Another shadow greeted it, detaching itself from the gloom gathered about the walls.

'Good evening, mighty necrarch lord,' the sardonic voice of the necromancer broke the silence of the improvised crypt. 'I trust this night shall be more productive than last.'

Sibbechai's burning gaze fell upon Carandini. It had had enough of this conniving little mortal, and his usefulness was at an end. The vampire would find some less truculent wretch to serve it now. Shrivelled flesh fell away from its grotesque fangs as the vampire snarled at its deceitful ally.

'I grow weary of your baiting, little man,' Sibbechai growled. Its fingers cracked as it spread its hand into a claw. But almost at once, it relented, folding its arms back around its body. The necromancer was baiting it because he believed he had the upper hand. It might be dangerous to kill Carandini before learning why.

'You failed to secure the book,' the necromancer stated. 'And you let that witch hunter live. Not what I expected when I proposed this alliance of ours.'

'I will deal with the witch hunter in my own time,' Sibbechai hissed. 'Twice he has dared to interfere. Every breath he takes now is borrowed from Morr.' The vampire snapped its fangs, as though crushing its enemy's throat between its jaws. Sibbechai turned its eyes again upon Carandini. 'The book shall be mine again. I know where it has been taken. And by whom.' The vampire suddenly smiled. There had been a faint smell in the cellar, a subtle taint to the air. Sibbechai had been trying to remember where it had smelled it before. Now it knew – it was the strange ink Carandini used when consulting the mummy claw he carried. Sibbechai could readily guess what the necromancer had asked of the oracular talisman. 'But this is already known to you.'

Carandini nodded his head. 'Castle von Gotz,' he said with a note of pride. 'Taken there by a wizard named Furchtegott.'

'The wizard will not stand in my way,' Sibbechai snarled, moving toward the cellar's trapdoor. Suddenly it turned – springing on Carandini before the necromancer could react, pouncing on him like a wolf upon an unsuspecting lamb. Sibbechai could read the minds of most mortals, plucking their thoughts from thin air if it concentrated hard. But Carandini was too well versed in the black arts, his mind guarded from the vampire's intrusion. Yet such protection was not complete. Sibbechai could still sense the emotions oozing from the necromancer's grimy soul. And as the vampire gave voice to its intention to kill the wizard, an intense joy gripped Carandini.

'What else do you know?' Sibbechai hissed into Carandini's face. The vampire held the sorcerer pinned against the wall, one talon gripping his neck, the other closed about the arm in which sleeve he kept a vial of holy water. 'What else did that daemon's paw show you?'

Carandini struggled to sneak air into his lungs. 'It… you will… the castle…' Carandini forced himself to make the words before Sibbechai crushed his neck. 'You'll die… if you go.' Sibbechai let the necromancer slide to the floor, the vampire's horrible gaze burning into his body.

'The castle is protected,' Carandini gasped as he sucked in huge lungfuls of air. 'Almost as potent as what the Klausners were using. Try to climb the castle's walls or fly up to its roof and the magic protecting it will destroy you.'

Sibbechai's skeletal features contorted into rage. Its withered claws smashed into the wall, crumbling the old brickwork as though it were sand. Carandini watched the vampire vent its anger. The vial of holy water had shattered when Sibbechai dropped him, removing his best defence. Now he was desperately trying to remember a spell that might work against such an undead horror.

'If the book is not mine, then neither shall it be yours,' Sibbechai snarled, fangs bared. The vampire advanced upon the cringing necromancer. Death was at hand.

'Wait!' Carandini cried out. 'There is a way! Listen to me!' The vampire halted, suspicion in its eyes. 'The wards are not infallible,' Carandini continued. 'There is a way to elude them, something their creators never accounted for.'

'You say it is protected from without and from above,' Sibbechai said. Carandini nodded in hasty agreement.

'Yes, but not from below,' the necromancer declared. 'It would be possible to dig into the castle's dungeons and bypass the wards.' Sibbechai grinned at the Tilean.

'A clever plan,' the vampire conceded. 'It is almost a pity that you won't be around to see it employed.' The vampire closed in upon him.

'You still need me,' Carandini insisted. 'It will take an army to dig up into the castle. I can raise that army for you.' Sibbechai shook its head in amusement.

'I am a necromancer too, remember?' the vampire laughed. 'I am very capable of raising a few zombies.'

'But the magic will be much more potent, faster, with my help,' Carandini pointed out. 'The witch hunter is looking for the book too. If he finds it before we do, then it belongs to neither of us. Are you willing to gamble that you have enough time to deal with this alone?'

Sibbechai stepped back. It nodded its head and folded its arms once more. 'Well spoken, necromancer. It seems your usefulness to me is not at its end after all.'

'THE GREAT AND good of Wurtbad,' Baron von Gotz scoffed between swallows of wine. 'The leaders of the Empire's greatest city besides Altdorf.' He tore a scrap of mutton from the plate set before him, stuffing it into his swollen face. The meeting he had called was held in the smaller of the castle's three dining halls. With the baron's return to health had come a vigorous appetite. The nobleman felt it would be unseemly to appease that appetite during the meeting if it were conducted in any other environment.

Not that any of his prestigious guests displayed any trace of hunger. Choice wines from the cellars, plates of expertly prepared meats, mutton, veal and venison, sat untouched. The baron was oblivious to the fact that it was he who diminished their appetites. He was no longer able to smell the loathsome stench of the salve Furchtegott applied to his skin, so accustomed to it had his senses become. He did not seem to appreciate the ugliness of the boils that peppered his face and hands, grateful only that they were not those of the deadly Stir blight. But the man sitting beside him did. Had the baron condescended to look in his direction, he would have seen his trusted Furchtegott grow pale.

The assembled, abstemious diners represented the ruling elite of the city. The richest merchants, the most powerful nobles, the masters of the largest guilds. Commanders of the river guard, the city watch, and Wurtbad's standing army regiments. Even the Lord High Justice, Igor Markoff, who made a show of moving peas around his plate whenever von Gotz's gaze drifted toward him. They had been discussing for the better part of two hours how to destroy the plague before winter set in. If the quarantine was not lifted by then, if more supplies of food were not brought in, then the famine that would result would claim far more than the pestilence itself.

None of them had any answer. Indeed, several of them had openly decried the measures von Gotz had already taken, herding those infected into Otwin Keep. The heads of the different temples were particularly vocal on that point, furious that von Gotz had ordered the sanctity of the Temple of Shallya violated. The baron grumbled as he lifted a steaming bowl to his lips and began draining it of soup. Miserable, pious zealots, they'd all stand around waiting for their precious gods to save them while the entire city rotted away beneath their feet!

'A pack of pampered idiots.' von Gotz snarled, slamming his fist against the table. Several of his more timid guests jumped in surprise. 'Not a single one of you has any ideas? Not one? Maybe the Stir Blight isn't the only rot that I should confine to Otwin Keep.'

'Begging your pardon, excellency,' a tremulous voice called from the end of the table. 'But I may have a solution.' All heads turned to see the swinish countenance of Witch Hunter Captain Meisser. Many of those present had complained about the templar's inclusion in the meeting, the Lector of Sigmar among them. Fortunately, the witch hunter had kept silent, nursing some private trouble of his own. Until now.

'You spoke…' von Gotz hesitated a moment, trying to recall the witch hunter's name, '…brother templar. There is something you'd like to propose?'

Meisser stood, trying to look dignified despite his bandaged arm. He had the attention of every person in the room. 'We must convince the elector count that the plague has been exterminated,' he said, redundantly repeating the entire premise of the meeting. 'Now that we have most of those infected locked up in one place, why do we not exterminate the plague? It would be an easy thing to seal the doors and set fire to the keep.'

Gasps of horror and disbelief swept the room, along with muttered oaths of outrage. 'That's his solution to everything,' one elderly guildmaster called out. 'Put somebody to the torch!' It brought a round of laughter from the table.

One man was not laughing. Baron von Gotz hurled his wine glass to the floor, drawing all attention back to himself. The nobleman's face was turned toward the witch hunter. 'An inspired suggestion, brother templar,' von Gotz declared. More gasps and oaths greeted the baron's statement. 'Tell me what you will need to accomplish this.' Incredulous voices fell silent as the hideous reality of the situation became apparent.

'I'll need a goodly supply of oil and timber,' Meisser replied. 'And some men. My own are… otherwise occupied for the moment.'

'You shall have them,' von Gotz declared, stabbing his knife into a loaf of bread. The fat nobleman grinned at his shocked guests. 'Eat up gentlemen,' he laughed. 'No need to be timid now. Once the quarantine is lifted there will be plenty more where this came from!'

CHAPTER SEVEN

MATHIAS THULMANN FOUND Streng waiting for him just outside the alchemist's shop. The bearded thug had even less of a taste for magic than the witch hunter. Thulmann supposed that it might be another reason why the man had entered his employ. The foremost, of course, being the Temple's gold. There was a keen look in Streng's eyes that Thulmann recognised as agitated excitement. Clearly Streng believed he had found a worthy subject for his barbarous talents.

'You have the demeanour of the orc that swallowed the halfling,' Thulmann commented. The mercenary detached himself from the wall he leant on. He still moved stiffly, Thulmann noted, but at least the colour had returned to his face. Either he was somewhat improved or had managed to slither his way into a tavern on his way from the chapter house. Either possibility was equally likely.

'They caught one of my plague doktors,' Streng grinned. 'That young templar, Emil. Had a bit of trouble bringing him in, but they got him.' Thulmann digested the report.

'Has he said anything?' he asked. 'We don't know that this fellow is one of those we want. There might be any number of thieves and charlatans posing as plague doktors as well as Weichs and his scum.'

Streng gripped Thulmann's shoulder, forcing the witch hunter to stop. 'You're certain it's Weichs then?' he demanded. Thulmann gave a solemn nod.

'The alchemist found traces of warpstone burned into the glass of that bottle you found. We followed Weichs's trail to Wurtbad and now we find men posing as healers using warpstone. It does not take an overly analytical mind to accept that two and two make four.'

'Makes sense at that,' Streng agreed. He hurried to match pace with the witch hunter as Thulmann walked down the street. What little traffic there was parted before the templar. Thulmann wondered if it was the natural trepidation people felt in the presence of such grim agents of justice, or testament to the contempt and fear they felt towards Meisser's methods. He realised sadly that it was most likely the latter.

'Captain Meisser,' Thulmann said, 'has he caused any more trouble?' Streng shook his head.

'No,' the mercenary laughed. 'Hasn't showed his face. Still skulking in his room. Don't suppose you could ask old Sigmar to make that weasel stay there until after we leave?'

Thulmann chose to ignore his associate's casual blasphemy. 'This plague doktor Brother Emil apprehended, has he said anything?' he returned to the topic at hand.

'Just the usual nonsense about being innocent,' Streng replied. 'We've got the wrong man and all that. Never mind the fact that he tried to gut Emil with a fair-sized pigsticker, or that he's got pasty green stuff oozing out of the bullet hole Emil put in his shoulder.' Streng grinned again. 'Fair number of pint-sized tentacles, too, wriggling round his armpits. Be a bit of fun pulling those out.'

Thulmann sighed. His henchman's enthusiasm for the more violent aspects of his employment often troubled him, perhaps more so than the deeds themselves. Still, they were a necessary evil. This man was, by Streng's account, an obvious mutant and would need to be destroyed lest his corruption spread to others. But before that, Streng would need to extract the information Thulmann required from the wretch. By whatever means necessary.

'I don't care a damn for your vile amusements, Streng,' Thulmann stated. 'As long as you can make this animal talk, that is all I care about. If his information leads me to Weichs, there will be a bonus in it for you.'

Streng spat into the gutter, causing a mangy cur to flinch away. 'If we find Weichs, you can let me have a go at that bastard scum,' the mercenary swore. 'I don't know if I can think of anything horrible enough for him, but I'll enjoy trying to find out.'

FATHER SCHOENBECK HAD been a servant of the Temple of Morr for most of his forty years. He had seen much death in that time and buried many. But in the last few weeks, he considered he had seen more death than in all the years preceding, more bodies consigned to the plague pit than he had ever interred in Wurtbad's cemeteries. He shook his head at the massive pit, filled almost to the brim with a tangle of arms and legs. Soon they would need to dig a bigger one, the priest observed. The plague showed no sign of satisfaction with the toll already taken on the city.

Father Schoenbeck turned away from the morbid vista of the pit, shuffling over to the small fire where his fellow servants of the Temple warmed themselves. Three of these were lesser acolytes, initiates who wore the same black robes as the elder priests. There had been many new converts to the Temple, men whose lives had been destroyed as they consigned their families to the plague pit. There was great need of them, for the rituals and prayers required to sanctify the dead were important. The dead had suffered enough indignity by being cast into a mass grave; if they were not properly consecrated the corpses could become a terrible threat. Sylvania was not so far away, and the sinister tales of that cursed country were well known in Wurtbad – legends of the restless dead rising from their tombs to avenge themselves upon the living. Among the duties of Morr's priesthood was to ensure that such an abomination never occur.

Not all of his companions were priests, however. Two sombre black giants stood near the fire, their bodies similarly covered by the hooded habit of Morr's servants. But beneath their black robes they wore armour, plates of blackened steel as strong as obsidian. These were the dour templars of Morr, the fearsome Black Guard. These terrifying warriors were charged to ensure the sanctity of the pit was not violated by grieving relations, desperately trying to steal back their loved ones.

Father Schoenbeck clapped his hands together above the little fire, trying to force warmth back into his numbed fingers. The priest's attention was pulled away from the flames as the sound of a creaking cart grumbled out from the darkness. It was a sound he had heard far too many times, a plague cart emerging from the city to deposit its cargo. He walked away from the fire, motioning for the acolytes to remain where they were. There were rites to perform before a body could be consigned to the ground, but the priest felt fully capable of performing them on his own. It would help break up the tedium of another night camped beside the pit.

The plague cart was as dilapidated as the others Father Schoenbeck had seen, drawn by a sorry-looking mule that might have been lying inside the death wagon rather than pulling it. The man who drove it was similarly repulsive, scrawny and sickly. The priest nodded in greeting to the carter, circling toward the back of the wagon to begin removing its cargo of corpses. The sickly man dropped from the seat of the cart, brushing a ratty lock of hair from his face as he followed the priest.

Father Schoenbeck stopped, puzzled, when he reached the rear of the cart. The bed of the wagon was empty. 'Where are they?' he asked aloud. His mouth dropped open in a gargled scream as the pallid man cast a handful of dust into his face. The foul powder sizzled where it struck, its unholy energies withering the life from his flesh.

'I am afraid I came here to collect, not deposit,' Carandini said as the priest withered and writhed at his feet. The necromancer spun around, eyes glowing as terrible energies gathered within his corrupted soul. One of the acolytes rushed forward, a shovel gripped in his hands as though it were a battleaxe. Carandini smiled and uttered a word that was obscene centuries before even Sigmar was born. The dark energies responded. The acolyte crumpled into a screaming pile of rags, steam rising from his skin as the blood boiled within his veins.

The two templars of Morr reacted no less quickly than the shovel-wielding acolyte, but, weighed down by their armour, they were several paces behind. Carandini conceded they were a fearsome sight, black giants with cloaks billowing, the naked steel of their swords gleaming in the starlight. But there were far more fearsome things at large this night than mere mortal man.

From the darkness, a gaunt shape emerged, interposing itself between Carandini and the templars. The Black Guardsmen came to a hasty stop, hesitating to consider this new foe. Sibbechai's eyes burned from the pits of its face. Even the most ignorant peasant could not fail to recognise the vampire for what it was. Carandini was mildly impressed when the templars pressed their attack, instead of fleeing into the night as the surviving acolytes had done. Not that their bravery would count for anything.

The knight to Sibbechai's right slashed at the vampire with the edge of his massive broadsword. The undead creature did not so much evade the blow as shift position, the steel cleaving only through the edge of the vampire's shroud-like cloak. However, in avoiding the first knight's attack, Sibbechai left itself open to the assault of the second. It was a manoeuvre that the Black Guardsmen were very accomplished in, to allow their numbers to overwhelm the preternatural speed of the creatures they were called upon to destroy.

If the black helmets of the templars had left their faces exposed, perhaps they would have showed satisfaction as the second knight's sword crunched into Sibbechai's spine; as the force of the blow knocked the gaunt, cadaverous apparition back toward the first knight. The first Black Guardsman raised his sword upward, ready to deliver a decapitating blow to the vampire's neck.

Sibbechai had underestimated its adversaries. These were men who displayed no fear before it, whose wits and skills were not dulled by the clumsiness of terror. But they had underestimated Sibbechai as well. The simple tactics that allowed them to dispatch the debased, bestial strigoi vampires they discovered hiding in Wurtbad's Old Cemetery three years before were not enough to overcome a necrarch. Even as the first knight's sword slashed towards the vampire's neck, it was twisting around, claws gripping the blade lodged in its spine, spinning the second Black Guardsman around with it.

The first knight's reflexes were far quicker than those of most men. As the vampire used his comrade for a living shield, the knight changed the course of his blow, lowering the cutting edge. Instead of slashing into the other templar's neck, the blade glanced from his shoulder guard. However, even if the action preserved the life of his comrade, it left the guardsman momentarily defenceless. Sibbechai exploited the opening, hurling the overbalanced templar into the other who had thought to decapitate it. The two knights crashed against the earth in a pile of clattering steel. Sibbechai glared at them as it ripped the sword from its body and hurled the weapon away into the night.

'Servants of death,' the vampire hissed, extending its clawed hand. The templars struggled to regain their feet, dragging daggers from their boots as they rose. 'I send you to meet your master,' the vampire sneered. A hideous force seemed to erupt from its palm, a bolt of darkness that struck the armoured knights. The screams of the warriors echoed within their helmets as the necromantic force began to crush them, crumpling their armour as though crafted from paper, pulverising the bones within. Soon the screams stopped, leaving only two piles of twisted metal. Sibbechai regarded the sanguine pool slowly spreading from the mangled wreckage with satisfaction.

'You might have left them in some condition to be of use to us,' Carandini's whining voice complained from beside the corpse cart. Sibbechai gestured to the vast expanse of the plague pit.

'We have more than we can use already,' the vampire declared. 'It would be well if you got started. There is work to do here.'

Carandini glared at the vampire, then turned and dragged the boathook he had brought with him in anticipation of the night's labours. He might have expected the filthy coffin worm to leave all the dirty work to him. The necromancer moved toward the edge of the pit, sinking the boathook into one of the nearest bodies.

WINTER HAD ALREADY laid claim to the dungeons beneath the Wurtbad chapter house. Thulmann's breath turned to cloud as he stalked along the dark corridor. The water seepage that oozed from the brickwork had turned to frost, clinging to the walls like icy cobwebs. The chill of the dungeons matched the witch hunter's mood as his mind recollected the events of the past hours. Returning to the chapter house, he'd found that if the hunt for the plague doktors had gone well, then the search for Sibbechai's lair had not. Reports had come back from the templars with no favourable results. Thulmann was not surprised – in a city as large and old as Wurtbad, the cemeteries were both numerous and vast, offering an enormous amount of hiding places. He was certain that, given enough time, they would turn up whatever crypt Sibbechai had laid claim to. But the witch hunter did not know how much time they really had.

Neither had there been any word from Silja. Not that Thulmann expected anything favourable from that quarter. The Lord High Justice had impressed him as a man of resolve and determination; if he was set upon draconian measures, then not even the disapproval of his daughter would make him rethink his decision. Besides, Thulmann did not believe their origin lay with Igor Markoff. It had been decided upon by a still higher authority.

Thulmann dismissed his concerns about Silja and Sibbechai. Those had to be dealt with later. Now there was the plague doktor to consider. He was of the same ilk as the one Streng had fought against. The same ghastly leather mask, a lilac pomander stuffed into its beak. More importantly, he had carried a black bottle very similar to the one Streng had found. Only this time it was full. Thulmann had taken the vessel to the alchemist, though the scholar assured him it would take several days to make a definitive test of its vaporous contents. On one count, however, he had been ready to deliver a guarantee – there was, he assured, certainly more than a trace of warpstone within the bottle.

The plague doktor had spoken only little, giving Thulmann little choice but to leave the scoundrel in the capable hands of Streng. The professional torturer had been hard at work for the better part of the day. He had a particularly harsh system, tormenting the subject until he lost consciousness then awakening him minutes later. In the near-perfect darkness of the torture chamber, the prisoner had no idea of the passage of time. Streng had an amazing talent for making hours seem like days. Thulmann knew that the longer a man believed himself a captive, the weaker his resolve became.

Thulmann paused outside the door to the torture chamber, delivering his coded knock. Streng pulled the solid oak portal inward. The bare stone walls inside were lit by the diabolic glow of a brazier. A large wooden beam crossed the ceiling, chains dangling from rings set along its length. Within two of these manacles the wrists of the plague doktor had been bound. His back was red, raw, strips of ragged cloth dripping from his shredded body. Thulmann could see livid scars and burns running along the mutant's limbs. The witch hunter's gaze did not linger upon the plague doktor's visage. Unless Streng had spent an inordinate amount of time pounding the prisoner's features into their present lack of symmetry, the doktor had more than enough reason to hide behind a mask.

'Is the prisoner ready to confess his sins?' Thulmann demanded, his voice a theatrical snarl. Streng scowled at his master.

'Still as tight as a clam,' the mercenary spat. 'Might take another week or two to break this stubborn swine.' Thulmann could hear a soft moan of horror seep from the plague doktor's ruined mouth. Streng's acting ability wasn't exactly subtle, but given the right stage he could be as convincing as Detlef Sierck.

'M-mercy...' the thing that hung from the manacles groaned. Thulmann turned slowly toward the wretch, face twisted with scorn and contempt.

'Mercy? For a diseased, mutant heretic?' The witch hunter stooped to glare into the ruined face. 'For an unrepentant, murderous beast that revels yet in his misdeeds and blasphemies?'

'P-please...' the plague doktor whined, his voice cracking with the effort.

'What is your name, scum?' Thulmann demanded. This filth was desperate to make him stay, knowing full well that if Thulmann left, Streng would be set upon him again.

'Han... Hanzel... Gruber,' the prisoner said. 'I... I've done... nothing!'

'Nothing.' Thulmann growled back. 'Nothing. You carry a bottle of foul poison, telling unsuspecting innocents it will cure their ailments. You call that nothing?' He was guessing about their methods. But if Weichs was behind the plague doktors, such treachery was of a piece with his usual techniques. 'Your mind is as riddled with corruption as your filthy body, mutant cur!'

'Mercy... pity...' Hanzel implored. Thulmann started to pace the small chamber.

'Mercy? Pity?' the witch hunter repeated. 'Only a decent man warrants such favours, not murderous Chaos-spawn. A good man would have destroyed himself when he learned what he was becoming. A decent man would have given himself over to the Order of Sigmar, to be exterminated rather than continue his polluted existence, exposing those about him to the same abominable taint that defiled his own body. And you have allowed your villainy to plumb even greater depths. How long have you been a disciple of the Ruinous Powers? How long have you knelt before the Dark Gods and done their unholy bidding?' Thulmann gestured to indicate the malformations visible on the man's tortured body. 'Is this the mark of their favour? Tell me, mutant, which of the Lords of Chaos do you serve?'

Hanzel's body shook within the grip of the chains, trembling at Thulmann's accusations, his words carrying the sting of Streng's whip. Tortured, abused, and now condemned, the twisted creature began to weep, tears falling from his swollen eyes.

'I… am no worshipper,' Hanzel croaked. 'I serve no Dark Gods.'

'We know better, heretic,' Thulmann snarled. 'I shall hear the truth from your lips. Streng will extract the words from your rotten soul! If it takes a week, a month, even a year, I will have the truth from you, mutant.' Thulmann stopped pacing. He listened to the sob of horror from the bound Hanzel.

'Of course, if there is some spark of humanity left within that deformed carcass, if you have the courage to defy your dark masters, you may be spared such an ordeal.' Thulmann could hear the sudden spark of hope ignite in the prisoner, a spark he hastened to quell. 'You are a mutant, the seed of Chaos flows in your blood. Such corruption cannot be allowed to live. But if you will speak to me of what I wish to know, the end will be quick. Prayers shall be made that Sigmar might purify your soul when it has been expunged from its diseased shell.' The templar strode toward Hanzel. 'If you speak, Streng will not touch you again. You have my word. Now. Which of the Dark Gods do you serve?'

Hanzel sagged in the chains, weighed down by a despair his failing strength could not support. 'I do not serve the… Dark Gods,' he repeated with as much force as he could. 'It was a man who… who did this to me. Who made me a… thing.'

'Which man?' Thulmann demanded. 'What is his name?'

'The doktor,' Hanzel said, the words dripping from his mouth. 'Herr Doktor Weichs!'

Thulmann grinned. He had suspected as much, but now there was no longer any question. Weichs was in Wurtbad. Only this time, there was nowhere for him to run. The witch hunter stabbed a finger at Hanzel's miserable frame.

'You shall tell me everything you know about this man,' Thulmann ordered. 'You shall tell me how I can find him. That is how you will redeem your filthy existence. That is how you shall earn the mercy of a quick death.' In reply, Hanzel nodded his head weakly. He was resigned to the inevitability of death, now that the witch hunter offered him a chance to strike back at the man who had made him a monster.

Before Thulmann could continue his interrogation, there was a knock on the door. The witch hunter motioned for Streng to see who it was. He complied, peering through the narrow slit in the portal.

'Emil,' the mercenary reported. Thulmann gestured for Streng to admit the young templar. He stepped inside, his face eager and anxious.

'Begging your pardon, Brother Mathias,' Emil said. 'A messenger from Silja Markoff to see you.' The templar's voice became grave. 'He says she needs you to come right away.'

'Please inform the messenger I have other concerns that demand my attention here,' Thulmann replied. It cannot have been a trivial thing that caused Silja to send for him. But he was so close to finally setting a noose about the neck of Freiherr Weichs.

'Brother Mathias,' Emil continued, 'you had best come. The messenger says that Captain Meisser is burning down Otwin Keep!'

Thulmann cursed, stalking from the torture chamber like a thing possessed. He was unsure of the purpose of Meisser's game, but still the swine would have to be stopped. 'Streng, you'd better come along too. I may need every man.' Thulmann cast one last infuriated look back at Hanzel. 'Lock this door. I want no one disturbing our guest until I return.'

HANZEL GRUBER'S BODY grew slack as the witch hunters left, sealing the door behind him. Within the gloom of the torture chamber, the cumulative effects of terror and despair left the prisoner's mind and body fatigued. Now both seized the opportunity to rest.

The tired man ignored the soft scratching sound that gnawed at the edge of his senses. He did not see the trickle of dirt falling from between the stone blocks in the wall, as sharp claws began to penetrate the witch hunters' dungeon. If he had, Hanzel would have screamed out for Thulmann to return. For there were far worse things than torture in the dark, and one of those things was now coming for Hanzel Gruber.

CHAPTER EIGHT

OTWIN KEEP TOWERED above the half-timbered structures of the district around it. Although the houses, shops and tenements were clustered so closely that the lanes slithering between them scarcely allowed two men to walk abreast, the imposing stone tower stood alone. None had been bold enough to build close to the forbidding prison, unwilling for his home or business to lie within the keep's black shadow. A stretch of some fifty yards lay empty and vacant all around the keep, its expanse all the more unnatural and intimidating for the cramped cluster of the surrounding streets.

The tower itself was six floors of dank cells and dark corridors, encased within grey stone walls as thick as a man's arm was long. Narrow slits peppered the face of the structure, angling downward through the outer façade before reaching the chambers within. It had been no compassionate attempt to provide the keep's inmates with daylight, but a cruder one to improve the circulation of the air and eliminate the stench of unwashed bodies and human filth. The little windows failed in both respects, acting only to funnel the cold grip of winter into the dungeons.

A crowd had gathered around the gruesome structure as Thulmann led his retinue of witch hunters towards the keep. Most of them wore the livery of Baron von Gotz's personal guard, although there were others in the colours of the city watch. As Thulmann watched, the soldiers busied themselves by adding to the pile of kindling that surrounded the keep, hurling broken furniture and splintered beams. Others prowled the edges of the heap, massive stone jars held in their hands, sloshing thick black oil onto the kindling. Some distance away a large bonfire burned, its flames illuminating the brutal tableau. Even through the thick walls, Thulmann's ears could detect the shrieks and pleas for mercy rising from those confined within the keep.

Meisser was standing near the bonfire, dressed in the same dark mantle he had worn when Thulmann relieved him of command. The deposed witch hunter captain barked orders to the soldiers constructing the pyre, waving his hands and gesturing wildly to punctuate his commands. The image of a maestro conducting his orchestra in one of Altdorf's elegant opera houses flickered through Thulmann's thoughts.

Thulmann approached the swine-faced Meisser. Some of the soldiers working on the pyre turned to watch. Meisser started when he saw Thulmann. But a smug look of superiority spread across his face.

'Come to help me in my holy work, Brother Mathias?' Meisser grinned. Thulmann paused, the flickering light of the bonfire casting his profile in sharp relief. He studied Meisser for a moment. Then his hand released its hold upon his sword, curling into a fist as it bridged the distance and smashed into Meisser's nose. Meisser staggered backward, a stream of blood oozing from his nostril, gawking as it stained his fingers, stunned that anyone should have the temerity to strike him. Dimly, Thulmann was aware of movement to his right. He spun around, ready to defend himself. Some of the tension eased as he saw that the men closing upon him wore the gold of the Ministry of Justice, and Silja Markoff was at their head.

'Mathias!' Silja cried out. 'He means to burn down the keep with all the inmates locked inside!' Thulmann nodded grimly, turning back to regard Meisser. The witch hunter captain was still nursing his injured nose. His lip trembled as he saw his nemesis approach him. A quick glance at the soldiers standing by the pyre informed him he could expect no help from that quarter. The oaths they had sworn to Baron von Gotz bound them to their orders, it seemed, but not to their overseer. Thulmann might beat him to a pulp and the soldiers would be content to do nothing more than watch.

Meisser's hand dropped away from his nose toward his tunic. At once he snarled in pain, as strong hands closed about his own and pulled his good arm behind his back. Meisser struggled in Streng's powerful grip, spitting invective at the brutish mercenary.

'Can't have you shooting the gaffer now, can I?' Streng growled, giving a tug on Meisser's arm that sent a fresh stab of pain through his body.

'Damn you...' Meisser hissed. 'I have a proclamation... orders... in my pocket.' He groaned again as Streng fumbled inside his tunic, his hand emerging with a folded sheet of parchment.

'This looks to be what he's whining about,' Streng said, proffering the document to Thulmann. The witch hunter unfolded it and began to read. As he did so, the greasy smile returned to Meisser's face.

'Release him,' Thulmann ordered. Streng stared at his employer, wondering if he had taken leave of his senses.

'He has orders from Baron von Gotz himself. The baron is very concerned about the concentration of disease in this keep. This, it seems, is the solution.' With a sigh of disappointment and a last savage twist of his arm, Streng pushed Meisser away. He fell to the ground, another cry of pain escaping as he landed on his bad arm.

'But Baron von Gotz was the one who ordered the sick to be brought here,' protested Silja. Thulmann handed the document over to her, allowing her to examine the seal and satisfy herself as to its authenticity. For his part, there was no need for further inquiry. A scheming rat like Meisser would never have been brazen enough for so bold a deception.

'No doubt he had this second order already in mind when he gave the first,' Thulmann commented. Which, he wondered, was the worst monster at large in the city now: Sibbechai, Weichs, or His Excellency the Baron von Gotz?

'It was decided at a meeting of all the great and good of the city,' Meisser spat as he regained his feet. He stabbed an accusing finger at Silja. 'Your father was the one who proposed this action to the baron.' Silja's face turned white. The Ministry soldiers to either side of her stepped forward to support her suddenly weakened legs. Thulmann glowered at the conniving captain, sorely tempted to finish the job of breaking his nose.

'I don't care who the orders come from,' Silja insisted. 'You can't do this! For Sigmar's sake, the Sisters of Shallya are still inside!'

'You would consign the holy servants of the goddess of mercy to a hideous death?' Thulmann demanded. His words were intended not only for Meisser's jaded ears. The soldiers around the walls of the keep began to back away, eyes downcast as an intense shame welled up within them.

'They refused to leave,' Meisser protested. 'They insisted on defying the baron's order.'

'Because they were foolish enough to think that even you would not set fire to the keep with them still inside,' Thulmann snapped back. He turned his gaze toward the soldiers. 'You men have honoured your oaths and displayed your willingness to obey your masters, no matter how distasteful the task they give you. But this order is an evil!' He leaned toward the bonfire, holding the baron's proclamation against the flames. 'Lords and masters may demand many things from the men whose loyalty they command, but no man has the right to ask another to damn his immortal soul!' Thulmann held the parchment high so that the soldiers could watch it burn. Their faces betrayed the uncertainty they felt. Not one of them had been without his doubts, but now each saw he was responsible for his actions to powers far greater than that of Baron von Gotz.

As Thulmann was beginning to think the baron's hideous intentions had been thwarted, there was a sudden movement close beside him. Meisser had seized his chance, lunging at the bonfire, ripping a burning brand from the flames. He had allowed Thulmann to usurp his authority once before, but not this time. Before anyone could react, Meisser hurled the burning stick into the oil-soaked pile surrounding the keep. The kindling burst into an upsurge of flames, swiftly racing away to spread across the rest of the pile.

Thulmann ripped the cloak from his shoulders, the witch hunters from the chapter house following his lead. A large number of the soldiers grabbed spears, swords and whatever else was at hand to attack the blaze. The screams from inside the keep rose into an ear-splitting din, distinct and terrible, despite the thick stone walls and the roar of the flames.

'Keep it from reaching the door!' a soldier wearing a sergeant's pectoral cried out, a look of horror on his face. The witch hunter threw down the smouldering cloak in his hands. The sergeant's voice was a piteous moan. 'Captain Meisser had my men cover the floors in straw soaked with pitch!' he declared. Thulmann's eyes mirrored the horror as he looked to the keep's iron-bound doors, the tiny serpents of flame slithering toward them from the piled kindling. Even as he called out for the men to redirect their efforts, he knew it was too late. The screams from the keep rose in intensity as the fire raced inside. A group of soldiers fought to force the massive doors open, trying to hack through the portal with axes until the heat of the conflagration drove them back. By degree, the men abandoned their efforts, retreating from the fire as it became obvious that their fight was in vain.

Thulmann stalked back toward the bonfire, trying to ignore the chorus of screams shrieking into the night. He looked for Silja Markoff, but could find no trace of her. Meisser's words had done their work well, penetrating her strength and determination, wounding the woman inside. Silja seemed to have few weaknesses, but her devotion to her father was beyond question. Thulmann hoped she would not do anything rash.

Nearby, Thulmann found Streng, grinning at him from above the crumpled form of Meisser. The witch hunter captain had been relieved of his weapons, presumably after Streng's fist had knocked the wind from his stomach.

'Keep your animal off of me!' Meisser demanded. The witch hunter glared back, ripping his pistol from its holster. The captain cringed away, eyes wide with horror.

'You should be begging *him* to keep *me* away from you,' Thulmann snarled. His thumb pulled back the hammer of his pistol.

'I was only following orders!' pleaded Meisser, pressing his face against the cobblestones so that he might not see the coming shot. Slowly, with an effort of will,

Thulmann released the hammer, slamming the pistol back into its holster.

'Gunning you down in the gutter like a dog is not disgraceful enough an end, Captain Meisser,' Thulmann declared, his voice dripping with disgust. He glanced aside at his henchman. 'Streng, take this parasite back to the chapter house. Get him out of my sight.'

Streng pulled Meisser back to his feet, shoving him across the plaza. 'Count yourself lucky he's the gaffer,' he hissed in Meisser's ear. 'I'd have no qualms about putting a bullet in that slimy brain of yours.'

Thulmann did not watch his henchman leave, turning instead toward the blazing Otwin Keep. Its flames rose into the night sky like some infernal hellfire. Some soldiers were still harrying the edges of the conflagration, but most of them had withdrawn. The witch hunter looked in the direction of the distant Castle von Gotz, wondering if the baron had a good view of the atrocity.

CROUCHED UPON THE tile roof of a three-floor riverside slum like some withered gargoyle, the grotesque shadow twisted, its undead eyes regarding the distant flicker of light as Otwin Keep burned. Sibbechai's corpse-face remained impassive. Fires were a common enough hazard in the cramped, overpopulated confines of the Empire's cities, common enough that they held little interest for a vampire after five hundred years of pseudo-life. The fire was too distant to interfere with the necrarch's plans.

Sibbechai turned its attention back to the looming grey walls of the Schloss von Gotz. So near, the vampire thought, that it could almost reach out and touch them. Though to do so would be unwise. Sibbechai had not endured five centuries to end its existence in a trap set for a pack of long-dead von Carstein butchers. Carandini had been telling the truth about the wards, of that it was certain. The necromancer had been far too pleased at the prospect of ridding himself of his undead partner to lie.

A chill slithered across the vampire's withered skin. Its gaze settled upon the dark, indistinct shape that had joined it upon the rooftop, nestled within the shadow cast by the building's chimney.

'You have come so very far,' Sibbechai sneered. 'Does your courage fail you now that you are so close to your desire?'

'No, monster. I merely wish to savour the moment.' The shape emerged into the starlight, revealing itself as a man. Gregor Klausner's pale hand held the sword he had liberated from Skorzeney's corpse, its naked steel gleaming. The youth's eyes were no less rigid, drinking in the corpse-like form of the vampire with an almost emotionless regard. Before, this monster had filled his heart with terror, now it failed to even make his palms sweat. Gregor wondered if it was because he was no longer human enough to know fear.

Sibbechai spread its arms wide, its shroud-like robes billowing about its lean frame. 'Strike me then,' it hissed. 'If you can.' Gregor needed no further invitation. He rushed at the vampire with a speed that would not shame a prize Arabyan stallion. Yet it seemed an eternity to Gregor's mind, as he sprinted across the slick clay tiles, as the gleaming point of his sword drew close to the vampire's putrid form. And in that eternity, Gregor learned that he was still human enough to know horror. Thrusting his sword at Sibbechai's heart, he felt his hand tremble, his arm hesitate. The vampire's leprous claws closed about his wrist, ripping the sword from him as easily as if he were a swaddling babe. Gregor's eyes filled with anguish as he glared into Sibbechai's rotten face. The monster's skull was distinct and vivid in a manner that the faces of the living no longer were.

'Your brother was a thuggish animal,' Sibbechai spat. The vampire's clawed hand smashed into Gregor's face, hurling the young noble across the rooftop. He landed on his back, feeling the tiles beneath him shatter as he fell. Gregor scrabbled at the broken shards as his body began to slide down the slope, arresting his fall only with a frantic effort. Looking up, he saw the burning eyes of Sibbechai glaring at him.

Sibbechai reached down, swatting aside Gregor's arm to grip his tunic. With an impossible strength, the vampire's withered arm lifted him into the air. Gregor tried to break the monster's grip, lashing out with his fists and feet. He knew prodigious strength was now his, equal to even the fiercest Kurgan warlord, yet the withered vampire did not so much as flinch under his blows.

'Your father was a doddering old coward,' Sibbechai snarled. Like a bundle of rags, the vampire hurled Gregor a dozen feet, across the expanse of the street and onto the roof of a neighbouring building. He landed hard. His hand groped at his surroundings to arrest his fall, finding purchase on an iron weather vane. Slowly, his every movement sending broken tiles crashing to the street below, Gregor crawled up the slope of the roof onto the narrow ledge that formed its peak. He was not surprised to see a thin shadow waiting for him. Gregor roared at the monster, ripping a tile from the ledge and flinging it. Sibbechai's claw effortlessly swatted the improvised projectile aside. Shrivelled lips pulled back in a contemptuous grin.

'I will kill you!' Gregor screamed, charging across the rooftop, intent on sending the vampire's withered form to the street below. Yet his desperate attack never connected with his intended victim. Displaying a still greater dexterity, and an agility that seemed impossible for a creature so frail, Sibbechai dashed ahead of Gregor, catching the youth's throat in its cadaverous claws.

'And you,' the vampire laughed, like the rustling of dead leaves, 'are a fool.' Sibbechai tightened its grip upon his neck, a clutch that would have broken the vertebra of any normal man. 'I had thought you could be of use to me. To aid me against the necromancer. But you are nothing.' Once again, Sibbechai tossed Gregor aside like a piece of garbage. This time, no rooftop stopped his fall.

The last son of the Klausners hurtled out over the street, plummeting down like a thunderbolt hurled from the heavens. Gregor's body slammed into the edge of the stone quay that overlooked the river, cracking the stonework as it pitched over the side. The dark waters of the Stir closed greedily about his lifeless form as it sank, only a few ripples marking his descent.

Sibbechai turned away, already dismissing the violent interlude. The thrall had been a disappointment, weak and impetuous. Gregor Klausner tried to fight against the curse, deny it sustenance. It bespoke a tremendous will, something that Sibbechai would once have found impressive. But in denying the curse the nourishment it craved, Klausner made himself weak, little more than a paper dragon. His defeat had therefore been contemptuously easy.

The vampire looked again at the Schloss von Gotz. It would deal with Carandini by some other means, when the time was right. For now, it had more important needs to satisfy.

'You ARE SO very good to me, Furchtegott,' the baron's words bubbled and gurgled like waters from a slimy pond. The wizard nodded at his patron, a forced smile frozen on his face. 'Smile,' Furchtegott thought, 'smile so he can't see the horror.'

'There is still a chance of infection,' Furchtegott advised. 'With your body expelling the remnants of the plague, we must be very cautious about allowing lesser afflictions to gain a foothold.' The wizard had no idea of that which he spoke of, but if it persuaded the baron to remain isolated in his room, allowing no one but Furchtegott to see him, then the falsehood would do its work.

The wizard wound bandages around the baron's body, trying not to picture the abomination they concealed. 'Your skin will be very sensitive for some time, excellency,' Furchtegott said. 'We must ensure that it is protected.' The baron nodded his bloated head, already becoming bored with his wizard's explanations. He reached over with a bandaged hand, ripping a chunk of flesh from the platter resting beside him on the bed. The carcass of an entire pig had lain on that platter when Furchtegott received it from the kitchen servant at the baron's door. Better than half of that now resided in the baron's swollen belly, and the nobleman showed no signs of being unable to finish the remainder. The smile faded from Furchtegott's features as he watched the baron cram the meat into his mouth, seemingly oblivious to the sickly pus seeping through his bandages and tainting his meal.

'You should perhaps watch your diet,' the wizard advised. He tried to tell himself that the baron's face was not undergoing changes, that his mouth did not somehow seem wider than it should, that the bruises over his eyes were just large boils, not some unnatural growth. Baron von Gotz grinned at his physician-mage, displaying the rotten brown stumps inside his face.

'Didn't you say a good appetite was healthy?' the baron chuckled. Furchtegott tried not to wince as the nobleman's obscene breath washed over him.

'Yes, quite so,' Furchtegott agreed, nodding submissively. He hurried to finish wrapping the baron's leg, wishing there was some way he could convince the nobleman to let him cover his face. The wizard had no idea what was happening to his patient. He had followed the rites laid out in *Das Buch die Unholden*, the spell that would preserve its recipient against the ravages of disease. But something had gone wrong, it had not worked as it was supposed to. True, the baron was certainly no longer in danger of his life, but he was sicker than ever. Furchtegott couldn't even begin to name the disease rampaging through the baron's body, much less its legion of symptoms. It was more like an army of sicknesses than a single ailment. How von Gotz could remain so oblivious to his deteriorating condition, the wizard could not understand, but it chilled him to the bone.

He would need to scour the book again, Furchtegott decided. There had to be an answer in there, a clue to what he had done wrong. If he could correct it, he could still salvage the situation. If not, he would need to find some way of disposing of the baron, destroying him before his condition became any worse, before he became something *unnatural*. There might not be any reward waiting for him if that came to pass, but at least he could avoid the attentions of the witch hunters and charges of sorcery. Furchtegott looked back at his patron as the baron shoved the better part of the pig's leg into his mouth, his ruined teeth crunching away at its bones.

He had to do something soon, but first he had to make sure that the baron did as the wizard told him and stayed in his room. If anyone were to witness the state of him now, Furchtegott was certain the witch hunters would not be long behind.

MATHIAS THULMANN STORMED into the Wurtbad chapter house. The old servant who moved to take the witch hunter's hat retreated before that merciless gaze, a judgmental ferocity that would have given the most courageous man pause. Thulmann's mood was dark, his thoughts murderous. During the long walk from Otwin Keep, he had struggled betwixt the lust for vengeance and his respect for justice. There was a set procedure to follow, chains of command to be adhered to. Certainly no official within the order could be executed without the permission of Altdorf. But would they see things as Thulmann saw them? Could they understand how Meisser had befouled the Temple of Sigmar, if they had not witnessed the atrocity of hundreds of men, women and children burning to death? Creatures like Arch-Lector Esmer and Witch Hunter General South Sforza Zerndorff might even sympathise with Meisser's attempt to ingratiate himself with the temporal ruler of Wurtbad.

'Mathias.' Streng emerged from one of the corridors that connected with the vestibule, Emil and the veteran witch hunter Tuomas close behind him. The bearded mercenary jabbed a finger over his shoulder. 'Some visitors to see you.'

Thulmann sighed with fatigue, rubbing his temples with his fingers. 'Anyone we know?' the witch hunter asked. The best scenario would be Silja, or perhaps her father, come to explain the madness Thulmann had tried to stop. The worst would be a delegation from Baron von Gotz intent on arresting him for interfering with the baron's edict.

'Actually, they came to see Captain Meisser,' Tuomas said.

'I reckoned that might be a bad idea under the circumstances,' Streng elaborated. 'Meisser's mouth kept flapping on the way back here. I had to shut it for him. It'll be a few days before he's presentable.'

'How fares the captain?' he inquired. Streng smiled back.

'In his study licking his wounds,' the mercenary said. 'Don't worry, this time I made sure he's locked in.' His grin widened. 'For his own good, of course.'

Thulmann did not share in the jest, his mind on more important problems. 'Our other guest?'

'Still in the dungeons, Brother Mathias,' Tuomas answered. 'Missing you terribly, judging by the way he's been carrying on. I don't think he screamed that much when your man was tickling his ribs with hot irons.'

'Reckon I'll have to try harder when I get my hands on him again,' Streng mused. He looked over to his employer. 'We pick up where we left off with Hanzel?' Thulmann closed his eyes for a moment, then shook his head.

'No. We'll leave him be for a time. If he's so eager to talk now, he'll be doubly keen to speak if we let him wait a little longer. I'll see these visitors of yours first.'

Streng led his employer to a garishly appointed chamber that had once been a training hall for Wurtbad's witch hunters before Meisser had transformed it into a reception hall for his many guests. The furnishings were sparse, but expensive, claw-footed chairs from the reign of Emperor Boris Goldgather reposing beneath tapestries woven in the time of Talebecland's Ottilia. Thulmann found the gaudy collection of antiques from disparate cultures as tasteless as it was flamboyant. It added another crime to Meisser's misdeeds. He wondered what kind of spineless sycophants Meisser had been courting that they were so easily impressed.

The two men now standing in the reception hall were clearly cut from a different cloth. Or perhaps shroud was a more appropriate word. The first was a stoop-shouldered wraith, his elderly frame cloaked in the heavy black robes of Morr's sombre priesthood, a silver pendent depicting an archway hanging from his wrinkled neck. The shaven-headed cleric's face was pinched and wizened, his eyes cold and dark. His companion towered behind him, a giant of a man with his body encased in a suit of obsidian plates and a heavy black mantle, a raven embroidered across the chest, his face concealed behind the enigma of his helmet. Thulmann could feel the menace exuding from the warrior, the aura of death that hovered around him. Here was an engine of death, a killing machine as near to perfection as any Tilean assassin or Norse berserker. The witch hunter nodded his head respectfully toward the unmoving Black Guardsman of Morr.

'Father Kreutzberg,' Tuomas announced, indicating the bald priest, 'and Captain-Justicar Ehrhardt of Morr's holy Black Guard.' The priest blinked as his name was spoken. The hulking shadow that was Ehrhardt did not so much as twitch a muscle.

'I am Mathias Thulmann,' the witch hunter announced as he stepped into the room. 'Captain Meisser is indisposed at the moment. I am acting as his surrogate.' A strained smile creased the ancient face of Father Kreutzberg.

'I care not for whatever games you people play among yourselves,' the priest said, taking Thulmann by surprise. Obviously Kreutzberg was more informed about Meisser's situation than he had expected. 'I have come here because there is a matter that mandates a more integrated cooperation between our temples.' The priest's voice dropped into a subdued whisper. 'Your vampire has been found.' The words brought gasps from the Sigmarite templars.

'You've discovered the vampire's lair?' Thulmann asked, hardly daring to believe it.

'No, but the monster was seen. Only a few hours ago, outside the city. It attacked the plague pits.'

'The plague pits?' Thulmann tried to imagine what the vampire had wanted there, what relevance it had to its hunt for Helmuth Klausner's grimoire. Even for a necrarch, it seemed a strange thing to do.

'Two priests from my order were killed,' Father Kreutzberg elaborated. He gestured toward Ehrhardt.

'Also two Black Guardsmen, crushed within their own armour.'

'But what would Sibbechai want at the plague pits?' Thulmann pondered aloud.

'It stole bodies, Brother Mathias,' Kreutzberg said. 'The corpses of my priests were taken, as well as an indeterminable number from the pit itself. The acolytes who escaped the massacre say the creature was not alone. It was helped by a heretic blasphemer, a necromancer.'

The priest's words did little to encourage Thulmann. The vampire alone was formidable enough, but if Sibbechai was working with a necromancer, the threat was doubled. The peculiar limitations imposed on the vampire by its profane state would not apply to a living sorcerer.

'The wheel marks of a cart were present,' Ehrhardt stated. 'It was heavier when it left than when it came.'

'Necromancers often profane the solemnity of Morr's realm by forcing the semblance of life back into dead bodies,' Kreutzberg explained. Gustl, one of the chapter house's templars, rushed into the room, his young face flushed with excitement.

'You'd better come quickly,' Gustl said as he tried to catch his breath. 'It sounds like your prisoner has got loose and is tearing apart his cell!' As if to punctuate the templar's report, a horrendous scream welled up from the depths of the chapter house, penetrating the thick stone floors. Even Streng was impressed by the violence of the act that could wrench such agony from a human throat.

'That was a cry of death,' Ehrhardt declared, his voice emotionless. Thulmann's hand fell to the hilt of his sword. He raced toward the stone stairway that descended into the depths. The other templars hurried after him, the metal-encased bulk of Ehrhardt easily keeping pace with the lightly armoured witch hunters.

The screams grew silent as Thulmann sprinted down the narrow dungeon corridor. A pair of templars stood outside the door to Hanzel's cell, drawn swords clutched in their white-knuckled hands. From behind the doors came the wet, visceral noises of a body being torn apart.

'Get that door open!' Thulmann snapped. Hanzel still offered his best chance to track down Weichs. He cursed himself. He should have done as Streng suggested, simply beating Hanzel until he spat out whatever they wanted to hear. Instead he had chosen the cleaner, more sophisticated approach of breaking the man psychologically. Sometimes, he considered, he was too timid for his kind of work.

'Out of the way!' barked Streng, pushing a rusty key into the iron lock. The mercenary ensured that he had a good grip on the dagger in his other hand, then flung the door inward.

Something leapt from the torture chamber, something spat out of a nightmare. The guards cringed, their minds refusing to accept the hideous apparition. The twisted shape moved with incredible speed, a blur of reeking rags and brown fur, its mangy hair caked in fresh blood. The thing hissed at Streng, filthy claws scratching at his face. The mercenary pulled away, the talons raking the heavy leather guarding his chest. The thing's muzzle snapped open, baring its chisel-like fangs, ropes of saliva drooling from its mouth. The abomination hissed again and lunged for Streng's throat.

Thulmann acted at once. He stabbed the point of his blade into the ratman's neck, tearing the steel out of its flesh with a savage sidewise motion. Putrid black blood exploded from the wound. With a pitiful mewing, the monster fell to the icy floor, its scabby tail quivering as life retreated from its malformed carcass.

'Skaven,' Thulmann pronounced. He could not blame the men for their shock and disgust. To most men in the

Empire, the ratmen were a legend, a story told to frighten small children. But Thulmann knew better, he had seen their kind before, the inhuman patrons of his uncle, the sorcerer, Erasmus Kleib. The witch hunter jumped over the shivering corpse and into the cell.

Hanzel Gruber's death was more ugly than anything Streng could have inflicted on him. The remains of the plague doktor's arms still hung from the manacles, but the rest of him was strewn across the floor. Thulmann had heard men describe bodies being 'hacked to pieces', but this was the first time that he found the phrase appropriate. The sound of scrabbling claws snapped Thulmann's attention to the far wall where a jagged hole gaped, dislodged stones and earth scattered about its opening. A naked pink tail swiftly disappeared into the darkness of the tunnel.

'They're getting away!' Gustl cried out, sprinting for the tunnel, a pistol gripped in his hand. Ehrhardt and two of the other witch hunters were right behind him. Thulmann cried out a warning, but they were already disappearing. The templar hurried after them, cursing under his breath. He had just reached the mouth of the opening when a terrible groaning sound rumbled through the tunnel. In an instant, the roof of the crudely burrowed passageway came crashing down, sending a cloud of thick grey dust billowing back into the torture chamber.

Thulmann retreated, trying to blink the dirt from his eyes. When he could see again, he found Tuomas and one of the guards, swords drawn, eyes filled with terror. Thulmann could appreciate their distress. It was a horrible moment when myth became reality, when the underfolk of childhood stepped out from the shadows. Their minds were probably trying to find a sane explanation for the ghastly body lying in the corridor. Perhaps they might even find one they could believe in.

'You can relax,' Thulmann said, slamming his sword back into its scabbard. 'They are gone – for now anyway.' He could see the men were unconvinced, eyes fixed on the blocked mouth of the tunnel. Thulmann pointed to Tuomas. 'Fetch shovels, picks, whatever you can find to dig with. If luck is with us, we may be able to excavate the hole and find their tunnels.' It was a forlorn hope, but it would give the men something to do. Thulmann could already hear more of the chapter house's denizens rushing along the corridor outside. 'Take a few of them to help you,' he commanded as Tuomas headed back to the hallway, striving to avoid nearing the ratman's carcass.

'Phew! Somebody didn't want him to talk.' Streng inspected the carnage, turning over what may have been a part of Hanzel's face with his dagger.

'The skaven are quite accomplished at covering their tracks,' Thulmann agreed. It seemed that Sibbechai wasn't the only evil at large in Wurtbad that had found powerful allies. Weichs and the skaven was a combination that churned the witch hunter's stomach – the inhuman and the unhuman.

Other witch hunters openly marvelled at the horror that had been done to Hanzel Gruber, many of them making the sign of the hammer as they studied his scattered remains. Thulmann was about to give orders when the man watching the imploded tunnel called out.

'Brother Mathias! They return!'

His sword leapt from its scabbard. Dirt began to fall away from the hole, spilling into the cell. The witch hunter considered evacuating the room. If the skaven were returning it would be in far greater numbers. Or perhaps only a few had been trapped and managed to survive the collapse of their tunnel. If they could capture one of the monsters alive, Thulmann might yet be able to uncover Weichs's hideout. He motioned for the other men to make ready, noting the glowing iron Streng held in his left hand to augment the dagger in his right.

'I want one alive,' Thulmann declared, giving Streng a sharp look who gave a noncommittal shrug of his shoulders.

The dirt continued to spill into the room. Suddenly something black emerged from the earth, clawing at the open air. Thulmann eyed the flailing fingers, then advised his men to stand down. It was no skaven paw, but an armoured gauntlet. Thulmann hurried to the hole, helping the man to dig his way free. Captain-Justicar Ehrhardt emerged, his plate armour caked in dust, his sombre raiment torn and ragged. As the huge Black Guardsman fought his way free, he dragged the insensible shape of Emil with him, tossing the stunned witch hunter to the nearest of his fellows. Ehrhardt lifted the steel helmet from his head, exposing a harsh, weathered countenance that would not have been out of place on a seasoned veteran of the Reiksguard.

'We had the vermin in sight all the time,' Ehrhardt snarled. 'But there must have been others deeper in the tunnel. The scum collapsed their run on top of their own.'

'Courage and honour are not trademarks of the rat-kin,' Thulmann said. 'They will happily kill dozens of their own to eliminate a single enemy.' The Black Guardsman nodded in understanding.

'When we have finished with this vampire,' Ehrhardt growled, 'then this vermin will wish they had made a better job of it.'

'I was unaware that the underfolk were the concern of Morr's Black Guard,' Thulmann observed. Ehrhardt turned his penetrating blue eyes on the witch hunter, shaking a pile of dirt from his armoured shoulder.

'They are now,' the knight said.

'Then I shouldn't worry about losing the ones in the tunnel,' Thulmann said. 'Because where one skaven is found, there are always others.'

FILTHY PAWS SCRABBLED in the murky water beneath the docks, struggling to wash the odour from their fur. The pungent lilac scent was chosen by Grey Seer Skilk because his minions could track it easily across great distances. In truth, the skaven found the smell unpleasant, even more intolerable than the odour of the man-things they were sent to collect for the grey seer.

The leader of the small pack of ratmen looked over at the bound form they had abducted from the little fishing boat he called home. The skaven's teeth gleamed as it snarled at the fisherman, punctuating its displeasure by nipping at the man's arm. Skilk's doktor-man wanted his subjects alive, but 'alive' did not mean 'unharmed'. The fisherman screamed into the linen his abductors had crammed down his throat. The creatures chittered with amusement as the wretch struggled against his bonds. His days of dreaming about a big catch were over, his nightmare as the big catch itself was about to begin.

The skaven leader resumed its fastidious cleaning. The vermin paused as it noticed a shape floating upon the water nearby. Its whiskers twitched as it tried to pick up the object's scent, the lilac stench making it more difficult.

'Man-person,' it declared in a whispered hiss. In reply, the belly of the skaven beside it rumbled with hunger. The leader lashed its tail in agreement. They were forbidden to nibble at the subjects they secured for Weichs, but there was no reason they shouldn't avail themselves of other man-flesh. The body floating beside the dock was almost like a gift from the Horned Rat. The skaven leader looked about it nervously, afraid that it would see the eyes of its god watching from the shadows.

'Fetch-bring,' the ratman snarled, shoving the skaven with the growling belly toward the body. The creature glanced about cautiously, then slithered into the water, swimming slowly and silently. Soon it was back under the concealment of the dock, dragging the corpse with it. Five sets of hungry eyes glared at the body. The leader snapped at its subordinates with a display of teeth and the pitted sword it held in one claw. It wouldn't do for them to snatch the most succulent meat until after the leader had eaten its fill.

The ratman jumped back, tripping over one of its subdued minions. The leader picked itself up, gesturing with a claw at the corpse they had dragged from the river. 'Man-thing live-move,' it squeaked. The other skaven cast suspicious looks at the body, drawing their own weapons. Life was a problem they could solve quickly enough.

'No!' their leader hissed, lashing its tail through the mud. 'Tie-bind, quick-quick! Fetch-bring for doktor-man!' The ratman paid little notice to the ugly looks its underlings cast as they sullenly complied with its orders. Their leader was already lost in thoughts of the reward for bringing two subjects to Skilk's doktor-man. Of course, it wouldn't be big enough to share with its fellow skaven. Rewards never were.

CHAPTER NINE

THE SITTING ROOM was dark, the dying fire insufficient to banish the shadows that devoured swan-legged tables, upholstered chairs and fur-strewn divans. The room's sole occupant did not stir to replenish the flame, content to sit and study the darkening wall as he drained the contents of the crystal goblet in his hand. The intensifying gloom was a perfect companion to the pall covering his heart.

Lord High Justice Igor Markoff did not stir as the door to his sanctuary opened. Dancing candlelight fought against the darkness threatening to engulf him. He did not care who this midnight violator of his tranquillity might be. It was much too late for that. He had devoted his life to making his name respected and feared throughout Wurtbad, in the murky dens of petty thieves and the polished halls of the nobility. It was only now that he truly understood how tenuous and fleeting such strength and power were. With their parting they had left little but the shell of a tired, frightened old man. Markoff took another swallow from his glass. It might not be possible to restore his strength from a bottle, but he knew he could find oblivion within one.

Dimly, words began to filter through the darkening haze. Harsh, angry words, accusatory words. How could he have let such an atrocity come to pass? How could he have engineered such a hideous scheme? Once he had been a man worthy of respect, even emulation. Now, the self he had shown to the world was revealed as naught but a sham, unmasking the murderous coward within.

'Enough, girl.' Markoff lifted his hand, begging his daughter to cease her tirade. He forced his eyes to remain fixed upon the wall. She had been there, at Otwin Keep, when Meisser carried out his orders. She would not be silenced. Markoff smiled thinly, a tiny ember of pride flickering in the gloom. There was so very much strength in her, so much more than the gods had seen fit to bestow upon her father.

'How?' Silja's words cut at Markoff like a dull knife. 'How could you have conceived such a horror? How could you allow such wanton murder to be perpetrated in the name of the baron?'

'What good would it do to deny your accusations?' Markoff sighed. 'Oh, I am not pleading my innocence. Far from it! I am as guilty as any of the others, those great and noble lords so very concerned with the welfare of their mighty city.' He drained the last dregs of schnapps from his goblet.

'It was the baron's great vision,' Markoff stated. 'It was Meisser who gave it form and substance, the rest of us who gave it life. I've always had a good head for logistics, for efficiency,' the magistrate said. 'The baron has always appreciated that. Left on his own, Meisser would still be wondering which direction the keep is in. *Was* in,' he corrected himself.

'Then it was your idea, your plan,' Silja hissed back at him. The fire in her gaze had little to do with her reddened face and the salty trails staining her cheeks. Her knuckles whitened as Silja's anger drained into them. 'All these years I've admired you, tried to follow your example. What a fool I was to be so blind!'

Markoff rose from his chair, turning to glare at his daughter. 'You would have me play the fool then?' he snapped. 'Stand aside and refuse to have anything to do with the baron's mad schemes, just let Meisser ooze his way ever deeper into his good grace? Would that please you? Would that make you proud?'

'But you are the Lord High Justice–' Silja began to object. Markoff shook his head, scoffing at his daughter's protest.

'Simply another instrument of the baron's will. What power I have, what authority I have, is because the baron allows it. A snap of his fingers, a stroke of his pen, and I am no more powerful than the rankest ratcatcher in the sewers.'

'There must have been someone you could turn to.' Silja's voice had lost some of its venom, her father's pain, frustration and disgrace touching her heart. Markoff shook his head.

'Who? The Grand Theogonist? The Emperor, perhaps? Or maybe our gracious elector count, who has set a ring of steel around this city and is perfectly content to sit back and watch it die? No, Silja, there is no authority I can appeal to.' Markoff's hand began to tremble. 'Baron von Gotz is the only law in Wurtbad. While the quarantine is in effect, he may as well be Sigmar returned.'

'Then madness rules Wurtbad!' Silja swore. Her anger flared as she looked upon her father's trembling frame. She had come here to confront a traitor, an archfiend who had engineered the deaths of thousands. Instead she had found only a broken, defeated old man. She

turned, striding from the chamber until she stood once
more upon the threshold.

'Tell me, father,' she said, her voice a withering snarl.
'When the baron next calls for his sycophants to endorse
whatever insanity stirs his rotten mind, will you crawl to
him on your belly like a dog, or will you have enough
dignity to stand before him like a man?'

Silja did not wait for an answer, disappearing into the
maze of hallways that formed the Ministry of Justice.
Markoff stared at the empty doorway for a time, then
contemplated the empty goblet in his hand. It would be
so easy to ignore her words, to sit out the storm. But she
was right. The baron was dangerously mad, more of a
threat to the city than the plague he was obsessed with
destroying. But Markoff's days of boldness and bravery
were behind him, all he wanted now was to live his few
remaining years in peace, to enjoy the rewards of his
labours in the time left to him. Someone else could try
to counter the influence of the baron.

He tried to forget the contempt in his daughter's
words. But, even with the schnapps dulling his mind,
Markoff couldn't banish her accusations. With a deep
growl, the magistrate hurled the goblet into the fading
fire, watching as it shattered into a hundred shards of
starlight. He grabbed up his cloak from where he had
thrown it across one of the divans.

If he was unable to forget, then the time may have
come to act in such a way that he would not be ashamed
to remember.

FURCHTEGOTT SLAMMED THE book closed, too furious to
experience the repugnance that crawled up his spine
whenever he touched the binding of the mouldy old grimoire. The mystic wiped his hands on his golden robes.
Das Buch die Unholden seemed to grin back at him with
a mocking smile. He had consulted many tomes of

magic since taking up the mantle of wizard, and learned many disquieting, profane secrets in his studies. Knowledge that some insisted man had never been meant to know.

But the ponderous volume compiled by the witch hunter Helmuth Klausner, from the writings of warlocks and sorcerers he had condemned during his career, was another matter. The book almost seemed to be alive, possessed by a malicious intelligence. Pages would turn of their own volition, even when weighted down by lead ingots. The book would never remain where Furchtegott remembered leaving it, always manifesting itself in some unusual spot within his laboratory, some place it had no right to be. Most frustrating of all, though, was the way in which it seemed to guard its secrets; the way text seemed to slither from one page to another, as though evading the prying eye that sought to decipher it.

At one hour of the clock, an ancient fertility rite of the Old Faith might be found beside the foul practices of the Arabyan snake cults. At the next, it might have moved much deeper within the book, lurking between a necromancer's spell for instilling vigour in undead automatons, or a Norse shaman's ritual for bestowing the curse of the werekin upon a warrior. The words themselves were cryptic, written in a dazzling array of languages, every sentence ridden with double-meanings and deliberate contradictions. Some of the ciphers the long-dead witches and enchanters had used to guard their spells were among the most complex Furchtegott had ever seen. Even without the book's malevolent trickery, dredging anything useful from its pages was a study in frustration.

He should have destroyed the damned thing, reduced it to slag with his own spells. But he allowed its power to seep back into the air around him. No, anger would not help him now. He had to keep his mind clear, to consider his best course of action.

Baron von Gotz was deteriorating at a faster pace than Furchtegott had imagined possible. Whatever the spell had been, it was working its unholy sorcery swiftly. The wizard reflected on how easily that first spell had revealed itself to him, that ritual said to preserve a man against the ravages of disease and plague. It had been almost as if *Das Buch die Unholden* had abandoned its usual tricks and misdirection in order to ensure Furchtegott's ruin.

Furchtegott looked over at the heavy beechwood shelves that loomed against the walls of his workshop. The accursed grimoire would not help him, but he had other resources to draw upon. A wizard of the gold order was an alchemist as well as a conjurer, and the array of chemicals, powders and elixirs resting upon those shelves represented the tools of his art. Among them were compounds and concoctions so deadly that even the most murderous Tilean poisoner would hesitate to employ them.

It had become a choice of life or death – the baron's life or his own. Furchtegott realised that there was really no choice at all. He walked to the shelf and removed an iron bottle. The way the baron was gorging himself, Furchetgott was certain that there would be ample opportunity for the contents to find their way into his stomach.

HERR DOKTOR FREIHERR Weichs sucked at his finger as he studied the prone figure lying on the floor of the cage. Quite an interesting specimen, he concluded, ignoring the unease that flickered deep within his subconscious. The skaven had dragged him from the river, so the claw leader that brought the man to Weichs had claimed. Not the most healthy of environments in the best of times, and with his manufactured plague still ravaging the city, these certainly were not the best of times. Still, mere sickness seemed an inadequate explanation of the man's many abnormalities. His temperature was far colder than it should have been. Respiration and pulse were so faint as to be almost imperceptible. And, of course, there was that thick treacle that oozed from the man's forearm when Weichs had cut him. The doktor had seen much blood in his life, but he would swear that the filth slopping through the specimen's veins was not blood. Even the black pollutant that coursed through the bodies of the skaven had more in common with human blood than what he had drawn from the man's wound.

A mutant, Weichs decided, but not like any he had studied, or even created. It was unfortunate that the specimen seemed to have lapsed into some form of coma. The sharp smell of rat musk drew Weichs from his thoughts. The scientist turned around to observe Skilk and his bodyguard scuttling through his laboratory, causing the skaven working the larger furnaces and the presses to abase themselves and squirt their pungent fear-scent.

'Doktor-man,' Skilk snickered as the horned skaven hobbled toward Weichs. 'Progress? Like-hear much-much.'

'I am trying some new compounds,' Weichs explained, unable to keep the fear from his voice. The words clearly did not appease his inhuman patron. Grey Seer Skilk's face split in a menacing smile, his fangs like daggers. Weichs took a step back, fearful that Skilk's patience had finally reached its limit. Suddenly, the ratman's head cocked to one side, whiskers twitching.

'Man-thing die-die soon,' Skilk declared as he peered into the cage. 'Doktor-man make bad-drink?' The grin was back on its verminous face.

'No.' Weichs protested. 'He was brought here in that condition by your people. My potions will help him, make him strong again.' Skilk chittered his laughter, shaking his head. Somehow, watching the skaven make such a common human gesture was more unsettling than his natural habits.

'Death-smell never false-speak,' Skilk stated, one claw tapping the side of his snout. 'Die-die quick-soon. Food for doktor-man's warren.' The colour drained from Weichs' face. Of all the disgusting habits of his skaven patrons, their penchant for human flesh was the vilest. Any meat would appease their voracious appetites, even that of their own kind. Man-flesh was no different. Weichs had long ago been forced to allow his subjects to be consumed when they expired from his experiments. The scientist averted his eyes, trying not to think any more upon the gruesome subject.

'I have a few new preparations I will be trying on the latest batch of subjects,' Weichs announced, gesturing for the skaven priest-sorcerer to follow him. Skilk waited for the man to lead the way. Skaven leaders were especially wary of allowing their underlings to linger behind them – at least those leaders who hoped to live very long.

Skilk listened as Weichs prattled about his latest experiments, his black soul secretly mocking the man. Weichs was clever, for a human, but stupid too. He really did believe Skilk was interested in finding a way to unlock the healing properties of warpstone. The idiot. Skilk was not sick. What did he care about curing disease? The doktor-man was too foolish to see that Skilk was studying the effects of warpstone upon the human form, learning how much or how little was needed to corrupt it. Men were a violent, frightful breed, their minds moved by strange motivations and imaginings. They could not endure the taint of mutation among their own, unless that taint manifested in one of the nestlings produced by their own breeder. Then they would try to defend what they would otherwise destroy, forming strange alliances to protect their own from those they had formerly called protectors.

It was another of the many weaknesses that pervaded the human race, their curious affection toward others of their kind at the expense of their own well-being. It made little sense to Skilk, and the grey seer had spent his entire life studying humans after the example of his mentor, Grey Seer Kripsnik. But Skilk did not need to understand it to exploit it, any more than Kripsnik had truly understood the human lust for the yellow metal when he conceived of flooding the lands of men with poisoned coins. It was enough to know that the weakness was there, waiting to be used. The world of men would tear itself apart from within.

Skilk would be the instrument of that final triumph, polluting their cities in ways that the plague monks of Clan Pestilens and the warlock-engineers of Clan Skryre had never dared imagine. Then it would be his name, not that of Thanquol or Gnawdoom or Skrittar, that would be pre-eminent among the Order of the Grey Seers, he who would be acknowledged as the one true prophet of the Horned Rat.

The grey seer's paws scratched at his fur as he listened to Weichs' explanation, its own secret dreams and ambitions kept secret behind the skaven's beady eyes.

THE DANK STENCH of the sewers was overwhelming, overpowering even that of the shambling shapes that silently marched alongside him. Carandini would have preferred the noxious reek of his zombies. To him, the stench of death and decay was comforting. It smelled like power.

The necromancer exerted his will, compelling the two zombies carrying him through the effluent river beneath Wurtbad's streets to stop. The former priests of Morr complied, their ungainly husks swaying slightly as Carandini's weight shifted. The Tilean scowled as he considered how very close he had come to being dropped into the mire that soaked the zombies' feet.

'The mighty deathmaster fears getting his feet wet?' a hissing voice laughed from the shadows. Carandini could see Sibbechai's smouldering eyes in the darkness. The necromancer silently cursed the vampire. Let it laugh, he told himself, for the necromancer would laugh louder when he spat on Sibbechai's ashes and stamped them into the dust.

'Are we near the castle yet?' Carandini demanded. Wurtbad's sewers were not extensive, certainly not so all-encompassing as those of Altdorf or Nuln, where the entire city was served by a network of underground canals and channels. The sewers of Wurtbad extended only beneath the wealthier districts, allowing the elite of the city to enjoy the same comforts they enjoyed when travelling to the Empire's other great cities. The brick-lined tunnels conducted the waste out into the Stir, spoiling the riverfront even as the noses of the wealthy were spared.

The vampire's skeletal face leered. It had been Sibbechai's plan to use the sewers. It had returned to its lair after reconnoitring the area around the Schloss von Gotz, its travels taking it close to the river and the culverts that drained the sewers into the Stir. Carandini had to reluctantly admit that Sibbechai's plan was well plotted, if odious.

'Not so far now,' Sibbechai pronounced. 'We are beneath the royal quarter.' Carandini did not bother to ask the vampire how it could know such things. The supernatural senses of the undead were impossible for a mortal mind to comprehend.

Suddenly, the vampire snapped around. Carandini could see its lips pull away from its fangs. Sibbechai seemed to glide toward the wall, its feet causing not even a ripple upon the foul waters. Its clawed hand reached out, pulling one brick free. Carandini expected mud or dirt to spill from the wall, but instead there was only darkness. Sibbechai tossed the brick into the filth at its feet.

'It seems we are not the only sappers beneath Wurtbad,' Sibbechai mused.

'Some thief's strongbox,' Carandini postulated. The vampire shook its head.

'I can feel the air stirring here. It must open into a tunnel of some kind, not some ruffian's hiding place.' Carandini snapped his fingers, motioning for the zombies to advance. The rotting workers began to chip at the wall with picks and hammers.

'This tunnel of yours may be an old escape route from the castle,' Carandini observed. 'If it is, our work shall be much easier.'

'There are many fell powers in the night, necromancer,' Sibbechai declared. 'Some of them older and more merciless even than the houses of the vampires.' His eyes shone with a terrible intensity. 'If you still pray to any of the gods of men, pray that we find only dirt and stone and nothing more.'

Carandini watched as the opening in the sewer wall grew, finding Sibbechai's words of warning more frightful than the monster's threats. It was not wise to ponder what manner of creature could evoke caution in a powerful vampire.

A CURSE ECHOED about the old torture chamber, as Streng tossed aside his shovel to remove the large stone that disturbed his digging. Thulmann could not quite kill the smirk that grew on his face; his henchman never did have the heart for manual labour. The heaps of dirt set against the walls continued to rise. The witch hunters might not be experienced miners, but their enthusiasm was a worthy surrogate. Stripped to the waist, the templars attacked the blocked tunnel with vigour, hacking away at the earth and stone as though it were the neck of an enemy. Captain-Justicar Ehrhardt stood in reserve, powerful arms folded across his chest, waiting for the diggers to uncover any large stones that his immense strength could remove.

Thulmann could well understand the drive that motivated these men. The skaven had violated the sanctity of their chapter house, caused the ignoble death of their comrades. Already the diggers had uncovered one of their brethren, crushed and suffocated by the tunnel's collapse. The steady pace of the diggers had increased after that discovery, more eager than ever to come to grips with the loathsome underfolk.

It was not thoughts of retribution that stirred Thulmann's mind. Hanzel Gruber was dead; whatever the plague doktor could have told had died with him. His killers were now the only link to Weichs. The witch hunter looked at the hole his men were tearing into, almost wishing to see a rodent's snout, furry bodies and clawed hands spill into the chapter house. Thulmann gripped the pistols in his hands. He would need to be careful with his shots. Some of the underfolk could speak and understand enough Reikspiel to converse with men. If Thulmann could capture such a beast, it might have some very interesting things to tell him. He looked at the two Wurtbader templars beside him, their pistols held at the ready. He had given orders to shoot to maim, hoping that they could master their emotions long enough to show restraint.

Thulmann spun around as a foot struck the stone floor behind him. It was not some rat-faced fiend, but one of the chapter house's young page boys. The boy's eyes were on the filthy carcass Streng had dragged from the corridor outside and thrown into a corner of the chamber.

'You should not be here,' Thulmann stated. 'Go back upstairs.'

'There is a visitor to see you, sir,' the page reported. 'Silja Markoff. Should I send her down?' The boy's eyes strayed back to the unnatural carcass of the skaven. Silja had seen enough horror for one night. The least that Thulmann could do was spare her the sight of such an abomination.

'No,' he replied. 'I will see her in the reception hall. Please tell her I will be come to her directly.' The page needed no further encouragement, hurrying from the subterranean chamber. Thulmann gave orders to the men to maintain their vigilance while he was gone, encouraging them to take one of the ratmen alive if at all possible.

His thoughts turned to Silja, and the purpose of her arriving so late. The witch hunter sighed as he mounted the steps. The last thing he needed to hear this night was more bad news.

CHAPTER TEN

'WE SHOULD DO something about the slums.' The voice of Baron von Gotz was like the sound of a dog slobbering into its water dish, a nauseating, wet lapping noise. Furchtegott cringed as the baron spoke, struggling not to picture that grotesque parody of a mouth. The wizard had drawn the heavy curtains about the baron's bed, advising the nobleman to avoid drafts, yet, even with that ghastly bulk obscured, he could not vanquish the image from his mind.

'They are a breeding place for the plague,' the baron continued, noisily biting into the plate of mutton that rested in bed with him. 'The sooner they are removed, the sooner my city shall be free of the Stir blight. Besides, they obscure my view of the river.' The baron laughed, causing Furchtegott to think of swine wallowing in a pigpen.

'As you say, excellency,' Furchtegott replied, trying to keep his dinner down. Why by all the gods was he not

dead? The wizard had chosen three of the deadliest substances known to his order, fairly drenched the
nobleman's food in the stuff, and still he would not die.
He didn't even seem to notice the poison, continuing to
glut his insatiable hunger upon an unrelenting tide of
dishes. He'd eaten enough to feed a battalion in the last
few hours, and ingested enough poison to kill an entire
army. And Furchtegott was becoming hard pressed to
keep the servants out, to intercept the baron's meals at
the door.

He shuddered, reaching for a bowl of soup the baron
had yet to slurp down. The wizard removed the iron
bottle from his bag, upending it and draining its contents into the soup. Troll vomit was one of the most
caustic acids a man could find, capable of gnawing
through just about anything if given enough time. Only
magic kept it from eating through its bottle, but no
magic would contain its deadly bite once it was resting
in the baron's bloated belly. It would chew its way
through the walls of his stomach, rip its way free of his
flesh. It was the most horrible way to die that the wizard
could imagine, aside from the loathsome metamorpho-
sis already consuming the baron. But the troll acid
simply had to work. It was his last hope.

The sound of angry voices outside the door turned the
wizard's attention away from the baron's bed. Furchtegott had just risen to his feet when the door swung
inward, a flush-faced Lord Markoff stalking inside like a
rabid wolf, the guards hurrying behind him.

'What is the meaning of this outrage?' Furchtegott
demanded. 'The baron is not receiving visitors.' The wizard lifted his hand, pointing imperiously at the open
door. 'Get out of here.'

'Save your crooked words and twisted spells, sorcerer,'
snarled Markoff, the fury in his voice causing Furchtegott
to involuntarily flinch. 'My words are for the baron, not

his simpering lapdog.' The two guards exchanged nervous glances, their halberds held at the ready. Furchtegott did not know what bribes or threats Markoff had used to force his way inside, but it was clear they were regretting their decision now. Two armed soldiers against the unarmed Lord High Justice might not be the one-sided affair they had imagined.

'Do I hear voices?' the baron slobbered. It was Markoff's turn to flinch, the colour draining from his face. Sigmar's grace, was that the baron's voice? 'Do I hear my dear Lord High Justice?'

'Yes, excellency,' replied Furchtegott. 'You must tell him to leave. He is disturbing your rest.' Sweat was streaming down the wizard's forehead. If Markoff threw aside those curtains, if he saw the thing lying upon the bed…

'I will not leave,' Markoff snapped. 'There are things I must discuss with your excellency. Crimes that must be addressed.' The magistrate's words dripped menace like the venom of an adder, his cold tone belying the terrible anger boiling just below the surface. Furchtegott could see the guards grow tense as Markoff spoke.

'Crimes?' The baron's swinish laugh grunted across the room. 'Crimes are your matter, Lord High Justice. Do not bother me with such petty details.' The baron continued to gorge himself, crunching bones as he broke them apart to suck the marrow within.

'I speak of the atrocity at Otwin Keep.' Markoff snarled. 'I speak of the massacre perpetrated on your orders, entire families slaughtered to appease your fear of the plague.'

'I rule Wurtbad,' the baron retorted, his voice like a boot sinking into mud. 'My word is law. My will governs the land. The city and all within it are mine. Mine. If they live to see the dawn it is because *I* have allowed it.'

Markoff took a step toward the bed. 'There are laws that are beyond those of any temporal ruler, baron. Laws even the Emperor himself must acknowledge and respect.' The magistrate gave no warning of his intentions. Even the soldiers, who had been watching Markoff closely, were unprepared when he ripped a dagger from beneath his clothing and leapt toward the bed. 'The thousands butchered in your name cry out for justice and by my hand they shall have it, monster.'

The curtains were torn aside. The sight they had concealed impacted upon Markoff like a brick wall. The dagger fell from his fingers, his knees crumpled as their strength withered. 'Monster,' he had called von Gotz – but in his darkest nightmares, Markoff could never have imagined how fitting the epithet truly was. A moan of horror surged from the magistrate's body as reason crumbled within his mind.

The soldiers rushed forward, eyes locked not upon the horror they called sovereign, but on the shuddering assassin. They drove the shafts of their halberds into the man's back, spilling him to the floor. Only then did they chance to gaze upon the source of Markoff's terror.

It surged forward, the thing sprawling across the bed like an enormous pustule. Arms that were twice the length of a man's reached forward, a clawed, scabrous hand closing about the neck of one of the guards like a hangman's noose. The soldier did not have time to utter the scream welling up inside him. As though it were killing a chicken, the thing twisted the soldier's neck, killing him with a sickening pop. His comrade shrieked, hurling his halberd into the thing's face and retreating back toward the door.

He might have escaped, for the thing baron von Gotz had become was not a thing of swiftness and grace. But Furchtegott could not allow the man to live, could not let him carry this episode of horror away with him before the wizard had a chance to correct the terrible mistake he had made. Furchtegott exerted his will and the door slammed close, held fast by invisible tendrils of irresistible force. The guard screamed again, smashing and clawing at the door, his nails digging deep scratches into the wood. The baron's corrupt bulk waddled slowly towards him, clawed hands outstretched.

'Traitors,' the baron spat. 'Murderers and assassins all!' The baron's obscene bulk loomed over the prone form of Igor Markoff. The once-feared Lord High Justice was mewing pathetically, his mind broken by the hideous thing he had dared to challenge. 'I am Baron Friedo von Gotz! Lord of Wurtbad, master of the Empire's most glorious city!' The baron's malformed claw drooped to the floor, snatching up Markoff's cringing form as though the man weighed no more than a doll. Furchtegott could hear the magistrate muttering and mumbling in his delirium, sobbing again and again the name 'Silja'. The baron pulled the magistrate toward the shapeless lump that served him as a face, the gigantic, gash-like mouth opening like the maw of a shark, displaying craggy, rotten teeth. Furchtegott closed his eyes as the baron's jaws snapped close and Markoff's muttering was silenced.

'This is a great day,' the baron said, when the sounds of flesh being ripped from bone had receded into Furchtegott's nightmares. Neither the guards nor Markoff would be telling anyone what they had seen. 'A terrible traitor to the Empire has been unmasked and destroyed. There must be celebration.' The grotesque mound resting atop the baron's shoulders shook up and down. 'Yes, all the city must celebrate. I shall make a proclamation and you shall record it for me, dear master wizard. I am going to declare a festival. The food stores shall be thrown open and distributed to the people as a reward for their loyalty. Anyone found not feasting shall be hanged as a traitor.'

The baron's voice trailed off into swinish laughter. 'I shall open the palace, too. It shall be a great festivity, such as Wurtbad has not seen since the last vampire count was destroyed at Hel Fenn.' A claw-like finger pointed at the wizard. 'You must make out the invitations, Furchtegott, I can trust no one else with such an honour.'

Furchtegott smiled uneasily at the hulking monster. The baron's mind was deteriorating even more swiftly than his body, but the wizard knew better than to challenge his insane notions. He obediently approached a writing table and readied quill and parchment. Out of one eye, Furchtegott could see the monster slurping down the bowl of soup the wizard had poisoned.

'One should always wash down meat with broth,' the baron burped, tossing the empty bowl aside. Furchtegott felt the last vestiges of hope curl up and die inside him. Even troll vomit seemed unable to kill the abomination! An even more horrible possibility presented itself as the baron began to dictate his decree. Perhaps the thing that von Gotz had become could not be killed.

IT HAD NOT taken long for their tireless workforce to excavate the compromised section of the wall. Beyond the broken brickwork, the zombies exposed a dank tunnel of earth, the walls uneven and crude, scratched as if by giant claws. The bricks they had torn down appeared to have been intended for removal, held by a simple clay that broke easily beneath the attention of an axe or a pick. Carandini did not like to think upon what sort of creatures had engineered such a tunnel and hidden it so cunningly. Goblins, perhaps, though they would have used tools more akin to those of men rather than the claw-like implements the diggers of this tunnel had employed.

'In that direction,' Sibbechai hissed, stepping into the tunnel beside Carandini. The vampire pointed to the north. 'The tunnel joins a crossroads ahead, we follow the left branch.' Carandini willed his zombies to lead the way. The passageway might be deserted, but the necromancer would not take any further chances. Sibbechai seemed to sense his fear, its skull-like face grinning at him from the darkness.

The tunnel continued for fifty feet before linking with the crossroads. Carandini was quietly impressed by the vampire's vision, the monster penetrating the darkness as well as a mortal man could see in the sunlight. It was yet another disturbing detail to add to Sibbechai's list of strengths, another obstacle to overcome when the time came to break their tenuous alliance.

Carandini watched the zombies shuffle deeper into the tunnel, disturbed to hear the sound of their feet sloshing through water. It explained the persistent stench of the sewer, even in the tunnel. The filthy water was seeping through the earthen walls. The necromancer noted that the low ceiling of the tunnel would prevent his undead porters from carrying him as they had before. Whatever had dug these tunnels was not disturbed by confined spaces.

The zombies completed the intersection, waiting for the puppeteer to tug at their strings and give them new tasks to perform. Carandini watched Sibbechai's gaunt shadow disappear to the left. At least if anything was waiting for them, the vampire would discover it first. It brought a greasy smile to the necromancer's face, which faded when he discovered the extent of the seepage. The tunnel ahead of them was like a subterranean swamp, a stinking quagmire festering between the crudely excavated walls. The Tilean snarled a curse on the unknown builders of the passage, willing his slaves forward before Sibbechai's skeletal shape vanished completely from view.

The reeking filth of the sewer lapped about his knees as he walked. Side tunnels opened onto the passageway, dark, cave-like openings that sent a chill of unease up Carandini's spine as he passed, wondering what might be watching their intrusion with malevolent, inhuman eyes. Several times, he fancied that he heard a soft, scuttling sound, or the hiss of bestial voices. Nervously, the necromancer willed several of his zombie slaves to walk behind him and protect his back.

They had proceeded several hundred yards through the darkness when the fear gnawing at his spine finally manifested itself. The necromancer stumbled into his fifth pothole, spilling himself into the filthy water. He rose from the muck, his cassock dripping stagnant brown water. Then he saw Sibbechai turn from where it stood a dozen yards deeper into the tunnel, its fiery eyes blazing. At first the Tilean believed the monster was simply gloating at his discomfort, but then he recognised an intense wariness. Sibbechai's voice rasped from the darkness.

'We are not alone,' it hissed. 'The underfolk are coming.'

No sooner did the vampire speak, than Carandini detected the squirming, splashing sound of many bodies racing up the tunnel behind him, a squeaking noise growing from a faint murmur into a distinct roar. Sibbechai returned its attention to the tunnel ahead as dozens of eyes gleamed at the vampire from the darkness. Carandini willed his zombies to form a defensive line around him. The vampire could attend to its own welfare.

Then they were upon them, a snarling, squeaking mass of vermin. The tunnel crawled with the verminous shapes, the pungent stink of their fur overcoming even the stench of the sewer water. Carandini saw a riot of shapes and forms, small brown rats swimming through the water alongside vermin the size of dogs. Most hideous were those that scuttled forward on two legs, loathsome mockeries of men carrying rusty knives and driftwood spears. Some of the creatures wore tattered rags about their furry bodies, others went naked, their fur pitted and marred where ugly symbols had been branded into their hides. These were hurled against the defensive line of Carandini's zombies like a living wave. The ratmen slashed into his undead guards with knives and claws, their fangs gnashing together as they chittered their fury.

Carandini drew back, with the words of a spell on his lips. Even in Tilea tales were told of the underfolk, the foul skaven. His native Miragliano had been repeatedly attacked by the creatures, plagued by their corruption for countless generations. There was little Carandini held in common with the men of his homeland, his dark studies setting him as a breed apart. But the necromancer remembered the old hatred of his race, the ancient enemy of his people. It was a hate deeper than his contempt for the men of the Empire, a hate that dwelled in his blood. The necromancer stretched forth his hand, invoking the terrible name of the Power. Several of the skaven shrieked, steam rising from their mangy fur. The vermin turned to scurry back into the shadows, but found themselves blocked by the spears and swords of their own kind.

The necromancer exerted his will once more. The skaven squealed as their fur fell from their bodies, as the flesh beneath shrivelled into leather, the blood in their veins turning to dust. Before the horrified eyes of their comrades, the creatures toppled into the filthy water, their bodies reduced to mummified husks. The skaven attack faltered, the vermin chittering in fear, then surged forward once more. Carandini urged the remaining zombies to close ranks around him while he called upon the Power once more. But nearly half of his undead guards had been dragged down by the ratmen's savage assault.

Further down the tunnel, Sibbechai confronted the advance packs of the skaven. Dozens of chittering monsters clawed and hacked at the vampire with an inhuman swiftness nearly the equal of its own. But if the vermin were fast, they lacked the supernatural strength of the vampire. While their claws and knives ripped ineffectively into Sibbechai's withered flesh, its talons tore open their throats, snapped their limbs and crushed their skulls. The vampire snarled its own rage and fury, licking black skaven blood from its talons. With seven of their number strewn about it, the skaven cringed, squealing in fright. Sibbechai saw a large, white-furred warrior, its scarred face scowling at the vampire, barking furious orders at the cowardly soldiers. The vampire glared back at the skaven leader. It had not come so close to achieving its destiny in order to let a mob of subhuman scum cheat it of victory.

Large brown rats milled about the tunnel, squeaking in confusion. Urged to attack by the musk-scent of the skaven, the rats had followed their more advanced relations. But the object of their aggression had filled their tiny minds with fear. The mind of an animal could feel the profane energies that gave the vampire its pseudo-life, the power that exuded from the undead monster. The rats quivered and whined, goaded to attack by the musk-scent of the skaven but repulsed by the unnatural life-force of the vampire. Then, almost as a single creature, the rats grew still. Their confusion was at an end.

Sibbechai extended its clawed hand, stabbing a talon in the direction of the white-furred skaven. 'Kill,' it hissed, its smouldering eyes glowing like embers in the darkness. The rats surged forward, their beady red eyes mirroring the glow of the vampire's. The skaven chittered in terror as the swarm engulfed them, gnawing and tearing at their flesh. The leader was barking orders to its warriors as a tide of brown death swept over it, tiny bodies worrying at its furred limbs, clawing at its rodent face. The skaven tore desperately at the wriggling, gnawing beasts, but for every one it ripped free, ten more leapt upon it. Soon, the creature's white fur was blackened with blood and it plummeted into the water about its feet, writhing weakly as the rats continued to chew on its ravaged flesh.

With the death of their leader, the remaining ratmen scurried back down the tunnels, squealing in fright. Sibbechai watched them flee, annoyed that it could not expend the power to destroy them all. Perhaps once *Das Buch die Unholden* was in its hands, the vampire would return to settle with the vermin. But that was for a later time. The vampire turned, looking toward where Carandini had made his stand. Sibbechai still needed the necromancer. It would have been inconvenient if the skaven had managed to kill him.

Carandini stood at the centre of a circle of charred, withered bodies. Only a handful of the necromancer's zombies remained, their rotten flesh torn asunder, many of them lacking arms and hands where the skaven had hacked them from their bodies. The Tilean met the vampire's gaze. Sibbechai could see the fear and loathing behind the necromancer's eyes.

'What do we do now?' Carandini demanded.

'We proceed,' Sibbechai replied, its voice a cold whisper.

'We cannot,' protested Carandini. 'What if they return? Neither do we have enough zombies left to dig our way into the castle.' Sibbechai sneered at the necromancer's fear.

'Then make more,' it hissed back. 'There is no lack of material to work with.' It gestured with its clawed hands at the twisted, mangled remains of the skaven floating in the stagnant water all around them. 'The vermin have not diminished our workforce, they have added to it.'

SILJA'S TIDINGS HAD indeed been ill. She had confronted her father at the Ministry of Justice, admonishing him for his role in the destruction of Otwin Keep. Rather than refuting her accusations, the old magistrate had quietly accepted the blame, with no more justification than fear of Baron von Gotz, sovereign ruler of Wurtbad, and the nobleman's growing madness.

Mathias Thulmann had listened to Silja, hearing in her voice only the palest echo of the strength and conviction he had become accustomed to. The Lord High Justice's complicity in the baron's hideous edict had crushed her spirit, her father's failure to stand firm before such horrendous misuse of power had broken her. The witch hunter knew that no words he could speak would comfort the pain in her heart. She looked upon him in pained misery, a desperate pleading in her gaze.

Thulmann took her in his arms, holding her tightly, willing the pain to flow out of her and into him. Silja's body trembled as the tension slowly faded, eased by the simple solace of the touch of another human being. The witch hunter's hand kneaded the back of her neck, trying to soothe the stress he felt tight beneath the skin. Almost against his will, he found trite words of comfort, promises that all would turn out for the best. Silja did not seem to notice their vapidity, or the emptiness of their reassurances. Her only reaction had been to hold the witch hunter still more tightly, her breath hot upon his shoulder.

Thulmann slowly pulled away, uncomfortable with where this moment might lead. He had claimed the affection of a woman once, and that love had ended in a tragedy that nearly destroyed him. Such things were for other men. Men who walked beneath the clean light of the sun, men who did not skulk in the shadows of night, chasing the dread Dark Powers. Silja deserved better than Thulmann could ever offer her, even if he dared. As he released the woman, a regretful smile cast its pall upon his face. He saw a brief flicker of fresh pain flash cross Silja's features and felt a twinge of agony somewhere deep inside himself.

'You need rest,' Thulmann said. 'I will have the servants prepare a room for you, Fraulein Markoff. Please accept the humble hospitality of the Order of Sigmar.' The witch hunter bowed before his guest, then turned. 'If you will forgive me, there are pressing matters I must attend to which I dare not delay longer.'

'Perhaps you might allow me to help,' Silja offered. The need in her eyes touched Thulmann's heart. She wanted something to distract her from the black thoughts clouding her mind, until the pain she was feeling became dulled. Against this he weighed the twisted, grotesque thing lying in one corner of the old torture chamber, the terrible horror his men were even now breaking their backs to unearth. The image of soft white flesh being torn by the claws and fangs of malformed monsters.

Thulmann shook his head. 'No, this is a matter for my order to resolve. I must decline your gracious offer.' The witch hunter opened the door, stepping into the corridor. 'Get some rest, we shall talk more in the morning.'

Then he was gone, leaving Silja alone with her doubts and fears. With no observer to steel her nerves, Silja dropped down into one of the antique chairs, her pretence of strength dispelled like a magician's illusion. She thought again of her father, hidden away within his fortress, drinking his soul numb. He had always seemed such a good and honourable man. She thought again of the witch hunter. He too seemed a good and honourable man. But if she had been so wrong about a man she had known all her life, how could she put any faith in a man she had met only days ago?

Doubt, distrust and fear clawed at Silja's thoughts as the hours of night wore on.

FREIHERR WEICHS RAN a cloth against his forehead, drenching it in sweat. Grey Seer Skilk was an unpleasant creature at the best of times, but the skaven sorcerer-priest was even more intimidating when angry. Weichs cringed every time the ratman's long, scaly tail slapped against the floor, writhing like some gigantic worm. Skilk ran one black-furred paw across the ghastly collection of trophies ringing his neck, the monster's teeth bared in a fearsome grin.

The source of the grey seer's ire grovelled on the floor before him, its belly resting on the bare earth. It mewed piteously at the horned ratman, chittering in its own shrill, piercing language. Whatever words were exchanged, they only seemed to add to the grey seer's fury and increased the creature's misery. Weichs could see that the skaven had already undergone some terrible ordeal, dozens of wounds marking its body, apparently bite marks, its foul black blood slowly dripping. Was there some disagreement among the ranks? From what Weichs had seen of the brutality that passed for society among the skaven, some schism among their own kind might explain both the messenger's wounds and the grey seer's ire.

'Dead-things?' Skilk suddenly snapped, turning his hostile gaze upon Weichs. 'Dead-things in tunnels?' he hissed. The grey seer reached down at the miserable wretch whimpering at his feet, grabbing the ratman by the scruff of its neck. With a savage shove, Skilk threw the messenger across Weichs's lab toward one of the iron specimen cages. 'Look-scent.' Skilk snarled, still glaring at Weichs. With horror, the scientist understood what Skilk was saying in his debased Reikspiel.

Something had invaded the skaven tunnels, something the messenger described as 'dead-things'. Skilk had connected this description to the strange comatose man lying in the cage, the one who had 'death-smell'. The grey seer was quick to suspect treachery, and now his distrust was focused upon Weichs. The scientist felt a wave of nausea as he contemplated what Skilk would do if he thought he had betrayed him.

'Same-same,' the messenger squeaked, scurrying away from the cage as though it held all the daemons of the Wastes within. Skilk's malevolent smile grew as he advanced on Weichs.

'Doktor-man plot-sneak,' the grey seer accused. 'Want-like Skilk kill-kill, yes?' Weichs could see the two armoured killers that always accompanied the priest slinking toward him from either side. The scientist glanced about his warren-like lab, searching for some means of escape. His own assistants were cowering behind their stations, even the malformed Lobo trying to hide behind one of the presses. The skaven that had been working with him were slowly creeping forward, their faithless hearts eager to see the drama play itself out. Guttural screams of excitement and glee roared from the cages, their twisted inmates rattling the bars at the prospect of seeing their tormentor destroyed.

'I've been loyal.' Weichs shrieked. 'I would not betray you.' He backed away from the snarling skaven, trying to place a worktable between himself and Skilk's guards. 'Someone is trying to trick you, trying to stop our work.' Weichs knew enough about the skaven mind to understand it was useless to try to appease its suspicious nature. If he was going to save his skin, he had to redirect its paranoia.

Skilk hesitated, almost visibly contemplating Weichs's desperate words. His bodyguards continued to stalk him, corroded swords clutched in their hands. Weichs

began to scan the table for anything heavy enough to
serve as a weapon. Suddenly Skilk lifted a black paw and
uttered a sharp hiss. The two skaven warriors backed
away, lashing their tails as they withdrew.

'Doktor-man true-speak, maybe,' Skilk said, his voice
still dreadful in its uncertainty. 'Other grey seers like-
want Skilk fail-fall,' the sorcerer considered. After what
seemed an eternity Skilk turned away. Weichs breathed a
deep sigh of relief as the grey seer barked orders to the
other skaven.

'Take-fetch dead-thing,' Skilk snapped. 'Burn-burn,' he
added, pointing a clawed finger to the largest of the
workshop's furnaces. Weichs would regret losing the
opportunity to study the strange man, but the loss was
more than balanced by the continuance of his own life.

Three of the ratmen scurried toward the cage, one of
them snatching the key to the lock from Lobo as the
malformed halfling emerged from hiding. The furred
monsters hesitated at the unpleasant smell of the cage's
occupant, but a glance over their hunched shoulders at
Skilk reminded the vermin who they were more afraid
of. The ratmen opened the lock, scuttling into the small
cell and dragging the unconscious man from his prison.
Weichs could see him move his arm slightly, a faint
groan rasping from his mouth. The man should have
stayed in his coma longer, Weichs considered. It was certainly no respite to wake up to discover the skaven's
intentions toward him.

The ratmen dragged the man across the laboratory,
toward the fiery maw of the furnace. One of the ratmen
was the mangled specimen that had brought word to
Skilk of the intruders in their tunnels. Black blood continued to drip from its injuries, trickling from the
monster's fur onto the pale skin of the prisoner's arm.

The prisoner shuddered into motion almost faster
than the eye could perceive, throwing aside his captors

as though they were made of straw. One crashed into the side of a cage, its back snapping on the unyielding metal. The ratman's pitiful cries became frantic, as limbs that had once been arms reached from inside the cage and began to tear the rest of his bones from its skin. Another of the skaven flew across a worktable, its body colliding with the delicate glass apparatus as fiercely as if fired from a ballista. The vessels exploded under the impact, bathing the hurtling skaven with their volatile contents. The ratman struck the floor screaming, the corrosive mixture melting the flesh from its bones.

The wounded skaven was not cast aside by the prisoner, but dragged close to the man's breast. Weichs saw the man throw back his head, mouth opened wide, displaying a set of serpentine fangs. The skaven held in his powerful grip shrieked as the fangs buried themselves in its neck. Blood exploded from the wound. Weichs was sickened to see even more of the foul liquid sucked up by the prisoner's leech-like mouth. He had always discounted the myths and legends that spoke of the Children of the Night, the creatures known as vampires. Now he knew better.

GREGOR DRANK DEEPLY, the squirming skaven he held clawing ineffectually at his face. The world around him had become red, his mind thundering with the unclean hunger that filled his entire being. He had denied it too long, so long that even the putrid smell of the ratman's corrupt blood was enough to make the hunger explode inside him. It was an avalanche, a tidal wave. He could no more resist it than an ant could resist the crushing tread of a giant. Now the skaven's blood surged through him, feeding the foulness he had tried to resist. Gregor could feel the strength rippling through his body, feel the power coursing through his ravaged frame. He howled in disgust as he tossed the dead skaven aside, feeling the triumph of the corruption within him.

More of the ghastly underfolk were surging toward him, chittering their wrath, knives and swords flashing in their unclean hands. Gregor knew them for the monsters they were, had heard his own father wake up screaming in the night as his dreams touched upon memories of the vile ratmen. But there was no room for terror in the shrivelled, dying thing that had been his heart. What were these noxious vermin beside the horror that he himself had become? Gregor roared back at the scurrying ratmen, not waiting to receive their charge but pouncing upon them, such was the unholy lust burning in his veins. Like a lion among jackals Gregor lashed out at his inhuman attackers, each blow crushing ribs or breaking limbs.

Above the cries and screams of the skaven, Gregor could hear a sharp, shrill voice shrieking commands. He turned his red-rimmed eyes, scowling at the verminous shape that barked orders to its kin. The horned skaven priest withered before Gregor's terrible gaze. He saw the creature lift a shard of black stone to its muzzle. As it gnawed the stone, profane energies gathered. The sorcerer stretched forth its hand, a sizzling bolt of black lightning leaping from its paw.

'The apparatus.' an elderly man hiding behind a cabinet screamed. 'Be careful of the apparatus.'

A normal man would have been struck by that terrible lightning, his body burned to a crisp. But Gregor was no longer a normal man. As swiftly as the priest's spell was unleashed, Gregor was faster still, diving aside an instant before it could strike him. The terrible energy struck like daemonic thunderbolts, smashing into the bars of the cage behind him, turning them into molten slag.

Gregor did not have the luxury of relief. Set upon by a pair of frantic men wielding heavy hammers, his unholy eyes could see the blood glowing inside them, a foul, corrupt purple. 'Mutants,' he decided as he broke the arm of one, and tore out the throat of the other, his filthy blood spraying across the cavern. Gregor grabbed the crumpled, shrieking shape of his wounded antagonist, pulling it toward him. Man or monster, blood or daemon ichor, Gregor would appease the hunger with the creature's life.

Across the workshop, Grey Seer Skilk gathered the terrible energies of the warpstone he had consumed, preparing to unleash another bolt of destruction. Then he watched the creature lift one of Weichs's human servants over his head and break the man's back like a twig, reconsidering the wisdom of drawing its attention.

Skilk backed away, promising his bodyguards a death far worse than anything the creature could do if they did not stop it. The armoured skaven hesitated, cautiously scuttling forward. Skilk watched them depart, then turned and scurried for the nearest tunnel, his infirmity forgotten in his flight. Skilk was dimly aware of others hurrying after him. The skaven was about to snarl his wrath at whichever of his kinfolk was endagering Skilk's life by deserting the fray. But his companions were not skaven.

'Follow-quick.' Skilk snapped at Weichs and his malformed halfling slave. They followed close behind the retreating skaven priest as he raced down the burrow-like passageway, leaving the carnage to unfold in the workshop.

As he fled, Skilk was already making new plans. Someone was concerned that Weichs's discovery might place great power in Skilk's paws. Skilk considered that the list of possibilities was almost endless, but only the plague priests of Clan Pestilens or another grey seer would be so bold as to strike in this manner. He had to keep Weichs safe, at least until the human had done what was required of him. And he had to find out who was unleashing these alive-dead man-people.

The resources of an entire warlord clan were at his disposal. Skilk would flood the tunnels with skaven warriors, bring down these horrible man-monsters, and unmask whatever foolish rival thought himself powerful enough to destroy Grey Seer Skilk.

'It's no use,' Streng protested. He hurled the shovel across the room, doubling his body over and sucking great gasps of breath back into his lungs. 'We've been working for hours and for every shovel we remove, three times as much dirt rolls back.'

Thulmann stared hard at his henchman, angered not by his words, but by the truth they held. The witch hunters had been working all night to excavate the skaven tunnel, yet their efforts had only exposed a few feet. At such a rate, the year would turn before they uncovered more than a few yards of the passageway.

'It is your decision, Brother Mathias,' old Tuomas advised, leaning on his pick to rest. 'You currently hold the authority of witch hunter captain.' Thulmann silently considered the problem.

'We serve no purpose here,' he finally relented. 'If we would find these creatures, we must do so in some other fashion. Though I confess that how we will do such a thing eludes me.'

'Sigmar provides,' Tuomas replied.

'And no debt owed to Morr is left unpaid,' Captain-Justicar Ehrhardt growled. The Black Guardsman stabbed his shovel into the earthen wall as though spearing the throat of an enemy and stalked from the chamber, pausing only to gather up the armour he removed when he started to dig.

'Friend Ehrhardt has the right idea,' Thulmann confessed. 'We all of us need rest. Then we shall plan our next move.' Days of searching for Sibbechai's lair had turned up nothing. Now he had lost his best chance of finding Weichs. All he had managed to accomplish in the last few days was an act that many within the Order of Sigmar would decry as mutiny, heresy and insubordination. His only hope to avoid censure was that perhaps Meisser was not entirely unknown to his superiors in Altdorf. His duplicitous character was Thulmann's best hope of exoneration.

He ascended the steps leading up from the dungeon, squinting as he emerged into daylight. It did nothing to diminish his grim mood. The witch hunter's mind turned over the many failures he had endured since returning to Wurtbad. He had failed to find *Das Buch die Unholden* and failed to destroy Sibbechai. He had spoiled his best chance at tracking down Doktor Weichs, the man who, his instinct told him, was responsible for the horrible plague ravaging the city. He had even failed to stop the atrocity at Otwin Keep, underestimating the lengths to which Meisser would go. The witch hunter shook his head. It was at such times that the power and grace of Sigmar were hard to perceive, when the might of the Dark Powers seemed unassailable.

The witch hunter saw Ehrhardt's huge figure filling the hallway. Beside him stood Tuomas and the old servant Eldred. There was an expectant air about the trio, as though they were waiting for him. As Thulmann approached, Eldred stepped away from his companions.

'A messenger from the baron left this in my care not five minutes ago,' Eldred announced. 'It is for the captain of witch hunters.' A conspiratorial smile spread on the old man's wrinkled features. 'Since Captain Meisser is unwell, I thought it would be prudent if I were to impart it to yourself.'

Thulmann took the scroll Eldred offered him. He broke its wax seal and slipped the ribbon that held the scroll from the document. His eyes raced over the precise, practised lettering that filled the page, outrage mounting within him as every word imprinted itself upon his mind.

'Brother Mathias?' Tuomas spoke, worried by his obvious distemper. The templar looked up, crumpling the scroll in his fist.

'It is an invitation from Baron von Gotz,' Thulmann declared. 'Herr Captain Meisser has been invited to a feast the baron is holding in his castle. Indeed, he has declared a city-wide celebration.'

'Celebrating what?' Ehrhardt dourly rumbled.

'The execution of Lord High Justice Markoff,' Thulmann spat, as though the words were poison. 'The baron names Markoff a traitor here, and says that he will not forget Meisser's noble and heroic action at the keep when he appoints a new Lord High Justice.' Thulmann slammed his fist against the wall, cracking the plaster with his fury.

'He can't do that.' protested Tuomas.

'He has the authority to do whatever he wants.' Thulmann scowled, then paused as a thought occurred. Silja had said her father was convinced that the baron was mad. If this could be proven, if someone was bold enough to level such charges against him in public, and had the power to enforce the baron's removal…

'Brother Tuomas,' Thulmann said, pointing a finger at the older witch hunter. 'Rouse Captain Meisser. Inform him that he has an engagement this evening and that he will be taking a number of guests with him.' Tuomas's brow knitted with puzzlement until he realised what Thulmann intended. The old witch hunter hurried to follow his orders.

'Whatever scheme is hatching in that crooked brain of yours,' Ehrhardt growled, 'make room in them for a Black Guardsman. The baron consigned all those poor wretches to the flames without allowing them the final grace of Morr. I would hear him answer for such sacrilege.'

Thulmann smiled and gripped Ehrhardt's hand. 'I am coming to believe that there isn't anyone the Black Guard of Morr doesn't have a grievance with.'

'Does the Order of Sigmar begrudge sharing its heretics with the templars of Morr?' Ehrhardt retorted.

The smile faded from Thulmann's face. There was one other person he would need to inform of Baron von Gotz's message.

Of all the trials he had endured in Wurtbad, telling Silja Markoff that her father had been executed as a traitor was going to be the hardest.

CHAPTER ELEVEN

AWARENESS BEGAN TO fight its way through the red mist that filled Gregor's mind. He looked at his surroundings, the subterranean laboratory of the plague doktor, Frei-herr Weichs, seeing it clearly for the first time. The cavern was a shambles, fires burned unchecked where chemi-cals and volatile compounds had been scattered during the fray. Broken glass and splintered wood lay strewn all about.

Scattered amidst the debris were twisted, inhuman bodies, the corpses of Weichs's malformed human assis-tants, the hideous forms of his skaven patrons. Blood, black and foul, stained the earthen floor. Gregor felt an intense loathing turn his stomach, as he realised that it was on such filth that he had gorged himself. That it was upon such vermin that the hunger raging within him had satiated its thirst. If he had believed he could fight Sibbechai's curse, if he had thought he could remain a man, he knew better now. He recalled the cold, evil gaze of the vampire, and the life that he had been cheated of. Miranda, with her soft tresses and passionate kisses, his ancestral home with its ancient setting and noble history. He thought of his father and his brother, both slain by the vampire. Sibbechai would suffer for what it had done. Nothing would stop him from having his revenge.

Gregor abased himself upon the charnel house floor of the cavern, begging for Sigmar to hear his plea. To grant him the determination to pursue his revenge. To do what had to be done in order to redeem his soul from the darkness. As he opened his eyes again, he saw a shaft of splintered wood torn from one of the tables during the battle. He grabbed it with an almost tender embrace, holding it as though the crude spear were some holy relic.

He could sense the vampire lurking somewhere nearby. The hideous curse that bound Gregor to Sibbechai would also lead him to it. Gregor walked forward into one of the gaping tunnel openings. However crooked the burrows of the underfolk, he would not lose himself. The profane light of Sibbechai's foul existence would lead him on.

And when he found the vampire, he would drive his spear through its shrivelled heart. Only then could he allow his own corruption to be purged from him by stake and hammer and flame.

Silja Markoff had returned to the garishly appointed reception hall. This time, however, the young woman's reserves of strength were depleted. She could not hold back the emotions raging within her. Tears flowed freely from her reddened eyes, her body trembling with terrible sobs. Thulmann's comforting hand rested on her shoulder. He knew that no empty words of comfort would provide solace now. It was much too late for platitudes. He found himself wishing that Father

Kreutzberg had not returned to the Temple of Morr. The old priest was well versed in the ways of death and offering succour to the bereaved. But Kreutzberg did not seem to share Ehrhardt's opinion that skaven were of concern to the disciples of Morr. Indeed, he had left the chapter house in almost unseemly haste after the ghastly events in the torture chamber, preferring the hunt for vampires to a confrontation with the under-folk.

'I shamed him into it.' Silja wept. 'He tried to explain and I wouldn't hear him.' She looked up at the witch hunter. He winced as he saw the pain in her face. 'The things I said to him. The hideous things I said, the last words he ever heard from my lips! I may as well have put the sword to his throat myself.'

Thulmann remained silent, letting her anguish fill the air. What could he say? That because of her, Igor Markoff had remembered his duty and his honour? That he had died the death of a hero, striving against a maniacal tyrant? Later such words might be of help, now they would only feed the misery of her loss.

Thulmann's hand tightened about her shoulder. His voice spoke firm and grim. 'He will be avenged, Silja. Your father's murder will not go unpunished.' A faint shadow of hope tinged the pain in her eyes, her hand closing over his own. 'By Sigmar's holy name, I swear it,' the templar added, feeling the power behind his words. Thulmann was a devout Sigmarite, some might go so far as to call him a zealot. He did not make oaths in his god's name lightly.

There was a sharp knock at the door. Slowly the portal opened, revealing Streng's unkempt visage, dust from the aborted excavation still covering his clothes. Thulmann noted that the mercenary had found time to raid the chapter house's armoury, a brace of pistols hanging from his belt.

'We're ready, Mathias,' Streng said. 'If we're to go through with this, we'd better act now.'

Thulmann extracted his hand from Silja's grasp. She looked from Thulmann to Streng and back again. The old cunning and suspicion that had allowed her to act as her father's agent returned to her eyes.

'Go through with what?' she demanded.

'It would best if you did not know,' Thulmann replied, smiling weakly. Silja rose to her feet.

'That was the only answer I needed,' she said. 'I'm coming with you.' Seeing the disapproving light in the witch hunter's eyes, Silja's voice grew soft, at once stronger and more vulnerable. 'He killed my father, Mathias. Surely that gives me the right.'

'I don't think they'll let the daughter of a man the baron executed as a traitor anywhere near the castle,' Streng pointed out.

'And how are you planning to approach the baron?' she asked.

'We have an invitation,' Thulmann admitted. 'Captain Meisser has been invited to attend a social gathering. Naturally a man of such importance is not going to attend such an event without his own functionaries to hand.'

'Then I'm coming with you,' she repeated. 'You can furnish me with one of those oversized cloaks and horrible hats you people always wear. Even the baron's own guard don't like witch hunters. They make them uneasy. They won't look too close at the face beneath the hat.'

Thulmann realised there was to be only one resolution. He nodded at Silja. 'Streng, have Eldred provide Fraulein Markoff with an appropriate raiment and see that she doesn't lack in the area of armaments.' He didn't like the lewd wink Streng gave as he loped off to implement his employer's commands, nor the way it brought colour to his own face. He was allowing Silja Markoff to accompany their expedition because it was the right thing to do. There was no other reason.

'I should warn you that Captain Meisser will be accompanying our excursion,' he said. 'You might say he's our walking invitation.' He raised an admonishing hand. 'Tempting as it might be, try not to kill him. At least not until after we're safely inside the Schloss von Gotz.'

'I REALLY MUST advise against such exertion after such a trying recovery, excellency.' It had been some time since the wizard Furchtegott had known stark, utter terror, but now he was fully reacquainted. He trembled with a helpless fear far beyond the child watching the shadows in its room assume monstrous shapes, or the woodsman who hears the scratching of a wolf at his door in the dead of night.

When the baron's proclamation had been made, Furchtegott had been too overwhelmed by the aftermath of Markoff's death to consider the consequences of such a whim. The food stores of the city were to be thrown open, the rabble allowed to plunder them to their hearts' content. If Graf Alberich Haupt-Anderssen did not lift the quarantine soon, if he could not be satisfied that the plague had been eradicated, Wurtbad would starve. There had been little chance of making it through the winter before, now von Gotz had ensured that there was none at all.

However, there was something of more immediate concern to Furchtegott. Something he cursed himself for not realising when he wrote down the baron's edict and hastily passed it on to his steward. Von Gotz was hosting a grand feast to celebrate the destruction of the plague, a great festivity to which all the notables of the city had been commanded to attend. The wizard should have realised that the baron would hardly host such an event without attending it himself.

The wizard regarded the abomination rummaging about its wardrobe, trying to find some piece of finery that would still fit its bloated bulk. Furchtegott pondered the horror of the baron's mind: how could he not see what he had become, not realise what was happening to him? Yet he carried on as though he were still as he once had been. Was it madness, Furchtegott wondered, or something even more unnatural?

'You take good care of my welfare, dear Furchtegott,' the baron's voice bubbled. 'But I am a robust man, a man who needs to be active and vital. I have been too long locked away in these rooms, my mind craves diversion. Do not trouble yourself, my friend, I shall not expire from overexertion, I promise you.'

Furchtegott could readily agree with that sentiment. He had tried every poison known to him, and quite a few deadly improvisations with the chemicals in his workshop, and still the baron lived. His constitution was not even remotely human now, his appearance even less so. Perhaps clean steel or a little battle magic might still destroy the monster, but after witnessing what the baron had done to Markoff and his own guards, the wizard knew it would take a heart much stouter than his own to put such a theory to the test.

'Why so glum, magician?' The sound that slopped from the baron's mass more resembled the gagging of a cat than human laughter. 'If I suffer a relapse, you will simply have to doctor me back to health once more. It would prove beyond a doubt your prowess in the arcane arts.'

The wizard forced himself to look on the baron, at the pools of black bile that had replaced the nobleman's eyes. 'I will take no responsibility for your health if you dismiss my admonition,' Furchtegott said, with all the disapproval he could muster. 'You have recently recovered from a most virulent pestilence and your body is still weak, even if you do not feel it. In your present state, you are highly sensitive to the ill humours of others. That is why you must keep to your room and allow no one in.' The wizard threw up his hands. 'Yet now, you seem intent on undoing all of my work, attending a feast where there will be hundreds of people from all over the city, each of them bringing with them who knows what diseases and foul airs!'

Baron von Gotz, or the creature that used to be him, wore an almost childlike look of contrition. The thing nodded its head almost sheepishly. 'I apologise, magister,' the Baron croaked. 'You know best, of course.' The thing shuffled toward its bed, letting the ermine cloak it had been fondling trail behind it like the tail of a slug.

'Stay here and rest,' Furchtegott replied, all conviviality now. 'I shall be back in a few moments with a restorative for you to drink.' The wizard retreated, pleased to see von Gotz draw back the curtains of his bed to keep any foul airs from lighting upon him when the door was opened. More importantly, it kept anyone in the corridor from accidentally catching a glimpse of him.

The baron was becoming more and more unpredictable, more unstable. Furchtegott could not be certain how much longer he would be able to control the thing. The time had come to escape, before he found his way onto the gallows or the witch hunter's pyre. He would gather up his most precious paraphernalia and slip from the castle while the feast was taking place. The guards would be too intent on checking the people flooding into the castle to pay much heed to someone leaving.

In the baron's bedchamber, an obscene puddle of rotting flesh and protruding bones waddled the floor once more. The baron's clawed hands fondled the soft, rich fur of his ermine cloak. He always looked so splendid in this pristine garment. He turned his viscous eyes toward the floor, imagining the gathering in the halls beneath his feet. It was his celebration, after all. It would be the height of impropriety for the host not to show himself to his guests.

The baron's talons fumbled at the clasp of his cloak, trying to fasten it about his swollen neck. He wanted to look his best when he made his entrance.

'WELL, COLLECTING THESE was a waste of time.' Carandini hefted the pick he had taken from a zombie, hurling the tool back down the tunnel. He wrinkled his nose at the ragged fur that hung from the reanimated skaven's shoulders, where the fangs of Sibbechai's rats had done their work. Removing a dagger from his cassock, Carandini began to cut away the flapping length of fur-covered flesh.

The necromancer and his living dead attendants had followed Sibbechai for hours through the wandering network of tunnels and passages. They had not been troubled again by the skaven, but Carandini was certain that the hideous underfolk had not forgotten the invaders. The hairs of his neck prickled every time he considered inhuman eyes watching their every movement, waiting for the opportune moment to strike.

They faced a stone wall, already breached long ago and resealed in a hasty fashion. Like the bricks in the sewer wall, the stones were intended for easy removal to afford access from the skaven tunnels. It made sense for the rat-men to extend their network to include the castle itself, allowing their spies to creep into the halls of power to observe the world above their own shadow kingdom.

'Do not complain, necromancer,' Sibbechai's sardonic voice intoned. 'The mutants have done our work for us. We need only remove a few stone blocks and the prize shall be in my grasp.' The vampire pointed a clawed finger at the wall. 'Set your creatures to work. I grow impatient.'

Carandini was chilled by the fanatical tone in its words. For centuries the monster had striven to recover the book compiled five hundred years ago by its brother, the witch hunter Helmuth Klausner, bound in the skin he had flayed from Sibbechai's undead husk. Now the flames of its desire glowed beneath the vampire's withered hide, even greater than the bloodthirst of its kind. Sibbechai would tolerate no more failures.

The zombies shambled forward, clutching and groping at the stone blocks. Carandini could sense the vampire's frustration and impatience mounting by the moment. The necromancer retrieved the claw of Nehb-ka-Menthu from his bag, crouching in the filthy earth that covered the tunnel floor. He drew signs and symbols in the dirt, the words of ancient Nehekhara slipping from his tongue. The already damp air of the tunnel suddenly became colder, the mud clinging to the fur and rags of the zombies crackling as frost appeared upon it. In response to the necromancer's invocation, they jerked and twitched with new life, attacking their labours with increased speed and strength. A cold sweat peppered Carandini's brow as he struggled to complete the complicated litany of words and gestures. Calling upon the malevolent spirit of the dead tomb king to bolster the strength of his own spells was not without its cost, or its dangers.

If Sibbechai noticed the necromancer's ordeal, it gave no indication. As still as the skeleton of a blackened tree, the vampire's unclean anticipation grew as each block was pulled away. Often the grip of dead fingers would prove insufficient for the task at hand, the huge stones tumbling free, crushing bones and breaking limbs. Those still able would rise again, limping back to their labour with the same silent obedience with which they endured mutilation. Others remained trapped beneath the stones, feebly trying to wriggle free and continue their work with broken spines and shattered skulls.

It was not long before the opening was large enough to admit a man's body. The vampire stepped forward, gesturing with its claw for Carandini to cease his spell. The zombies were instantly still as the necromancer's voice stopped, standing like grisly statues. Carandini rose slowly to his feet, breathing deeply as he tried to replenish the air in his starved lungs. Even with so potent a talisman as the hand of Nehb-ka-menthu, Tomb King of lost Khareops, drawing on the dark magic of necromancy had its price.

Sibbechai regarded the recovering sorcerer, its eyes smouldering in the darkness. The creature lifted its skeletal hand and gestured at the opening. 'You first, deathmaster,' it hissed. Carandini heaved himself upright, stumbling toward the hole as his weakened body recalled the mechanical exercise of moving his legs. Carandini stepped through the hole in the wall, into the darkness below the Schloss von Gotz.

His sensitive eyes pierced the shadows. The skaven had chosen their entry point well. The room was large, with only a single ironbound door leading from it. Much of it was empty, the rest occupied by stacks of wooden planking, bricks and clay roof tiles. Clearly it was some manner of storeroom, but the layer of dust showed it had not been entered for some time.

Sibbechai had made a terrible mistake in allowing the Tilean to precede it. Carandini was a black sorcerer versed in the magic of death and undeath, but he was still a man, living blood still flowed through his veins. Sibbechai was one of the undead, a child of the night. Strange were the limitations placed upon its unholy kind. The castle was a human abode, and no vampire could gain entry to such a residence without being invited across the threshold. Carandini smiled at this flaw in Sibbechai's plan. The vampire would still be scratching at the door when Carandini retrieved *Das Buch die Unholden* from whatever fool now possessed it.

Sibbechai's eyes glowed in the dark like dancing flames. Even as Carandini opened his mouth to hurl a parting jibe, he realised his mistake. The vampire had helped Carandini turn the corpses from the plague pit into zombies, but had lent no aid in restoring their ranks after the skaven attack. It had not helped Carandini control the automatons, nor lent its own dreadful power to the creatures' penetration of the castle wall. It had conserved its power while letting the necromancer expend his. Now, Sibbechai turned its hypnotic eyes upon the Tilean, forcing its thoughts into his weakened mind.

Like a puppet, Carandini drew closer to the hole. Words came unbidden to his lips, words that did not originate in his own mind. In truth, any living, human being could gain entry for a vampire to a human dwelling. It was for this reason that the dread vampire counts had kept living slaves among their undead households, to steal into places their masters could not go, to unlock doors a vampire could not open. It was for this reason that Sibbechai had allowed Carandini to come so close to the prize.

'Enter, master,' Carandini heard himself say. Sibbechai's malevolent laughter crackled about the underworld like lightning. With a flourish of its shroud-like robes, the vampire swept forward, its gaunt shadow falling upon the sorcerer. As its fiery eyes burned into his own, he knew he gazed upon his death. Sibbechai had spared him only so that he might invite the monster across the threshold. Now his usefulness was at an end. Raw terror threatened to explode his heart as he realised there was nothing he could do to stop it.

'No, deathmaster,' Sibbechai laughed. 'You will live a short time yet. You will be granted the privilege of seeing Sibbechai in all his magnificence. You shall see the

treasure you thought to cheat me of before I allow death
to still your screams.' The vampire laughed, gliding away
from the necromancer as though it were nothing more
than mist and shadow. Carandini watched as the ranks
of zombies followed the vanishing fiend toward the
storeroom's only door. But Sibbechai had not finished
with its treacherous confederate, placing another oblig-
ation upon Carandini's weakened mind.

'Remain here, necromancer,' it hissed. Carandini
watched the vampire's claw close about the heavy door,
tearing it from its hinges as though it were crafted of
paper. 'Do not fear,' it said as its shadow drifted away
into the cellars beyond the storeroom, 'I shall not be
long.'

THE CASTLE VON Gotz was alive with activity. Servants
dressed in their garish livery bustled about, seeing to the
care and comfort of the small army of guests that filled
the castle's halls. They represented the very best the city
had to offer – the scions of the ancient families of the
nobility, the wealthiest of the river merchants who
brought trade and prosperity to the city, guildmasters
representing virtually every lawful vocation in Wurtbad,
and several that existed upon the grey fringes of the law.
Foppish aristocrats in powdered wigs rubbed shoulders
with grizzled army officers who wore their scars as
proudly as their medals.

Young baronets dressed in silk shirts hobnobbed with
ageing countesses, their wrinkles buried beneath layers
of powder and perfume. Above them all the marble walls
of the castle gleamed, alabaster cherubim frolicked, and
the faces of barons long dead and forgotten glowered
from massive canvases. But above all else there hung that
intangible pall of dread and foreboding that reached out
and clutched at every soul. Among the gathering, conversation was either idle or far too desperate, the

laughter nervous or raucous. The music of the orchestra assembled in the castle's grand ballroom was too precise, too dispassionate, as though even the notes felt subdued by the weight of the atmosphere.

There was no one who did not submit to that tension hovering in the air. The baron claimed that the plague had been vanquished, but few would verify his boast. The baron said that Graf Alberich would soon lift the quarantine, and that food from all across Stirland and the Empire would be brought into their city, but most were sceptical of such assurances. The assembly was perhaps the largest the castle had ever paid host to, but it was not from jubilation or gratitude that the throng had manifested. Each had received the note asking them to the castle. The baron had not invited his guests, he had commanded them. Now each nervously waited for whatever misery would unfold next, or else gave way to reckless abandon, to deny the dread numbing their hearts.

Like the music, the festivities were hollow and lifeless, a moth heeding the call of the flame and knowing it to be its death knell.

'For a city on the brink of winter, plague and starvation, they certainly know how to suffer in grand style,' Streng said, tearing into a goose leg appropriated from one of a dozen long dining tables in the castle's cyclopean ballroom. The mercenary patted his belly, letting a loud belch rumble.

'If the quarantine isn't lifted soon,' Thulmann stated, 'these people will be boiling boot leather and tree bark in a month.' Streng shrugged his shoulders, taking no interest in what befell the populace of Wurtbad. 'You might do well to remember that we are in this together, friend Streng. Until the quarantine is lifted, what happens to the city, happens to us.' Streng shot a sour look at his employer, then set the plate down on a nearby divan. The witch hunter's words went far toward ruining his appetite.

'I could do without remembering that sort of thing,' he grunted. 'Now I have to go and find enough ale to let me forget.'

'Keep your wits about you and your eyes open,' Thulmann warned. 'Don't forget why we are here.' The mercenary gave Thulmann a sour glance, but he understood.

It was a mad plan. If Thulmann was completely honest with himself, it was akin to bearding a dragon in its lair – arresting Baron von Gotz in his own castle, stealing him from the midst of a veritable army of guards, retainers and sycophants. The witch hunter's only hope was that the baron's madness was just as obvious to his guests as it was to him. From the few snatches of subdued conversation he had heard, he felt that perhaps his hopes were not idle ones. The great and the good of Wurtbad might be perfectly happy to see von Gotz deposed, so long as someone else risked his neck to do so.

There were seven of them in the group Thulmann had led into the castle. No, eight, the witch hunter corrected himself, though he wasn't counting on any help from Meisser. True to Silja's prediction, the baron's guards had barely even looked at them, passing them on after only the most perfunctory examination of Meisser's invitation. Thulmann was mildly surprised that the delegation from the Order of Sigmar had not been asked to relinquish the weapons they so openly wore, but then, nobody would expect the pious templars, sworn servants of Sigmar and the Empire he founded, to raise arms against its highest representative in Wurtbad. Besides, with the execution of Markoff, Thulmann suspected that Baron von Gotz might be expecting Meisser to protect him from other elements within the Ministry of Justice.

If the sentries at the gate had been anxious not to offend the witch hunters, they had been even more careful not to disturb the imposing black giant, Captain-Justicar Ehrhardt. Morr was a god who was worshipped not out of devotion, but fear. That fear encompassed the god of death's morbid servants, the Black Guard of Morr. The baron's soldiers had not been courageous enough to ask Ehrhardt for the massive sword hanging from his belt. Even now, with the castle's ballroom playing host to such a crowd as it had never seen before, the Black Guardsman was given a wide berth, afforded a level of fearful respect Thulmann doubted even the Emperor himself would be able to evoke. Ehrhardt stood poised against a fluted column, his hard eyes surveying the crowd like a wolf studying a flock of sheep.

'I still say this plan of yours cannot work.' Meisser had not left Thulmann's side since leaving the chapter house, perhaps sensing that the witch hunter was the only one preventing Streng from smashing in his skull and Silja from slitting his throat. Of course, Meisser was hardly thrilled by the prospect of challenging Baron von Gotz, especially after all the pains he had suffered to ingratiate himself to the nobleman. He found Thulmann's notion akin to the dangerous ravings of a lunatic. It gave him no joy to share in that danger. It had taken a few overt threats from Streng to close his mouth, but Meisser would not forsake one last attempt to sway Thulmann. 'Arresting the ruler of Wurtbad in his own castle? Maybe you should rethink which of you is the insane one.'

'Your concern is duly noted, Brother Meisser,' Thulmann replied in a low ·hiss. 'You might, however, consider that if anything runs afoul, there are certain members of our group who will make sure you are in no condition to gloat about it afterwards.' The smug look that had flashed across Meisser's face every time he observed a soldier wearing the baron's colours now evaporated. Thulmann decided to drive the point deeper. 'Besides, if my plan does fail, the baron will not take any chances. He will execute anyone who played a role in trying to depose him. And it was your invitation that opened the door for us.' Meisser's eyes widened with horror at the truth of it. When the time came, he would have even more to fear from von Gotz than he did from Thulmann and his associates.

'You... you may be right,' Meisser admitted, sweat trickling down his face. 'You should allow me to aid you. If von Gotz is the monster you think him to be, you will need all the help you can get.'

Thulmann gave the witch hunter captain an incredulous stare. Did Meisser really believe him so stupid as to misplace his trust, or was the man simply so desperate that he would switch loyalties at the eleventh hour? 'I take comfort in your conviction,' he sighed. Meisser nodded his head like an excited vulture.

'Oh, you will not regret your confidence in me,' Meisser assured him. 'All my skills are at the disposal of this bold enterprise.' He held his hand out to the witch hunter. 'But of course I should be much more helpful with a weapon.' Thulmann rolled his eyes.

'I'm afraid I'll feel better for not looking over my shoulder,' he observed. He looked past Meisser, at the slender, black-clad figure close behind. 'Though I'm certain that Silja Markoff would happily give you one of her blades.' Meisser almost jumped out of his skin at the woman's presence, and the violent hatred burning within her eyes.

'Worry not, toad,' Silja spat. 'I desire the baron's head more than I do yours.' Her gloved hand patted the sword hanging from her belt. 'But his is the only head I want more than your own.'

Thulmann looked across the crowd of burghers and aristocrats, seeking out the dark-garbed figures of the other witch hunters. They were scattered about the fringes of the room, as Thulmann had instructed them. From their vantage points, they should have been able to observe anyone entering or leaving the room, as well as maintaining eye contact with at least one of the other conspirators. When the baron made his entrance, one of them would give the signal to the others. Events such as the feast were coordinated to a strict regime dictated by centuries of tradition. Tradition held that the first waltz would be reserved for the baron and the baroness. Thus far, the musicians had busied themselves with less elegant melodies, awaiting the appearance of their patron. The baroness was a handsome woman entering the borderland of middle-age, despite her elaborate wig and the low neckline of her sapphire-hued dress. She had remained seated on a throne-like chair upon a dais at the centre of the north wall, engaged in idle chatter with courtiers and casting sullen glances at the empty chair beside her.

Then the screams began. Sharp and piercing, they were the cries of men and women who felt the chill of Old Night clawing at their souls. The cacophony of terror sounded from the main hall, rising in pitch and volume as more voices joined the chorus of dread. Soldiers sprinted from the ballroom, hastening down the marble corridors to the extravagant great hall. Thulmann shouted sharp commands to his own men, signalling them to follow his lead.

Death and decay filled his nostrils as the witch hunter raced toward the great hall, the reek of profane and unclean powers. It evoked the filth and perversion of the most obscene cults he had uncovered, the horror of men who grovelled before a god that was nothing but foulness and corruption. Thulmann felt the writhing of invisible worms upon his skin, the air grow heavy with spectral filth. As he ran, he could see less stalwart men doubled over, emptying their bellies onto the marble floor as the atmosphere of disgust overwhelmed them. He prayed that he was wrong, that the horror his mind told him was loose within the castle was only a nightmare conjured by his macabre recollections.

He forced his way through the shrieking, fleeing mass of perfumed finery into the main hall and lifted his eyes to the grand stairway, upon the visage of Baron Friedo von Gotz, and knew that his worst fears paled beside the reality.

The hand of Nurgle was upon Wurtbad.

WITHIN THE DARKNESS of the cellar, Carandini shivered, pulling his heavy cassock tight about his body, though he knew the chill that gripped him was not of the flesh, but of the soul. Somewhere in the castle above his head, Sibbechai was even now moving toward its desire, the abhorrent *Das Buch die Unholden*. Once the vampire had the dread tome in its undead claws, it would return for him. Then the death Carandini had hoped to cheat forever would reach out and claim him.

A sound from the yawning mouth of the tunnel opened his eyes wide with fear. So intent had he been upon the impending triumph of Sibbechai, he had neglected to remember an enemy just as horrible, and just as near. Carandini's eyes searched for any sign that the underfolk had returned. He breathed a sigh of relief when the object of his fear showed himself, not a twisted figure covered in fur and filth, but the shape of a man like himself.

'Stand aside,' the cold voice rasped from out of the darkness. As he came closer Carandini was surprised to find that the man's face was not unknown to him. The necromancer smiled at the pallor of Gregor Klausner's skin, the lustreless quality in his eyes. So, Sibbechai had chosen to let both of Wilhelm's sons share in the necrarch's curse? How very thoughtful. But why had the vampire waited so long to summon its thrall to its side?

'I know the vampire is here,' Gregor snarled as he continued to advance. Carandini was startled by the crude wooden shaft clutched in his hand. 'Don't try to stop me.'

Understanding suddenly dawned in the necromancer's mind. The vampire did not have complete control over its creation. Gregor had not been reborn as some dutiful slave, but as a vengeful revenant, determined to destroy the monster that had damned him. Spectral cords bound the two together, allowing Gregor to sense the presence of the elder vampire.

'Stop you?' Carandini laughed, making an elaborate show of stepping from Gregor's path. 'What makes you think I'd even try?' Gregor eyed the necromancer suspiciously as he stalked past. Carandini was amused by the irony of it all.

'Good hunting,' he shouted, as Gregor vanished into the corridor beyond the storeroom. It would be terribly fitting if Sibbechai were to be destroyed by one of its own creations, if all its foul dreams were foiled by its own twisted schemes. There were few thralls with the strength of will to rise against their masters. Carandini hoped that Gregor was one such man. If he were, the necromancer would know soon enough. The compulsion Sibbechai had placed upon him would die with the vampire.

But then, the necromancer's attention was arrested by the din of a vast host flooding through the tunnels. The Tilean shuddered at the chittering squeals of rats, the verminous speech of the underfolk. He slid back into the shadows of the storeroom as the squeaking horde drew closer, the clatter of swords and spears became distinct.

The necromancer called the darkness to him, wrapping the shadows about him like a cloak, willing himself to become one with the night.

The skaven spilled from the tunnel, a tide of rancid fur, ragged leather armour and rusted steel. Rodent muzzles sniffed at the air, red eyes scoured the darkness, eager for any sign of life. More and more of the slouching beasts crept forward, urged on by the force of bodies behind them. Carandini watched in silent horror as the skaven began to fill the room, chisel-fangs bared as their sensitive noses discerned the scent of those whom they hunted.

Then a creature more horrible than a thousand of those that preceded it stole into the cellar. It was a grey furred ratman, wearing a dark robe and fur collar, an iron-tipped staff clutched in its paws. From the sides of the vermin's skull, great horns protruded. Carandini could sense the power of the hideous creature, could almost see the obscene energies swirling about him. The skaven wizard barked a command and the entire host surged forward, squeaking as they pushed and shoved their way into the corridor, following in the very footsteps of Gregor Klausner. The horned ratman turned its head, glaring directly at Carandini before scurrying after the horde it commanded. The necromancer cringed. Even a man used to the dead fires of Sibbechai's face was unsettled by the inhuman malevolence of the ratman.

A tremendous relief washed over Carandini as the rodent cacophony faded. He would never forget the hateful look the horned ratman had directed at him. Then the Tilean's eyes happened to look downward toward the floor. Hundreds of tiny red eyes looked back at him. The floor had become a living carpet of scrawny, furry bodies. Dozens of mouths snapped open hungrily, displaying sharp fangs.

Carandini wondered if Sibbechai would have at least inflicted a more dignified death upon him, as the army of rats swarmed forward and a living tide of vermin engulfed the necromancer.

CHAPTER TWELVE

THULMANN'S EYES WATERED at the stench of the walking putrescence. It may once have been a man, but it was such no longer. Dark Powers had been invited into the flesh and they had consumed it utterly. Perhaps the mind of a man, the tattered, broken fragments of a human soul, yet shrieked within the hulking heap of filth and corruption, the mass of bloated, shapeless flesh. Gangling arms, disproportionate to the body of a man, fell from what might be called shoulders, the green-tinged flesh of each broken by pus-dripping boils and livid red rashes. The abomination's body was like a pile of unformed meat, folds of fat rippling against each other, filth drooling from its sores and lesions filling the crevices between each ripple, making a wet, smacking sound as it moved. The daemon's belly was an open wound, devoured from within by some powerful acid, displaying its purple intestines with the pride of a general displaying his medals. The brown muck of partially digested food stained the monster's belly as it walked, its broken guts spurting more of the filth across its body. Peering from behind the monster's organs, tiny yellow eyes glistened. It seemed to Thulmann that small, daemonic things moved within the host.

Its head, if such the ghastly blob rising above its shoulders could be called, was swollen beyond any semblance of humanity. Features were stretched and distorted, the eyes askew and lacking symmetry, two pools of blue putrescence amidst the decayed green flesh. The mouth was a gigantic maw, stretching from ear to ear, ragged rows of rotten, brown tusks jutting from its jaws, a writhing yellow tongue wriggling between the fangs like a great maggot. Antlers, broken and decayed like the rest of the monster, sprouted from the sides of the beast's head, like some profane parody of a saint's halo.

The final ghastly touch was the ermine cloak that fluttered from the beast's neck. Thulmann recognised the emblem that the clasp bore, on the seal that had been fixed to Meisser's invitation, the seal of Baron Friedo von Gotz, ruler of Wurtbad, now a child of Nurgle.

The obscenity continued its descent, dribbling, babbling and oozing. Thulmann had no intention of listening to whatever blasphemies the daemonic horror might be struggling to give voice to. Disgust unseated the fear in his breast. With one fluid motion, the witch hunter drew one of his pistols. Almost screaming a litany from the *Deus Sigmar*, Thulmann aimed and fired, sending the bullet crunching into the monster's skull.

For a moment, the unclean one was still, its eyes rolling about as though unfixed within its head. Grimy black sludge spilled from the gaping wound at the centre of what was once its forehead, leaking across its face in a stream of filth. As the sludge dripped down into the beast's mouth, the maggot-tongue flickered outward, licking the muck from the daemon's diseased visage like some exotic delicacy. The daemon's corrupt flesh sizzled as the tongue passed over it, putrid smoke rising from its decay. Then the eyes became focused, the tongue retreated back into its cavern-like dwelling, and the monster continued to slither down the stairs.

Thulmann threw the spent pistol aside, drawing two more from the bandolier that crossed his chest. Perhaps the shambling monster could not be harmed by clean steel and lead, but the witch hunter was determined to put the possibility to the test. From the corners of his eyes, he saw movement all around him, as people raced back into the main hall. One of these he recognised as the old templar Tuomas, another was the huge shape of Ehrhardt, his enormous blade gripped firmly in his armoured hands.

There were many more who owed no particular allegiance or loyalty to Thulmann. Perhaps emboldened by the witch hunter's display of defiance before the monstrosity, perhaps feeling the strength and courage of Sigmar coursing through their blood, or trying to purchase time for their families and loved ones to escape, they all came. Thulmann saw halberdiers in the colours of von Gotz stand beside elegantly dressed noblemen, slender rapiers and longswords filling their perfumed hands. One man, his brown hair and beard wild and unkempt, his flowing robes a deep rust red, began to utter strange words, words that were old when mankind was young. Thulmann felt the temperature in the hall rise as the wizard drew power into himself, the fires of sorcery gathering about him. The bronze-hilted sword grasped in the wizard's leathery hand began to glow, lit by an internal fire. The sorcerer glanced respectfully at the stalwart templar, a gesture that was returned.

Wizards and witch hunters were uneasy allies, their mutual fear and loathing too great for either to ignore. But, standing before the obscenity that had once been

Baron von Gotz, it was enough for Thulmann that the sorcerer was human.

The unclean one hesitated as its bilious eyes glowered at the armed men arrayed against it. The daemon's mouth dropped open as it slobbered a guttural noise that sounded too much like 'traitors' to be coincidental. It surged forward and, from its mutilated belly, tiny shapes burst forth, miniature horrors much like itself, spilling down the steps like a tide of slime, capering and squealing as they bounded across the stairs. Thulmann pointed a pistol at one of the gibbering imps, exultant when the bullet exploded it into a splatter of muck and excrement. A moment later, Tuomas fired his weapon and another nurgling exploded.

'Kill the small ones.' Thulmann shouted. 'One scratch from their claws will kill just as surely.' Thulmann fired his other pistol, then drew his sword as the creatures swept forward, slashing at them, hearing their pained squeal as their diseased limbs were cut away, as their pus-filled bellies were split open. All about him, the other men desperately hacked at the daemonic vermin, screaming out as diseased claws broke past their defences and tore into their flesh.

Above it all, the unclean one waddled forward, opening its gigantic maw to spew a stream of stinking liquid corruption into the armoured figure of a soldier. The halberdier shrieked as the steaming green filth sizzled upon his armour, gnawing through his flesh. He toppled forward, his weapon clattering across the floor as the unclean one's vomit hungrily dissolved his very substance. A foul liquid laughter rumbled from the daemon, its swollen head mocking the men desperately struggling to stave off the assault of its nurglings.

ALL WAS CARNAGE as Furchtegott emerged from his chambers. As the screams reached his ears, as he saw the fleeing crush of bodies filling the corridors of the castle, the wizard knew there could be only one cause. Baron von Gotz had decided to ignore the advice of his physician and meet his guests. Furchtegott cursed his own stupidity for waiting so long to escape. Even now, the abomination that von Gotz had become was prowling through his castle, killing Morr only knew how many. And, even worse, leaving others alive to bear witness to the obscene consequences of the wizard's spells. Furchtegott could almost feel the flames of a witch hunter's pyre slithering up his legs.

But they would have to catch him first, and Furchtegott was determined to make that as difficult as possible. He firmed his grip upon the heavy leather bag he carried, his spell books and the rarest of his material components safely concealed within. He had cast aside his golden mantle, assuming a silk tunic and leather breeches, polished black boots with silver buckles and a shapeless velveteen hat. Amidst the finery of the baron's shrieking guests, the wizard would become just another face in the mob.

Furchtegott stepped from the doorway, into the tide of panicking humanity. He could dimly hear the sounds of combat above the screams and cries. It seemed a few valiant foes were trying to make a stand against von Gotz in the main hall. Furchtegott silently wished them luck, he himself having done everything he could to kill the abomination. The wizard joined the exodus swirling around him, the mass of frightened men and women fleeing toward the servant's wing and the kitchens. It was as good a direction as any, and there was a small side entrance near the kitchens through which stores were brought into the castle. The little side door would make an undignified but useful exit.

Even as such cheering thoughts occurred, Furchtegott's hopes of escape were dashed. More screams sounded from up ahead. The fleeing mob became frozen as those at the front of the pack tried to turn back and those behind them tried to press forward. The wizard struggled to see beyond their bodies, to discover what was happening. There was no possibility it could be von Gotz, even if he had managed to overcome the forces fighting him in the main hall. Then the wizard saw an arm covered in fur and clutching a bloodied meat cleaver. One of the bodies obscuring his view was cut down. As she fell, her hideous killer stood revealed.

It was a giant rat. An enormous rodent standing upon its hind legs, wearing a ragged leather tunic and wielding a butcher's blade. As if the very existence of such a monster were not horror enough, the creature's furry hide was torn and mangled, ripped apart by fangs and blades. From its throat, a dagger protruded and its eyes were lifeless orbs of emptiness. The ratman was dead, its carcass animated by some abominable will. Beyond it, Furchtegott saw a fleeting glimpse of other zombie creatures, some as verminous as the first, others the mutilated husks of men. The walking dead slowly, emotionlessly and inexorably hacked their way through the crowd.

Furchtegott reached into his travelling bag, removing the *Das Buch die Unholden*. In scouring its pages for the spells that damned von Gotz with something more horrible than Stir blight, the wizard had seen many rites and incantations related to the living dead: spells to summon them from their graves, and spells to control them. The wizard's frantic hands flipped through the pages. As he did so, a terrible chill seemed to wash over him. The world seemed to grow darker, reality twisting into a soundless shadow.

The wizard looked up from the abhorrent tome and found himself staring into the eyes of ageless evil. Furchtegott could feel the malevolence emanating from the tall, gaunt shadow, feel the ancient hate of all things living burning in its eyes. The vampire exposed its fangs in a bestial snarl. A clawed hand rose, a talon pointed. In a moment of ultimate horror, Furchtegott realised the awful spectre had come to the castle for one purpose. It had come for *him*.

Furchtegott clutched the dread book to his chest, somehow sensing that the vampire would not risk using its unholy magic upon him while he still held the book. But that grace did not extend to the cowering masses between him and the necrarch. Even as the zombies began to redouble their attack with frantic haste, Furchtegott could feel the winds of magic shifting as the vampire drew upon their darkest energies.

The wizard turned, his voice roaring, one hand clutching *Das Buch die Unholden* to his breast, the other gesturing madly as he wove the heavy substance of the sorcerous wind Chamon to his will. The crowd pressing upon him from behind suddenly fell, wilting to the floor as their limbs became as heavy as gold. Furchtegott dare not risk looking back to see what fell power the vampire was unleashing upon the mob, but sprinted back down the corridor, leaping from one prone, screaming victim of his magic to another as if they were a living carpet.

Sibbechai watched the wizard flee, snarling. With a gesture, the vampire unleashed the dark magic it had summoned to itself, sending a withering spectral wave into the mob. As the ghostly light struck living flesh, the victims screamed and fell, their hearts bursting within their chests. The vampire was heedless of the energy it now expended, restraint the farthest thing from its mind. It willed the ghastly force to grow, to hasten its harvest of shrieking souls. It had seen the mortal fool who dared violate the vampire's grimoire with his filthy touch. Sibbechai would pay him the price for such audacity, when it strangled the wizard with his own dripping entrails.

As the wall of screaming flesh withered before it, the vampire swept forward, gliding amidst the havoc like a hungry vulture. Its shadow-like form flitted across broken corpses and twitching bodies, its eyes fixed upon the fleeing wizard as Furchtegott fled back down the corridor. The vampire snarled a command to its zombies, ordering them to follow after it. But Sibbechai had little need of such miserable slaves. It had seen the terror in the wizard's face. There was little it had to fear from such a man. Sibbechai spread its arms wide, willing its body to change. The loathsome substance of its form twisted and contorted, bones snapping and remoulding themselves. Soon, where once the vampire's gaunt frame had stood, a great bat hovered. Its grotesque face spread in a shrill shriek and then it streaked down the hallway, a black blur of shadow and menace.

The wizard's flight carried him to the great hall, but no further. Furchtegott froze as he saw the carnage he had only heard before. Soldiers struggled against hideous, decaying imps, their rotting fangs and diseased claws caked in blood and filth. The immense hulk of von Gotz lashed out at a dozen adversaries, massive claws scraping the marble walls when his clumsy blows failed to connect. A wizard of the bright college slashed at the horrible daemon with a burning blade, while a huge giant in the armour and surcoat of a Black Guardsman hacked at the monster's flank as though chopping into a tree trunk. But it was the sight of nearly a half dozen men in the dark cloaks and hats of the Order of Sigmar that caused him to freeze, to magnify his terror even beyond that evoked by the vampire. The private dread that lurked in the back of every wizard's mind had at last taken shape, the witch hunters had come.

Paralysed by fright, Furchtegott spilled to the floor as the gargantuan bat swooped upon him. Sibbechai's shape twisted and shuddered back into its corpse-like state, cruel talons closing upon the wizard's neck, forcing his head back, striving to expose the book crushed against the man's chest.

The vampire snarled in rage as cold steel raked its face. Burning eyes glared at the ashen-faced woman who had slashed at Sibbechai with her sword. The necrarch hissed at Silja. Silja returned the monster's glare with a defiant glower.

'Mathias.' she shouted, slashing at the vampire again. 'Sibbechai is here.' The woman's sword cut into its dead flesh once more, but no blood swelled from the wound. With a savage growl, the necrarch slammed Furchtegott's head into the stone floor and leapt toward Silja.

Sibbechai's leap was caught in mid-pounce, a heavy sword smashing into its body, severing its spine and flinging it across the hall like a sack of straw. It crumpled against the far wall of the room, limbs twisted about its broken carcass like the crooked legs of a spider. Captain-Justicar Ehrhardt strode toward the vampire's body. Thulmann's gloved hand restrained him.

Both men had heard Silja's cry. Ehrhardt had detached himself from the combat with von Gotz in time to rescue the woman from the vampire's attack. Thulmann gave thanks to Sigmar that Ehrhardt had been able to intervene, but now it was his duty to ensure Sibbechai's destruction.

'Help them against the daemon,' Thulmann ordered. Ehrhardt saw the determination in the witch hunter's eyes and did not argue. The Black Guardsman had a debt to settle with Sibbechai, but Thulmann staked an even greater claim. He pulled the vial of holy water hidden within his tunic and, oblivious to the melee swirling around him, stalked toward the vampire's body.

Silja moved to follow him, but, as she did so, her eyes fell upon the soiled and befouled cloak hanging from the daemon's neck, the gold clasp sparkling from

between the folds of flesh. She felt a red rage blaze
within her as she noted a ghastly familiarity in the creature's distorted features, a twisted echo of the face of
Baron von Gotz, the man who murdered her father. All
thoughts of Thulmann and the vampire vanished as Silja
charged into the fray, slashing at the corrupt monstrosity
with all the ferocity of an Arabyan dervish. One thought
now filled her mind, one purpose moved her hand. Silja
Markoff would be the one to still the diseased heart of
the baron and send his soul shrieking into eternal night.

THE WITCH HUNTER closed upon Sibbechai's carcass,
watching for any sign of movement. The swords of
Morr's Black Guard were enchanted by the dark priesthood, enchanted to strike sure and certain against the
undead. But Thulmann had seen for himself that vampires were hideously difficult to destroy, and would rise
again so long as their profane spark endured. He would
only be satisfied when the necrarch's body was ashes and
its dust scattered into the fast-flowing waters of the Stir.

'Mathias.' Thulmann turned away from the vampire's
corpse at the sound of his name. He turned to see Streng
and a number of soldiers struggling against a ragged
pack of shuffling, shambling figures. Zombies. Slaves of
the vampire. Nor were all of them human, but a number
of skaven were included among their ranks. Streng struck
the head from the shoulders of one of the ratman zombies with a huge axe. Even as the zombie tottered, its
clawed hand lashed out, ripping the warrior's sleeve. The
furred paw was cut away by the clean, deft stroke of a
broadsword. Thulmann was startled to find Meisser's
hand gripping the blade. Clearly Streng had not been the
only one to liberate a weapon from the suits of armour
ranged about the hall.

Meisser stabbed once more, ripping open the rotting
chest of another zombie, spilling its festering blood

across the floor. He attacked an undead creature that was menacing a flush-faced aristocrat with powdered wig dangling from his frilled collar. Enough of Wurtbad's great and good had lingered behind to confront the von Gotz daemon. They would witness Meisser's bravery and remember it in the years to come. The lust for power had won over the weasel's sense of self-preservation.

Suddenly, a grim, bloody figure tore its way into the hall, flinging soldiers and zombies aside with equal disregard. Thulmann felt his soul sicken as he saw the sanguine apparition, its once handsome features now contorted into the visage of a monster. Gregor Klausner glared back at him, his eyes already beginning to lose the last flicker of humanity within them.

'Get away from him, Thulmann,' Gregor growled, brandishing the jagged wooden spear he carried. 'Sibbechai is mine!'

Thulmann stood silent, sword in one hand, holy water in the other. What could he say to this creature, this thing that had once been a man? This abomination that he had permitted to exist? He had known such a thing might happen, had shuddered at its possibility on the long road back from Wurtbad. He should have killed Gregor while he had still been a man, while his soul remained untainted. Now it was too late. Thulmann begged Sigmar's forgiveness for the selfish timidity that allowed such a fate to befall Gregor Klausner. The witch hunter knew there could be but one way to atone for his failure.

Gregor watched Thulmann prepare to meet him. Watched the witch hunter lift his blade. He did not want to fight this man, but he could not allow Thulmann to stand between him and the creature that had polluted his very existence.

'Your fight is not with me, witch hunter,' Gregor said. 'Let me pass.'

'I cannot suffer you to live,' Thulmann replied. 'I should never have allowed this to happen.' The guilt tore at him. Gregor cocked his head, listening intently to something. A wicked smile spread across his face.

'You have more pressing concerns than myself,' he stated. Thulmann believed the vampire's words merely a trick to lower his guard. Then he heard it, a low murmur beneath the sounds of battle. The scratching of claws on stone, the chittering voices of inhuman throats. Its source grew nearer. Cold dread filled the witch hunter as a horde of furry bodies and gleaming fangs burst into the great hall.

The skaven had come.

THE HORDE OF vermin spilled into the great hall, a living flood of inhuman evil. Rusty, crooked swords slashed out, hacking into living and undead flesh with equal disregard. Caught between the soldiers and the skaven, Sibbechai's zombies had their rotting bodies crushed beneath the tide of frenzied ratmen, cut to ribbons until no sign of unnatural life remained. Their living foes proved more difficult, mustering a hasty defence to meet the assault. Halberds impaled squealing skaven bodies as the creatures threw themselves at their human enemy, sizzling black blood mixing with the filth streaming across the floor.

Streng hacked into one ratman's collar, splitting the creature almost to its belly, losing his axe as the corpse toppled away and ripped the weapon from his hands. The mercenary cursed as more of the vermin surged forward to take the place of their slain comrade. He snarled defiance at the hideous creatures, throwing himself at them, letting his larger mass crush the small ratmen to the ground. Streng's fingers closed around a furry throat. The ratman clawed at him, frantically trying to push his weight from its body. Before life could completely fade from the creature, Streng's world was hurled into darkness as the blade of another ratman struck his head, pitching him across the floor.

Grey Seer Skilk scurried behind the horde of clanrats, the warriors he brought to destroy the undead forces he believed were created by his enemies and rivals. Madness was engulfing the great hall of Castle von Gotz. Man struggled against skaven, even as capering, imp-like daemons slashed and gnawed at their legs. At the foot of the stairs, a number of human warriors struggled to combat a greater, even more obscene form. Some of the ratmen drew too near this hulking monster. Skilk saw a pair of them disembowelled by a single sweep of the daemon's claw. He cringed as he sensed the hideous energies emanating from the monster, an aura of such vileness that he had felt only in the presence of the diseased plague priests of Clan Pestilens. Skilk watched as a huge black knight chopped into the monster with his sword, only to have the wound close upon itself as he withdrew his steel. Only the burning blade of a wild-haired human magician seemed to inflict any lasting hurt upon the behemoth.

Skilk snapped commands to his bodyguards. The sooner he destroyed the creatures he pursued, the sooner he could scurry back into the safety of the tunnels. A half-dozen black-furred warriors snarled back, spears gripped in their paws. One pair of skaven scuttled forward from behind the protection of the larger black ratmen. Both of the ratmen wore heavy leather cloaks, the garments glistening with moisture. One of them had a large wooden cask lashed to his back, the other carried a massive, wide-mouthed instrument of iron and copper like an oversized blunderbuss. Heavy tubes of insulated ratskin connected the barrel carried by one to the weapon wielded by the other. Skilk gleamed with feral glee as they scurried forward. There was no quicker way to clear a path to one's prey than the employment of a warpfire-thrower, one of the most ghastly products of skaven technosorcery.

The grey seer snarled for the fury of the weapon to be unleashed. The leather-clad ratmen hissed and squeaked in response, swinging the wide mouth of the weapon towards the combat raging before them. With a wild roar it was loosed, a gout of liquid fire rushed from the mouth of the weapon, spraying flaming ruin across a wide stretch of the hall. The black, viscous fire clung and burned, charring flesh and fur, blackening steel and melting skin. Soldiers, zombies, nurglings and ratmen alike were consumed by the horrific discharge, for the skaven cared little for their fellows caught in the flame. It was enough that the enemy perished alongside their own.

Skilk chittered happily as he watched the warpfire-thrower do its ghastly work. But the sorcerer's glee turned to horror as his eyes darted back to the huge, plague-ridden monstrosity that slobbered and roared at the foot of the stairs. The hulking monster had been surrounded by dozens of enemies, both human and ratman, the blades of both sides doing little more than scratch its polluted surface. Only the burning sword of the man-thing wizard seemed to deal the daemon any harm, and that threat was ended when a sweep of the monster's claw lifted his head from his shoulders. With that single threat destroyed, the unclean one's diseased gaze fixed upon the black flames spewing from the warpfire-thrower. Uttering an inarticulate, slobbering bellow, the bloated daemon barrelled through the ring of foes that surrounded it, smashing aside those too slow to react to its charge, ignoring the half-dozen blades that sank into its body as it thundered across the hall.

The skaven sorcerer shrieked to the warpfire holders to turn it upon the bellowing daemon. The gunner dutifully

turned, fear of Skilk overwhelming the urge to flee, but
the skaven carrying the fuel tank wanted no part of it.
Desperately, the ratman struggled to free itself of the
wooden cask strapped to its back, succeeding only in
snagging the fuel tube. As the gunner pulled back the
lever that would bathe the unclean one in devouring
flame, only a pitiful trickle dribbled from the nozzle. The
ratman stared incredulously at its weapon, then
squeaked in terror as the massive paw of the daemon
smashed into it, throwing its broken body a dozen feet
across the hall. Still connected to the gunner by the thick
ratskin tubes, the fuel carrier hurtled after it, landing with
a sickening crunch as the heavy cask crushed the ratman's
spine.

Skilk snarled at the daemon, his sorcerous energies
gathering in his black paw. Warpfire-throwers were difficult and expensive to obtain, and could only be had
from the warlock-engineers of Clan Skryre. Monster,
man or preternatural abomination, Skilk was determined that the daemon would suffer for this
inconvenience. The grey seer unleashed the crackling
energy, sending a bolt of swirling black lightning stabbing into von Gotz, scorching a hole clean through its
chest, shocking the gibbering horror's heart into a crusty
cinder. Smoke and steaming filth rose from the crater in
the daemon's chest, Skilk admiring his own marksmanship when his glands suddenly spurted the scent of fear
into the air. The abomination was still moving, still
alive, even with its heart cooked! Worse, the formerly
wavering, vacant gaze of the daemon was now focused
on the skaven sorcerer-priest.

Awed by the power and strength the monster had
shown, Skilk backed away from the monstrosity, barking
orders at the mob of black-furred warriors to defend
him. The armoured ratmen demurred, cringing alongside their master. Skilk hissed angrily, unleashing

another charge of black lightning, directing its baleful energies not at the daemon but at the nearest cowering warrior. The ratman squealed in agony as a gaping hole the size of its own head was blasted through its torso, tearing through flesh, bone and armour as easily as wet paper. Their terror of the grey seer restored, the black skaven firmed their grips on spears and shields and surged forward, attacking the hulking monster in frantic desperation.

Skilk hid behind the protective wall of steel and fur, lips writhing as he muttered spells to bolster the flagging courage of his defenders, filling their minds with a reckless bloodlust that would swiftly burn out their brains. But the loss of a few dozen warriors mattered little, especially if it kept his own hide intact.

THULMANN FOUND HIMSELF swept up in the skaven assault, desperately slashing and thrusting at the inhuman warriors of the underfolk. Rodent muzzles snapped and chittered inches from his face as the vermin pushed deeper and deeper into the hall. Beside him, valiant soldiers screamed and died, noble aristocrats spilled their blue blood upon the floor as curved skaven blades gnawed hungrily into their bellies. For every man that fell, two furry corpses littered the ground, but still it was not enough. They could not fight a battle of attrition with the skaven, for the vermin might lose ten of their own for every man they killed and still carry the day.

Then the witch hunter saw the warpfire-thrower brought forward. Alone amongst the men who struggled against the monsters, Thulmann recognised the weapon for what it was. He threw himself to the floor as the skaven fired, as a blast of sizzling fire incinerated those around him. The screams of dying men and ratmen filled his ears, as the incredible heat, the stench of singed fur and burnt flesh filled his other senses. Thulmann felt the dripping mass of a charred skaven topple onto his prone body. He rolled away, ripping his cloak from his shoulders as some of the liquid flame from the ratman's corpse began to devour it. Only the mind of an inhuman monster could have conceived so ghastly an invention, could have imagined fire that clung to its victims like paste and would consume flesh down to the bone.

Even as Thulmann recovered, he was borne down to the ground, his sword flying from his fingers. A shrieking, clawing, rodent shape straddled him, slashing him and snapping at him with its fangs. By luck or cunning, the skaven warrior had survived the fratricidal blast of the warpfire-thrower, but the nearness of such a death had unhinged the creature's mind. Like a mad beast, it clawed at the witch hunter, frenziedly trying to bury its fangs in his neck. Thulmann tried to hold the snapping jaws away, pressing upward on the underside of the ratman's muzzle. His other hand groped across the marble floor, struggling to reach the sword just beyond his reach. The skaven's frenzied strength was starting to win, despite the creature's slighter mass.

Thulmann struggled to shift his attacker's weight and stretched once more for his sword.

GREGOR KLAUSNER STOOD above the withered ruin of Sibbechai's body, glaring down upon it with a cold, lifeless hate. He held the crude wooden spear in his hands, poised for the final, lethal stroke that would impale the vampire's heart and end its profane existence forever. But he found that his limbs would not obey him, that his body would not heed his command. A terrible will beyond his own held him frozen in its grip, a force just as powerful as the vile thirst that coursed through him, just as alien to the mortal being he had once been.

Sibbechai's wilted form began to shift and move, leathery lids rolling back from smouldering eyes. The

Black Guardsman's blow had been a killing stroke, even
for a vampire. But the foul breed of the necrarchs were
more than mere vampires. They were powerful sorcerers,
versed in all the black arts. Where another of its kind
might have perished, Sibbechai had merely retreated
until it could call its shadowy energies back into its
body, could magically repair the damage done to its
dead husk. A cruel smile spread across Sibbechai's skeletal visage as it saw Gregor standing above it. Like an
expanding shadow, the vampire rose from the floor, its
gaunt frame looming before him.

'Now you understand,' it laughed. 'Few there are
among men with the will to resist that of an immortal.
Fewer still are those thralls with the strength to harm
their masters!' Sibbechai's cruel laughter grew as it saw
despair fill Gregor's features. 'Perhaps in a few hundred
years you may be strong enough to try again. If you are
still human enough to care, that is.' The vampire ripped
the wooden shaft from Gregor's frozen hands, hurling it
against the wall with such force that it shattered into a
shower of splinters.

Sibbechai's gaze scoured the chaotic battle for the man
it sought. It found him staggering toward one of the corridors connecting with the great hall, blood streaming
from a gash in his forehead. Furchtegott moved awk-
wardly, his wits rattled by the blow to his head inflicted
by the vampire. He had somehow escaped the notice of
the opportunistic skaven. But the only thing that mattered to the vampire was the forbidding tome still
clutched in the wizard's arms.

THE WRITHING SKAVEN pressed itself downward, fangs
designed to gnaw through wood, to chew solid earth
asunder, now eager to worry the witch hunter's throat.
Thulmann's fingers groped at the hilt of his sword, his
fingertips brushing against the cold metal pommel.

Desperately he tried to close even a single finger around the sword, to pull it back towards him. The ratman's efforts were growing more desperate too, more frenzied and frantic with each passing breath. The monster understood the deadly game it played with the man pinned beneath it and was just as determined to survive. Claws raked through the templar's chest, digging deep furrows in his skin. Blood welled up from the wounds, spilling across the skaven's paws. Thulmann could feel his strength fading, could feel the arm that held the rodent muzzle away from him begin to falter.

Abruptly, the contest was decided. Steel erupted from the ratman's forehead as a sword was thrust through the back of his skull. The twisted, inhuman corpse flopped to the floor, twitching as death spasms racked its nerves. Thulmann breathed deep, staring up into the face of his rescuer. Gregor Klausner glared down at him, kicking the witch hunter's sword within reach of his grasping hand.

'It is time to finish this farce,' Gregor snarled. He waited for Thulmann to gain his feet, then thrust at the witch hunter's throat. Thulmann swatted the stroke aside with his own blade. Gregor gave him little time to recover, thrusting at him with inhuman speed. The battle unfolding all around them no longer existed for Thulmann and Gregor, their world narrowed to the clash of steel, thrust and parry, attack and counterattack. Gregor's strength was tremendous, his speed incredible. Thulmann had been hard pressed in his duel with the vampiric monster that Sibbechai had made from his brother Anton, now he discovered Gregor had been far better with the blade than his sibling. The witch hunter found himself increasingly on the defence, giving ground to his foe, retreating before his strikes. He knew that retreat was death, that there was no chance of survival unless he could mount his own assault and put his enemy on the defensive. But his struggle against the von

Gotz daemon, against the nurglings and the skaven, had already tried his strength and endurance. Soon he would tire, his guard would falter and Gregor's sword would spill his life onto the floor. Thulmann was experienced enough a swordsman to be under no illusion that there was any other outcome.

Then, as Gregor overextended his thrusting sword, Thulmann saw an opening. There was no time for thought, no time to ponder the providential moment. The witch hunter's sword stabbed into Gregor's chest, crunching through ribs to transfix his heart. Thulmann pressed his weight into the attack, forcing the point of his weapon deeper until it emerged from his enemy's back. It was only then, as he heard Gregor's sword fall from his dying fingers, that the templar considered the amateurish sloppiness of the manoeuvre that left his enemy exposed for the attack.

'Why?' he asked as darkness began to creep into Gregor's eyes.

'I could not... destroy Sibbechai... could not destroy myself,' Gregor's voice rasped. A faint tinge of respect briefly flickered in his eyes, a last gleam of friendship and admiration for the man who had killed him. 'Could not... could not give you time... for pity...' Gregor's body trembled. Thulmann watched it topple to the floor.

The witch hunter shook his head sadly, bending down to retrieve Gregor's sword. With a savage thrust, he stabbed the dead man's blade into his chest, then withdrew his own sword from Gregor's heart. Without the penetrating steel transfixing it, there was the possibility that unholy life might return to the vampire. Thulmann would leave no chance for that to happen. Gregor Klausner had earned the peace of the grave.

The templar looked to the wall where Sibbechai's body had lain, not surprised to see it gone. His fist tightened about the grip of his sword, fatigue vanquished from his body as a fresh surge of fury filled him. This time the necrarch would not escape him.

FURCHTEGOTT STAGGERED across the great hall, his bleary senses regarding the battle with cold detachment. The wizard tried to focus, to clear the clouds from his mind, but the discordant din within his skull would not be silenced. Even the pain pulsating from his shattered nose seemed numb and unreal, as though he were remembering rather than experiencing the injury.

The wizard's mouth suddenly dropped open, a dry rattle sounding from deep within his body. Furchtegott's limbs grew slack, his head lolled downward. Only the thin, skeletal claw buried deep in his back held the conjurer upright. The gaunt shade of Sibbechai twisted its hand, ripping still deeper, puncturing his lungs with its sharp talons. The vampire hissed a curse upon the dying wizard, tossing him away like rubbish. The wizard was of only minimal interest to the necrarch, it was the treasure he had thought to steal that blazed within its brain.

Almost reverently, Sibbechai crouched before the massive tome, gazing upon it with the same intense fascination as might shine from the eyes of a weirdroot addict. *Das Buch die Unholden*. Long centuries had passed since the grimoire had been stolen, and many had been the secrets Helmuth Klausner had added to its already copious store of profane knowledge. With those secrets, Sibbechai might become the most powerful of its sorcerous breed, its mind filled with arcane lore that few minds had ever known. The vampire's hand stretched forward to grasp the book, trembling. For the first time in centuries, Sibbechai felt nervous anticipation shudder through its veins. Flesh of its flesh, bound in skin flayed from the vampire's own body, now it would reclaim its own.

A piercing scream ripped from its withered lips as the necrarch's hand touched the evil binding. Crackling green light rippled up its arm, scorching and consuming the vampire's body. Even as Sibbechai tried to pull away, its arm crumbled into ashes, the charred corruption spreading to its chest as the fell sorcery worked its horrific magic. Long had the Klausners known the nature of their nemesis, and long had they prepared for Sibbechai's moment of triumph. Potent wards had guarded Klausner Keep from Sibbechai, but still more potent were they that protected *Das Buch die Unholden*.

The vampire slithered back, legs crumbling into dust as the green light devoured them. Sibbechai's skeletal jaws gnashed and cursed as its withered face cracked and crumbled. Its clawed hand fell apart, fingers dropping to the floor as the flesh burned away. Finally, its entire body seemed to collapse upon itself, into a pile of corpse dust from which the vampire's skull glared, before it too fell into ruin and ashes.

From behind the defence of his bestial warriors, Grey Seer Skilk observed Sibbechai's destruction with deep satisfaction, but also a keen malice. The skaven sorcerer had seen the magical tome the vampire had killed in order to claim. Had felt its power as its protective wards consumed Sibbechai. Feral greed gleamed in Skilk's beady eyes as the ratman considered to what purposes he might put such potent magic. He dragged one of his warriors from where it stood jabbing at the daemonic von Gotz abomination with an iron spear.

'Fetch-bring, quick-quick!' Skilk snarled, gesturing with his claw at the book of sorcery lying beside the ashes of the vampire. The black-furred warrior demurred, sensing the unnatural energies it exuded. Skilk lashed the ratman's face with his tail, repeating his command in a low growl of fury. The warrior scurried forward, recalling all too vividly the black lightning that devoured one of its comrades. The strange book might very well kill him, but the grey seer most definitely would.

Trickles of saliva fell from Skilk's muzzle as he watched the warrior pick up the book. The armoured skaven hesitated, as though waiting for a strange and ghastly death to fall upon it. Skilk snapped an impatient command and the warrior scurried back. The grey seer snatched the book from his slave, squeaking happily as his furry paws caressed the skin-binding. He could feel the fell energies trapped within the tome, taste the dark sorceries crying out to be released. Skilk had invaded the human fortress for revenge and had instead found power. Surely the Horned Rat was smiling upon his humble servant.

Many of his warriors still stood, forming a wall of shields to contain the bloated daemon's advance. Skilk could also see a number of humans waging desperate combat against the abomination. He watched as an older man with one arm bound against his chest slashed his sword into a skaven corpse still smouldering from the warp-fire attack. A length of burning rag from the corpse's tunic was cut away by the stroke as the blade swirled through the air, wrapping the burning cloth around his weapon. He returned to his attack, opening a sizzling wound in the monster's back. The daemon roared in anger, returning its attention to the humans.

Skilk had little interest in which side would win. It was enough that the foolish humans had diverted the daemon's attention. The grey seer barked another order, commanding his warriors to retreat back into the tunnels, an order the terrified ratmen lost no time in obeying. Skilk hastened to slip into their midst, scurrying along as they raced back along toward the castle's cellars. One of the oldest axioms of skaven wisdom was that of safety in numbers. Skilk wanted plenty of bodies

between himself and any lingering foes they might
encounter as he made good his escape.

THULMANN WATCHED WITH impotent rage as the skaven
scurried back to whence they had emerged. He had seen
the horned grey seer retrieve *Das Buch die Unholden* from
its resting place beside Sibbechai's ashes. The witch
hunter did not like to ponder what purpose so loathsome a being might put the tome to, but there was
nothing he could do to thwart the monster's escape. The
unclean one stood between him and the skaven. There
seemed little hope of destroying the daemon before the
ratmen disappeared back into their subterranean world.

The thing that had been Baron von Gotz showed no
sign of tiring. Liquid filth that might have been its
internal organs drooled from the gashes in its diseased
hide. Still it clawed and slashed at its foes. Only the
touch of flame seemed to pain the beast, and it lashed
out at all who threatened it with purifying fire. The
pyromancer who had joined the attack was dead, his
head ripped from his shoulders by the daemon's claws.
The skaven warpfire-thrower had been similarly dis-
patched. Now, it was the crude expedient of burning
cloth wrapped around steel that troubled the monster
as it lashed out with enraged, if clumsy, swipes of its
enormous hands.

Meisser's courage had not broken, doubtless because a
few of Wurtbad's notables had not yet fled or been
killed. Thulmann had to reluctantly credit the scheming
Meisser for improvising his fiery weapon, a tactic many
of the remaining defenders were quick to emulate. Yet
the stabbing flames could do little more than annoy the
bloated monster. If they would destroy the beast they
had to find a way to engulf it in fire.

The skaven with the fuel cask lashed to its back was
writhing upon the floor, trying to crawl away. Inspiration

suddenly gripped Thulmann. He reached a gloved hand out, pulling the fighter beside him away from the battle.

'We've got to try and work that damnable machine!' he yelled, pointing at the skaven weapon. The witch hunter dashed toward the crippled ratman, smashing his foot into the creature's neck and stilling its mangled form. He cut the rat-gut straps binding the cask to the ratman's body. Beside him, the other warrior removed the wide-mouthed fire-thrower from the creature's companion. Thulmann was surprised to find that his helper was Silja. She nodded grimly to him, handing the witch hunter the arcane device.

'Do you have any idea how to work it?' she asked as he made a hurried study of the weapon.

A grim smile flashed upon his face as he hefted the heavy metal cylinder and directed its nozzle toward the rampaging beast. 'None at all,' the witch finder admitted. 'It may be wise to step back.' Whispering a final prayer to Sigmar, Thulmann's fingers tightened around the brass lever protruding from the underside of the weapon and pulled it back.

The unclean one's gaping mouth twisted in a burbling moan of agony, as liquid fire bathed its gruesome bulk in flame. The abomination staggered and swayed, slithering about the great hall as the flames greedily devoured its obscene flesh. In its agonies, the creature's fiery touch set tapestries and carpets burning, its pain-maddened tread grinding corpses into cinder beneath its splayed feet.

Thulmann dropped the unclean skaven weapon, appalled by its horrific power. A daemon beast that had slain over a dozen men, whose unnatural flesh had resisted hundreds of blows from sword and axe, had been consumed in an instant by the technosorcery of the ratmen. He watched the thing fall, shuddering upon the floor as its polluted hide blackened and blistered.

'Justice for my father.' Silja's words were as chill as ice. Thulmann acceded.

'Yes, and justice for Wurtbad,' he announced, as the thing that had been Baron Friedo von Gotz shrivelled and died.

WITCH HUNTER CAPTAIN Meisser advanced on the daemon as it burned, intending to bury his sword in its dying bulk. It was as good as dead already, a fact even the grim Black Guardian seemed to accept as he stepped back, but Messier was determined to impress the handful of soldiers and noblemen still able to bear witness. When Meisser cut the head from the dying abomination, it would be he, not Thulmann, who was named slayer of the beast. In the weeks to come, it would be important for Meisser's name to be held in higher regard than that of Mathias Thulmann, if he were to wrest back control of the Wurtbad chapter house.

But, as Meisser stepped forward, thunder roared across the room and the witch hunter captain's schemes exploded from the back of his skull. A shock of disbelief contorted Meisser's face as his body crashed forward into the burning carcass of the daemon.

'Shit! I missed.' Streng snarled, from where he lay crumpled upon the marble tiles. The mercenary let the smoking pistol fall from his fingers, reaching up to dab his hand against the gash that the skaven had torn across his scalp. Thulmann hurried to his henchman's side, Silja following close behind him. The witch hunter removed linen bandages from a pouch on his belt, kneeling to treat Streng's injury.

'Very slovenly marksmanship,' Thulmann reprimanded him. 'I don't think you'll ever master the pistol.'

THE FIRES FROM the dying daemon had spread from the main hall, racing through the castle as though possessed of a malevolent intelligence of their own. Or perhaps a benevolent intelligence, Thulmann considered. Everything the daemon horror had touched might have become tainted by contact with it. The fires would consume the taint as certainly as they had consumed the walking pestilence that had been Baron von Gotz.

Thulmann wondered how the baron had come to such an end, how he had so swiftly changed from a mortal man into a living effigy of the Lord of Decay. Doubtless the answer lay with *Das Buch die Unholden*. He shuddered to think what awful uses the underfolk might find for such a work of arcane knowledge.

Beside him, Silja turned her eyes from the inferno. 'Is it over?' she asked. Thulmann shook his head sadly.

'It is a beginning, not an end,' he replied. 'We've won the battle, but the war rages on. The skaven have retreated back into their tunnels, but the threat they pose is more terrible than before. And Doktor Weichs is still out there, somewhere. While he lives, sickness and plague could run rampant at any time.' Thulmann sighed deeply, returning his gaze to the castle.

'Small victories are sometimes hard to accept, Fraulein Markoff, but sometimes they are the only ones the gods see fit to offer us.'

ABOUT THE AUTHOR

C. L. Werner has written a number of Lovecraftian pastiches and pulp-style horror stories for assorted small press publications. More recently the prestigious pages of *Inferno!* have been infiltrated by the dark imaginings of the writer's mind. Currently living in the American south-west, he continues to write stories of mayhem and madness set in the Warhammer World.